D0407852

CHRONICLE OF A BLOOD MERCHANT

ALSO BY YU HUA

To Live

The Past and the Punishments

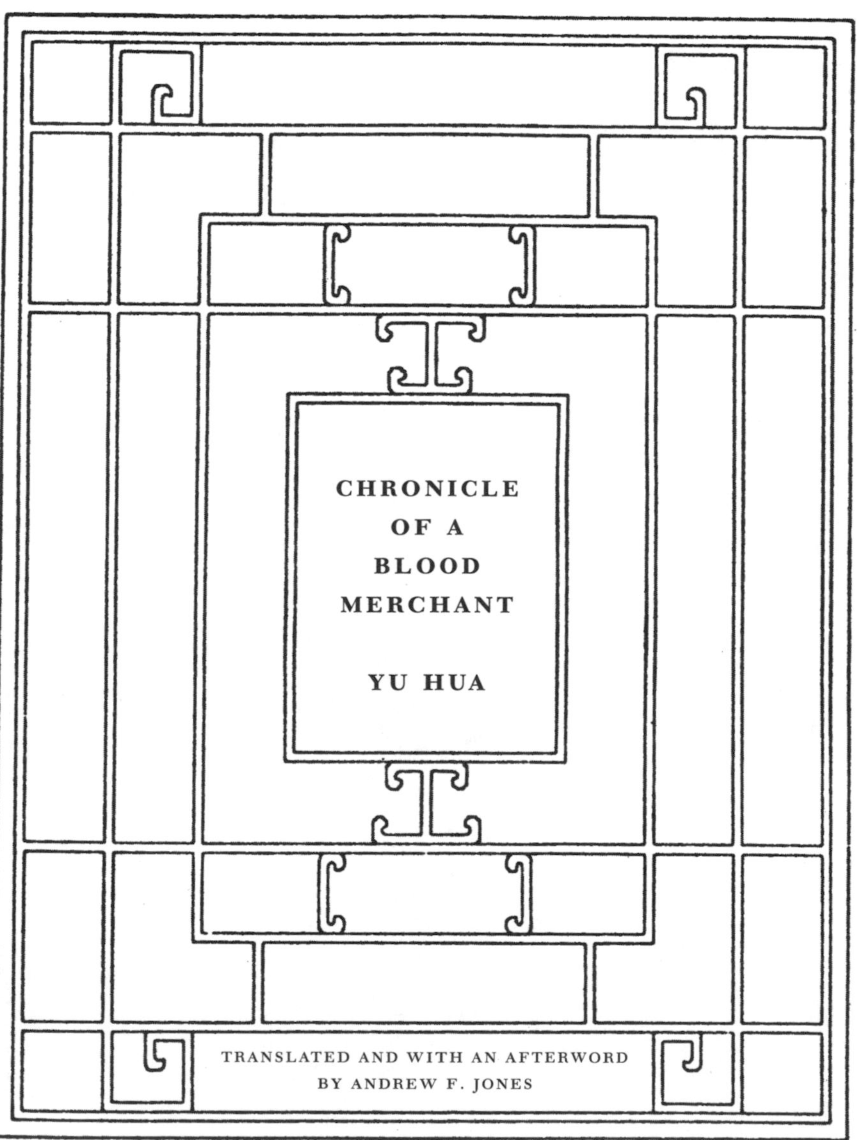

CHRONICLE OF A BLOOD MERCHANT

YU HUA

TRANSLATED AND WITH AN AFTERWORD BY ANDREW F. JONES

PANTHEON BOOKS NEW YORK

 Published in the United States by Pantheon Books, a division of Random House, Inc., New York, and simultaneously in Canada by Random House of Canada Limited, Toronto. Originally published in China as *Xu Sanguan mai xue ji* by Jiangsu Wenyi Publishing House, Nanjing, in 1996, and by Nan Hai Publishing House, Haikou, in 1998.

Library of Congress Cataloging-in-Publication Data

Yu, Hua, [date]

[Xu Sanguan mai xue ji. English]

Chronicle of a blood merchant / Yu Hua ; translated from the Chinese by Andrew F. Jones.

p. cm.

ISBN 0-375-42220-X

1. Yu, Hua, 1960—Translations into English. I. Jones, Andrew F. II. Title.

PL2928.H78X813 2003

895.1'352—dc21 2003048808

www.pantheonbooks.com

Book design by Iris Weinstein

Printed in the United States of America

First American Edition

2 4 6 8 9 7 5 3 1

CHRONICLE OF A BLOOD MERCHANT

CHAPTER ONE

Xu Sanguan worked in the silk factory in town, distributing silkworm cocoons to the spinners. But today he was out in the country visiting his grandpa. His grandpa's eyes had dimmed and blurred with age, and he was having trouble making out who it was standing by the door. He called for Xu Sanguan to stand a bit closer, looked him over for a moment, and then asked, "Son, where's your face?"

Xu Sanguan said, "Grandpa, I'm not your son, I'm your grandson, and my face is right here in front of you." He pulled his grandpa's hand over to his face, let him pat it, and then put it back in his lap. His grandpa's palms felt like raw silk yarn.

His grandpa asked, "Why doesn't your dad come and see me?"

"Dad died a long time ago."

His grandpa nodded, and a string of saliva slipped out from between his lips. He tilted his head and sucked until some of it came back in. "Son, how's your health?"

"Good," Xu Sanguan said. "Grandpa, I'm not your son."

His grandpa continued, "Do you sell your blood too?"

Xu Sanguan shook his head. "No, I've never sold my blood."

"Son," Grandpa said, "you're telling me that you're in good health, but you've never sold your blood. I think you're trying to make a fool of me."

"Grandpa, what are you trying to say? I don't understand. Grandpa, are you senile?"

Grandpa shook his head.

Xu Sanguan added, "Grandpa, I'm not your son. I'm your grandson."

"Son," his grandpa continued, "your dad wouldn't listen to me. Fell for some 'flower' or other in town."

"Golden Flower. That's my mom."

"Your dad said he was old enough. He told me he wanted to go into town and marry some 'flower' or other. I said, 'Your two older brothers haven't gotten married yet.' If the eldest hasn't even gotten married yet, how could I let the youngest go ahead and take a wife before him? Around here, that's not how you play by the rules."

XU SANGUAN sat on his fourth uncle's roof gazing at the horizon. The sky was a wash of crimson that seemed to emanate from the muddy paddies in the distance, shining across the fields, transforming the crops into a vast tomato-red expanse. Everything was bright red—the little streams and paths that crawled across the land, the trees, the thatched cottages and the fishponds, even the streams of smoke that poured crookedly out from village chimneys.

Xu Sanguan's fourth uncle was spreading fertilizer across the melon patch beside the house as two women, one older, one younger, walked past. Xu Sanguan's uncle said, "Guihua looks more and more like her mama."

The younger of the two women smiled, and the older one caught sight of Xu Sanguan sitting on the roof. "Who's that sitting on your roof?"

Xu Sanguan's uncle said, "That's my third brother's son."

The three people below all glanced up at Xu Sanguan. Xu Sanguan chuckled as he looked down toward the young woman called Guihua. Guihua lowered her eyes to the ground. The older woman said, "He looks just like his dad."

Xu Sanguan's uncle said, "Guihua's getting married next month, isn't she?"

The older woman shook her head, "Guihua's *not* getting married next month. We've broken off the engagement."

"Broken the engagement?" The fertilizing trowel in Xu Sanguan's uncle's hand dropped to the ground.

The older woman lowered her voice. "The boy's health is no good. He can only eat one bowl of rice at a time. Even Guihua can eat two bowls of rice at a time."

Xu Sanguan's uncle lowered his voice as well. "How did that boy go and ruin his health?"

"I really don't know how it happened. First I heard people say he hadn't gone to the hospital to sell blood for almost a year. That got me wondering if maybe he had some kind of problem, so I sent someone to invite him over for dinner, just so I could see for myself how much he could eat. If he could eat a couple big bowls of rice, I figured I could set my mind at ease, and if he could eat three, well, Guihua would have been his. He ate one bowl, but when I went to get him some more, he said he was full, said he couldn't eat any more. Imagine a big strong man like that not even being able to eat a little more. Well, I figured there's something wrong with him for sure."

Xu Sanguan's uncle nodded his approval. "You're a thoughtful mother."

The older woman said, "That's what mothers are for."

The two women glanced up once more toward Xu Sanguan, who was still chuckling as he looked at the younger woman. The older woman said once again, "Looks just like his dad."

The two women walked away, one in front of the other. Both of them had big rears, and as Xu Sanguan looked down on them from above, he had trouble distinguishing where their buttocks ended and their thighs began. When they were gone, Xu Sanguan watched Fourth Uncle continue to spread fertilizer across the melon patch as the sun set and his body grew increasingly indistinct in the haze of dusk.

"How much longer are you going to work, Uncle?"

"I'll be done pretty soon now," his uncle said.

"Uncle, there's something I don't understand that I want to ask you about."

"Go on."

"Is it true that people who sell their blood are really healthy?"

"That's right," Fourth Uncle said. "Didn't you hear what Guihua's ma said just now? Around here the men who haven't sold blood can't get themselves a wife."

"What kind of rule is that?"

"I don't know if there's a rule or not, but everyone who's strong enough goes to sell his blood. You get thirty-five *yuan* a shot. That's more than you make in six months in the fields. And blood's like well water. If you never go to the well, the source dries up, but if you use it every day, there'll always be just as much water as there was before."

"But Uncle, if what you say is true, then selling blood's a real money tree."

"That depends on whether or not you're in shape. If you're not in shape, you might as well sell your life away when you go sell blood. When you go sell blood, the hospital has to check you out first. First they take a tube of blood and check to see whether or not you're healthy. They'll only let you sell to them if you're healthy."

"Fourth Uncle, do you think I'm in good enough shape to sell blood?"

Fourth Uncle looked up at his nephew on the roof, who looked back at him, torso bared and grinning. The flesh on his arms looked solid, so Fourth Uncle said, "You could sell blood."

Xu Sanguan grinned to himself until another thought crossed his mind, and he looked down at his uncle. "Fourth Uncle, I want to ask you something else."

"What is it?"

"You said that when they check you at the hospital, they take a tube of blood, right?"

"That's right."

"Do they pay you for it?"

"No," Fourth Uncle said, "you give it to them for free."

THE THREE OF THEM walked down the road. The oldest was in his thirties, the youngest only nineteen. Xu Sanguan, who was walking in between them, was somewhere in the middle. He said to the two men walking beside him, "You're carrying watermelons, and you've both got a big bowl in your pockets. Are you planning to sell watermelons in town when you're done selling blood? One, two, three, four—you each have four watermelons. Why so few? Why not bring in a hundred pounds each? What are those bowls for anyway? Why didn't you bring any food? What are you going to have for lunch?"

"We never bring anything to eat when we're going to sell blood," the nineteen-year-old, Genlong, replied, "When we're finished selling blood, we're going to go to a restaurant to have a plate of fried pork livers and two shots of yellow rice wine."

The man in his thirties was called Ah Fang, who explained, "The pork livers build up the blood, and the rice wine gives it life."

Xu Sanguan went on, "You said you sell four hundred milliliters each time. How much is that really?"

Ah Fang took a bowl from out of his pocket, "See this bowl?"

"Yeah."

"Two bowls at a time."

"Two bowls?" Xu Sanguan sucked in a breath. "They say it takes a whole bowl of rice just to make a few drops of blood. So how many bowls of rice do you have to eat to make two bowls of blood?"

Ah Fang and Genlong chuckled. Ah Fang said, "It's no use at all if you only eat rice. You have to eat the pork livers and drink some rice wine."

"Xu Sanguan," Genlong went on, "didn't you say just now that we don't have enough watermelons? I'll tell you something. We aren't planning to sell any watermelons today. These melons are gifts."

Ah Fang added, "These melons are for Blood Chief Li."

"Who's Blood Chief Li?"

They had arrived at the head of a little wooden bridge. A stream stretched into the distance, widening and narrowing as it flowed through the fields. Green weeds poked out above the surface of the water, clinging to the banks of the stream and climbing up the edges of the surrounding rice paddies.

Ah Fang stopped and said to Genlong, "Genlong, we'd better drink some water now."

Genlong put down his melon-laden carrying pole and shouted, "Time to drink!"

They took their bowls out from their pockets and clambered down the embankment. Xu Sanguan crossed to the middle of the wooden bridge, standing to watch as they dipped their bowls into the stream, waving them back in forth in the water until they had swept away all the weeds and debris from the area directly in front of them. This accomplished, they noisily gulped down bowl after bowl of water—four or five bowls each.

Xu Sanguan, still standing above them, called out, "Did you two eat lots of salted pickles for breakfast?"

Ah Fang looked up. "We didn't have any breakfast. We drank eight bowls of water though. And besides what we just drank, we still have to stop in town and have some more, until our stomachs are so swollen that it hurts and the roots of our teeth start to ache. Because the more water you drink, the more blood there will be. The water sinks into the blood."

"When the water sinks into the blood, does the blood get watery?"

"Sure. But there's more of it."

"Now I know why you brought the bowls along," Xu Sanguan said, as he too climbed down the embankment toward the stream.

"Will one of you lend me a bowl? I'll drink some too."

Genlong handed him his bowl. "Take mine."

Xu Sanguan took hold of the bowl and squatted down by the stream.

Ah Fang said, "The water on top's dirty, and the stuff on the bottom is too. You want to drink from the middle."

When they had finished drinking from the stream, they continued down the road. This time Ah Fang and Genlong walked next to each other while Xu Sanguan walked to one side, listening to the rhythmic squeaking of their carrying poles.

Xu Sanguan said, "You've been carrying those the whole way. Let me take one."

Genlong said, "Take Ah Fang's for a while."

Ah Fang said, "A few watermelons don't bother me. When I go to town to sell melons, I usually carry a hundred pounds at a time."

Xu Sanguan asked, "Just now you mentioned Blood Chief Li. Who's he?"

"Blood Chief Li," Genlong explained, "is the bald man who's in charge of buying blood for the hospital. He's the one that decides who gets to sell blood and who doesn't."

"And that's why you call him Blood Chief Li," Xu Sanguan concluded.

Ah Fang continued, "Sometimes there's a lot of people who want to sell blood, but not very many patients in the hospital who need it. At times like those, everything depends on whether or not you're on Blood Chief Li's good side. Because the people who are on his good side are the ones who'll get to sell their blood."

Ah Fang added by way of explanation, "And what exactly does it mean to be on Blood Chief Li's good side? In Blood Chief Li's own words, 'When someone remembers me even when he doesn't need to sell any blood. When he remembers me from time to time.' And what does it mean to remember him from time to time?"

Ah Fang pointed at the watermelons dangling from the carrying pole, "This is what it means to remember him from time to time."

"We're not the only ones who remember him either," Genlong added. "That girl named Ying something or other remembers him *all* the time."

The pair burst into broad grins. Ah Fang told Xu Sanguan, "She gets on his good side under the covers. If she wanted to sell some blood, everyone else would have to stand aside, no matter who it happened to be. And if somebody should offend her, well, it wouldn't matter if his blood belonged to an Immortal, because Blood Chief Li wouldn't even let him *give* it away."

They arrived at the edge of town as they spoke. As soon as they got into the city, Xu Sanguan took the lead, because he was from town and knew his way around. They told him they wanted to find a good place to drink some more water. Xu Sanguan said, "Once you get into town, you shouldn't drink stream water anymore. It's dirty here. I'll take you to drink well water."

The two followed Xu Sanguan's lead as he guided them down a twisting narrow lane, saying as he went, "I can't hold it in anymore. Let's find somewhere to pee."

Genlong said, "You can't pee. If you pee, all that water will go to waste. And you'll have less blood to spare."

Ah Fang said to Xu Sanguan, "We drank a lot more than you, and we're still holding it in." He turned to Genlong. "His bladder's small."

Xu Sanguan, brows furrowed against the pain of his swollen bladder, began to move more and more slowly down the lane. "Can it kill?"

"What do you mean can it kill?"

"Kill *me*! I mean, could my stomach burst?"

"Do the roots of your teeth ache?" Ah Fang asked.

"My teeth? Let me check. . . . No, I guess they don't."

"Then there's nothing to be afraid of. As long as your teeth don't ache, there's no risk of the bladder bursting," Ah Fang affirmed.

Xu Sanguan brought them to a stone well near the hospital, which stood under the canopy of an old tree, its sides carpeted in green moss. A wooden bucket with a length of neatly coiled hemp rope tied to its handle lay to one side of the well. They threw the bucket into the well, where it hit the water below like a resounding slap in the face. When they had drawn a bucketful of water, Genlong and Ah Fang each drank two bowls. Ah Fang handed Xu Sanguan his bowl, and he too drank a bowl of water. Ah Fang and Genlong urged him to drink another, but after Xu Sanguan poured the water into the bowl and took a couple of sips, he poured what was left back into the bucket. "My bladder's too small. I can't drink any more."

They made their way toward the blood donation room at the hospital, moving as carefully as women in the final month of pregnancy, their faces tomato red with the effort of holding in the urine. Ah Fang and Genlong moved even more gingerly than Xu Sanguan, for they were still burdened by melon-laden carrying poles. Their hands were clasped around the cords from which the watermelons were strung so that the poles wouldn't wobble back and forth with each step. But the hospital corridor was a narrow one, and a few of the people squeezing past could not help but jostle the poles. The water distending Ah Fang's and Genlong's bladders wobbled along with the watermelons, and their faces went crooked with pain. Each time they were jostled, they had to rest until the watermelons stopped swaying, then continue painstakingly down the hallway once the poles had steadied.

Blood Chief Li sat behind a desk in the blood donation room, feet propped atop an open desk drawer, and his legs splayed to reveal his crotch. All the buttons on his fly had fallen off, and a pair of flower-print underwear peeked through the gap between. There was no one else in the room besides Blood Chief Li. As soon as Xu Sanguan saw him, he thought to himself, *So this is Blood Chief Li. Isn't he the bald guy who comes by the factory to sell fried silkworm chips?*

When Blood Chief Li saw Ah Fang and Genlong shuffle in with their carrying poles, his feet slid back onto the ground, and he gave out an affable chuckle. "So it's you two! You're back again." Then he glanced toward Xu Sanguan and gestured in his direction. "I think I've seen this one before."

"He lives in town," Ah Fang said.

"That must be it," Blood Chief Li said.

Xu Sanguan added, "You're the one who comes by our factory to sell silkworm chips, right?"

"You're at the silk factory?" Blood Chief Li asked.

"That's right."

"Damn," Blood Chief Li went on. "No wonder I've seen you around. Are you here to sell some blood too?"

Ah Fang said, "We've brought you some watermelons. Fresh picked this morning from the fields."

Blood Chief Li raised his buttocks from the chair to lean across the desk and inspect the watermelons more closely. He chuckled. "They're pretty damn big too. Just set them down in the corner."

Ah Fang and Genlong bent over in an effort to extract the watermelons from their baskets and set them down in the corner. But no matter how hard they tried, they were unable to bend far enough, and after several abortive tries, their faces went a fiery red and the sound of their panting filled the room.

The smile faded from Blood Chief Li's lips as he watched them struggle. "Just how much water did you drink this time?"

Ah Fang replied, "Just three bowls."

Genlong, standing to one side, corrected him, "He had three. I drank four."

"Bullshit." Blood Chief Li's eyes were fixed on them. "You think I don't know how big your bladders are by now? I know damn well that when you two really get going, your stomachs swell up as big as a pregnant lady's belly. Ten bowls, at the very least."

Ah Fang and Genlong broke into sheepish grins, and Blood Chief Li, won over by their smiles, waved his hand as if to dismiss the matter. "Forget it. At least you two still have a conscience. At least you two still remember me from time to time. You can sell this time, but don't do it again." Then he shifted his attention toward Xu Sanguan. "Come here."

Xu Sanguan moved over to the desk.

"Move your head a little closer."

Xu Sanguan lowered his head, and Blood Chief Li reached out a hand, grabbed hold of the skin around Xu's eyes, and forced them wide open.

"Let's take a look at your eyes. Let's see if there's any jaundice. No . . . then stick out your tongue, let me see your innards. . . . Doesn't look so bad. All right then, you can sell blood as well. And listen here. Usually the rule is that we're supposed to take a sample first and check if you have any diseases. But you're a friend of Ah Fang and Genlong, and I wouldn't want them to lose any face—especially considering that this is our first meeting. In short, just consider this as my little gift to you."

AFTER THE THREE MEN finished their transaction, they made their way, step by painstaking step, toward the hospital's public lavatory. Xu Sanguan followed closely behind the other two. They kept their eyes to the floor, silent and grimacing with pain, wary of the one false move that might cause their bladders to burst.

They lined up in a row in front of the hospital urinal, and as they began to pee, a wave of intense pain rolled across the roots of their teeth. Their teeth began to chatter so resoundingly that the splatter of their urine on the wall was very nearly drowned out by the sound.

Not long afterward they arrived at the Victory Restaurant. The

Victory Restaurant was nestled under an old bridge, and the peak of its roof barely reached the stone underside of the structure. A mass of weeds grew from in between the roof tiles, cascading over the eaves like eyebrows. The front door was almost indistinguishable from the tall windows, edged by wooden slats, that ran across the storefront. The three walked into the restaurant through one of these windows and took a table by another window that looked out over the creek that ran through the west end of town. A few discarded vegetable leaves floated past them on the current.

Ah Fang shouted to a waiter, "A plate of fried pork livers, and two shots of yellow rice wine, and make sure to warm up the wine for me."

Genlong shouted in turn, "A plate of fried pork livers, two shots of yellow rice wine, and warm up my wine as well."

Xu Sanguan had watched closely as they shouted out their orders and, impressed by the aplomb with which they had slapped the table for emphasis, followed suit with a shout, "A plate of fried pork livers and two shots of yellow rice wine. Oh, and warm mine up too."

In a twinkling three plates of fried pork livers and three pots of rice wine were delivered to their table. Xu Sanguan lifted his chopsticks and was just about to spear a piece of the pork liver when he noticed that Ah Fang and Genlong had lifted their wine pots instead. Squinting with anticipation, they slowly took a sip, and then simultaneously emitted a long hissing sound, upon which their facial muscles visibly relaxed and they both broke into satisfied smiles.

"That's the best part," Ah Fang said with a sigh.

Xu Sanguan put down his chopsticks, lifted his wine pot, and took a sip. The wine flowed down his throat, warming his insides as it went, and he too unwittingly emitted a long hissing sound.

Ah Fang and Genlong grinned. "Now that you've sold blood, do you feel dizzy?" Ah Fang asked.

"I'm not dizzy, but I feel like I don't have any energy left, and my feet and legs seem kind of rubbery when I walk."

Ah Fang said, "You've sold your energy. That's why you feel weak. What we sold just now is energy, understand? City people call it blood, but we country folks call it energy. There are two kinds of energy. One kind comes from the blood, and the other comes from muscle. But the kind that comes from the blood is worth a lot more money."

Xu Sanguan asked, "What kind of energy comes from the blood? What kind comes from muscle?"

Ah Fang said, "When you climb into bed, or when you pick up a bowl of rice from the table, or when you walk from my house over to Genlong's, you don't use much energy at all. That's the kind that comes from the muscle. But when you go into the fields and work, or you carry a hundred pounds of watermelon into town, when it comes to that kind of hard labor, you have to use the kind of energy that comes from the blood."

Xu Sanguan nodded. "I think I understand now. The kind of energy you're talking about is like money in your pocket. If you spend some, you have to go out and earn some more."

Ah Fang nodded and turned to Genlong. "These city folks are really pretty bright."

Xu Sanguan said, "You two work in the fields every day, but you still have enough extra energy to sell your blood to the hospital. You're really a lot stronger than me."

Genlong said, "We're not necessarily stronger than you. It's just that we country folks are more used to spending our energy. We depend on selling blood to make enough money to afford a wife, or build a new house. We make just enough in the fields to make sure we don't starve."

Ah Fang said, "Genlong's right. I'm saving the money I made today for a new house. Another couple of times, and I'll have enough to start construction. Genlong's selling blood because he's got his eye on a girl named Guihua in our village. Originally she was engaged to someone else, but then they broke it off, and Genlong ended up falling for her instead."

Xu Sanguan said, "I've seen Guihua. Her behind is too big. Genlong, do you like big behinds?"

Genlong grinned while Ah Fang explained, "Women with big behinds are nice and solid. Being in bed with them is like being on a boat—nice and comfy."

Xu Sanguan broke into a broad smile.

Ah Fang went on. "So, Xu Sanguan, have you thought it through? What you're going to do with the money you earned from selling blood?"

"I don't know yet," Xu Sanguan said. "I've only just learned what it means to sell the kind of energy that comes from the blood. What I earn in the factory is just sweat money, but what I earned today is blood money. You can't spend that kind of money on just anything. I have to find something important to spend it on."

Genlong interrupted. "Hey, did you happen to notice those underpants Blood Chief Li had on?" Ah Fang smirked as Genlong continued. "Do you think they might have been that Ying Something-or-other's panties?"

"Obviously. My guess is that they accidentally put on each other's underwear when they got up this morning," Ah Fang said.

"I would really like to see"—Genlong chuckled—"whether or not she's wearing Blood Chief Li's underwear."

CHAPTER TWO

Xu Sanguan sat in the melon patch eating watermelons. His uncle, to whom the melon patch belonged, stood, stretched his arms behind his back, and brushed the dirt from his rear. A little cloud of dirt swirled around Xu Sanguan's head and settled on the watermelon in his hands. He blew the dirt away as he continued to bite into the tender pink flesh. When his uncle was finished patting off his backside, he sat back down on the low bank of dirt at the edge of the plot.

Xu Sanguan asked, "What are those shiny yellow melons called?"

Just beyond the mass of tangled watermelon vines was a row of trellises fashioned from bamboo poles, from which dangled clumps of golden yellow melons, each about the size of a hand. On the other side of the trellis were an equal number of glossy green melons, which appeared to be a little longer than the yellow ones. The fruit sparkled brightly in the sunlight. When the wind blew, first the leaves, then the vines, and finally the melons themselves began to sway in the breeze.

Xu Sanguan's fourth uncle lifted his skinny, wrinkled arm to point across the melon patch. "Do you mean those shiny yellow ones? Those are Goldens. The glossy green ones to the side are Old Lady melons."

"I'm not going to have any more watermelon, Fourth Uncle. I think I've already eaten two whole melons."

His uncle said, "No, you haven't. I had some too. I think I ate half of one of yours."

Xu Sanguan said, "I know Goldens. The flesh smells really good, but they aren't actually all that sweet. But the seeds are sweet. People in town always spit out the seeds when they eat Goldens, but I never do. I figure if it grows in the earth, it's got to be good for you. I've had Old Lady melons too. They're not too sweet, and they're not very crisp either. By the time you open one up and take a bite, it's all mushy. When it comes to eating Old Lady melons, it doesn't matter if you have teeth or not. Fourth Uncle, I think I could actually eat some more. I think I'll have a couple of Goldens and then eat an Old Lady."

Xu Sanguan sat in his uncle's melon patch all day long and didn't get up to leave until the sun began to set. By the time he stood to leave, his face shone as red as pork livers in the light of the setting sun. Gazing toward the smoke curling up from the farmhouses, he patted the dirt from his rear and started to rub his stomach, which was swollen with watermelon, Goldens, Old Ladies, cucumbers, and peaches.

As he rubbed his belly he turned to his uncle and said, "I'm going to get married."

Then he turned back toward his uncle's melon patch and began to pee.

"Fourth Uncle, I want to find someone to marry. Fourth Uncle, for the past two days I've been thinking about the thirty-five *yuan* I made selling blood and what I ought to spend it on. I wanted to give some to Grandpa, but he's too old now, really he's so old he wouldn't even be able to spend it. And I wanted to give you some too, because of all my father's brothers, you treat me the best, but Fourth Uncle, I just can't give it to you, because I earned it by selling blood, not just ordinary muscle. That's why I can't bear to give it away. Fourth Uncle, when I stood up just now, I suddenly realized I should get myself a woman. Then my blood money wouldn't go to waste. Fourth Uncle, all I ate was a bunch of melons, so how come it feels like I drank lots and lots of wine? Fourth Uncle, my face is burning, my neck is hot, the soles of my feet feel like they're on fire."

CHAPTER THREE

Xu Sanguan's job was to push a trolley heaped with puffy white silkworm cocoons back and forth across a huge workshop, delivering them to the flock of young women who ran the spinning machines. He horsed around with them every day, joking and laughing amid the deafening roar of machinery. Often their hands would reach back and pat his head, or find their way to his chest and playfully shove him back a few steps. If he were to choose one of them to be his woman, to share a quilt with him on a snowy winter's night, then he would choose Lin Fenfang, the girl with the braids that dangled down to her waist, the girl whose smile revealed a row of straight, white teeth and a pair of dimples, because he figured that he would never tire of looking at her, even for a lifetime. And sometimes Lin Fenfang was among those who would pat him on the head. Once she even surreptitiously squeezed his hand. After that he always gave her the best cocoons, and he could never bear to give her any of the ones that had gone bad.

There was another girl who was very pretty. She worked in a little snack shop in town, standing every morning next to a giant wok full of oil, making fried dough for breakfast. She was constantly breaking out into exclamations: when some hot oil splattered on her hand, or when she discovered a spot on her dress, or when her foot slipped as she walked down the street, or when she noticed that it had begun to rain, or when she heard a thunderclap, he invariably heard her cry out, "Aiya!"

This girl was called Xu Yulan. Her work for the day was finished by breakfast, after which she was free to spend her afternoons strolling back and forth through the streets, chewing contentedly on melon seeds wherever she went. Sometimes she would stop to shout a hello to someone she knew who was standing across the street, bursting into giggles and a series of "aiyas" as she spoke. At these times there was usually a little piece of melon seed husk stuck to her lips, and if the people who walked by just as she opened her mouth were lucky, they would even smell the sweet vegetal fragrance that emerged from between her lips as she spoke.

After she had walked a few blocks, she would usually walk back to her house, reemerging ten minutes later clad in an entirely different outfit. Then she would once again begin to amble through the streets. She changed her outfit three times a day, because the fact was that she only had three outfits into which to change. And every day she changed into four different pairs of shoes, because she only had four pairs of shoes to wear. When there was nothing new left to wear, she would wrap a silk scarf around her neck.

In truth, she had no more clothes than anyone else, but everyone thought of her as the girl with the most extensive and fashionable wardrobe in town. Her strolls through the streets made everyone feel as if her pretty face were as familiar as the stream that flowed across town. And almost everyone in town knew her as the Fried Dough Queen. "Look, there goes the Fried Dough

Queen." "Did you see the Fried Dough Queen go into the fabric shop? She buys some pretty new pattern practically every day." "No, she just looks, she never buys." "The Fried Dough Queen's face smells so sweet." "The Fried Dough Queen's hands aren't very pretty. Too short, and her fingers are stubby." "So *that's* the Fried Dough Queen?"

One day Xu Yulan, the Fried Dough Queen, walked a few blocks with a young man called He Xiaoyong. They talked and laughed, and later they stood by the railing of a wooden bridge until the sun started to set and night had nearly fallen. He Xiaoyong was wearing a clean white shirt, sleeves rolled up to the elbows, and when he talked and laughed, he would cross his arms and wrap his hands around his elbows. Xu Yulan found this gesture enchanting, and when she looked prettily up at He Xiaoyong, her eyes sparkled with light.

Sometime later someone saw He Xiaoyong walk by Xu Yulan's front door just as Xu Yulan herself had just emerged from inside the door. When she caught sight of him, she called out, "Aiya!" Her face was wreathed in smiles. "Come in and sit for a while."

When He Xiaoyong walked inside, he saw Xu Yulan's father sitting at a table drinking some yellow rice wine. Xu Yulan's father, seeing a young stranger come in through the door with his daughter in tow, slid his chair and issued an invitation. "Have a drink?"

After that He Xiaoyong was often to be seen at Xu Yulan's house, huddled with her father as they spoke in low tones over a pot of yellow rice wine, punctuated from time to time with what sounded like conspiratorial laughter.

And thus Xu Yulan found herself walking out of her room and standing next to the table, demanding as loudly as she could, "What are you two always talking about? What's so funny?"

That very same day Xu Sanguan returned home from the country. As he reached town, night had already fallen. In those days there weren't yet any street lamps installed in the city; red lanterns hung from the eaves of some of the shops, shining in uneven bands across the stone-cobbled street. Xu Sanguan walked home, enclosed one moment in darkness and the next in light. As he passed the theater, he caught sight of Xu Yulan. The Fried Dough Queen was standing sideways by the front entrance of the theater in between two big lanterns, cracking melon seeds, her face glowing luminously red in the lantern light.

Xu Sanguan walked over toward her, hesitated, turned, and walked back. He stood across the street, grinning as he watched how prettily she pursed her lips as she spit out a melon seed husk. Xu Yulan saw Xu Sanguan too. First she glanced in his direction, and then she turned to watch as two passersby walked down the street. When they had gone, she glanced back at Xu Sanguan and just as quickly wheeled around to glance inside the theater, where a man and a woman were standing and talking about the show. When she twisted her head back around, she saw that Xu Sanguan was still standing in the same place.

"Aiya!" she finally exclaimed, pointing at Xu Sanguan. "Why are you staring at me like that? And smiling that way too!"

Xu Sanguan crossed the street and stood in front of the girl bathed in crimson light. "Let me treat you to some steamed dumplings."

Xu Yulan said, "I don't know you."

"I'm Xu Sanguan. I work at the silk factory."

"I still don't know you."

"I know you," Xu Sanguan said. "You're the Fried Dough Queen."

Xu Yulan giggled. "So you know about that?"

"Everybody's heard of you. Let's go. I'll treat you to some steamed dumplings."

"I've already eaten today." Xu Yulan smiled. "Why don't you ask me tomorrow?"

The next day Xu Sanguan took Xu Yulan to the Victory Restaurant. They sat at a table by the window, at the very same table where he had eaten pork livers and drunk yellow rice wine with Ah Fang and Genlong. And just like Ah Fang and Genlong, he slapped the table for emphasis as he called out to the waiter, "I'll take the steamed dumplings."

He treated Xu Yulan to the steamed dumplings. When she had finished, she told him she could still eat a bowl of wontons.

Xu Sanguan slapped the table. "Bring a bowl of wontons."

That afternoon Xu Yulan happily ate a plate of preserved plums, but after she ate them, she said her mouth was salty, so she ate some candied fruit, but when she was finished with the fruit, she said she was thirsty, so Xu Sanguan bought her half a watermelon. They stood together on the wooden bridge as Xu Yulan happily devoured the watermelon. Then she happily proceeded to hiccup.

As her body swayed with hiccups, Xu Sanguan counted on his fingers how much money he had spent. "Steamed dumplings twenty-four *fen,* wontons nine *fen,* preserved plums ten *fen,* two bags of candied fruit comes to twenty-three *fen,* half a watermelon a pound four ounces all together seventeen *fen,* the grand total comes to eighty-three *fen.* When are we getting married?"

"Aiya!" Xu Yulan cried out in surprise. "What makes you think I'm going to marry you?"

"I spent eighty-three *fen,*" Xu Sanguan explained.

"You're the one who invited me," Xu Yulan hiccuped. "I thought it was free. You never said I had to marry you if I ate your things."

"What's wrong with getting married anyway?" Xu Sanguan said. "After we get married, I'll love you and take good care of you, and I'll buy you this much food almost every day."

"Aiya!" Xu Yulan cried out again. "I wouldn't eat that much even if I *were* married to you. If we got married, I'd pay for my own food. And if I had known it was going to be like this, I never would have eaten anything at all."

"What's done is done," Xu Sanguan comforted her. "Everything'll be fine once we get married."

"I can't marry you. I have a boyfriend. And my dad would never agree. My dad likes He Xiaoyong."

And so it was that Xu Sanguan, cradling a bottle of yellow rice wine and a carton of cigarettes in his arms, arrived at Xu Yulan's door and sat down at the table across from her father. After he slid the wine and the cigarettes across the tabletop, he began a lengthy discourse.

"Do you know who my dad was? My dad was a famous carpenter. My old man made furniture for all the best families in town. No one else could make a table as fine as his. When you ran your hand across the tabletop, the wood was as smooth and shiny as silk. You know who my mom was? My mom was Golden Flower. You know who she was? She was the most beautiful woman on the west side of town. People used to call her the Westside Beauty. After my dad died, she married a Nationalist company commander, then ran off with him. I'm my dad's only son. I don't know if Mom and that company commander ever had any kids or not. I'm called Xu Sanguan. My uncles' two sons are older than me, so I rank third in the Xu family. I work in the silk factory, and I'm two years older than He Xiaoyong, and I started working three years before he did, so I definitely have a lot more money than he does. If he wanted to marry Xu Yulan, he'd have to save up for a few more years, but I already have enough to get married now. I'm ready now; all I need is your permission."

Xu Sanguan added, "Xu Yulan is your only child. If she were to marry He Xiaoyong, your family line would be broken for good, because no matter whether the kids were boys or girls, their last name would still have to be He. And if she married me? My last name is the same as yours, Xu, so no matter if we had boys or girls, they would all be named Xu. Your family line will remain intact, and you'll always have descendants to burn incense for you at the family shrine. Look at it this way—if I marry Xu Yulan, it would be just the same as if I agreed to take on your family name instead of making Xu Yulan take mine."

When Xu Sanguan's speech reached this juncture, Xu Yulan's father broke into a wide grin. He looked across the table toward Xu Sanguan and, drumming a tattoo on the tabletop with his knuckles, said, "I'm going to accept this bottle of wine, and the carton of cigarettes. What you say is absolutely right. If my daughter marries He Xiaoyong, my family line will be broken forever. But if she marries you, both of our family's futures will be assured for generations to come."

When Xu Yulan was informed of her father's decision, she sat on the bed, tears falling from her eyes. Her father and Xu Sanguan stood to one side. Watching as she wiped the tears from her face, Xu Yulan's father said to Xu Sanguan, "Take a good hard look. This is what women are all about. When they're truly happy, all they can do is cry."

Xu Sanguan said, "I'm not so sure it's because she's happy."

At this point Xu Yulan interjected, "What am I supposed to say to He Xiaoyong?"

Her father replied, "Just tell him that you're getting married. And that the groom's name is Xu Sanguan, not He Xiaoyong."

"How can I tell him something like that? What am I supposed to do if he can't take the news and he starts bashing his head against the wall?"

"If he does himself in, then there's not a whole lot more you could say to him."

In her heart Xu Yulan didn't want to let He Xiaoyong go so easily. He was the man who liked to fold his arms around his elbows as he talked, the smiling man who came to her house almost every day, the man who would bring her dad a bottle of wine almost every other day and sit drinking and chuckling at the table to keep him company. And there had been a couple of occasions when, taking advantage of the fact that her dad had gone around the block to the public toilet, he suddenly pushed her behind the door and pressed her body against the wall with his own. Each time it happened, she had been so scared that her heart leaped wildly in her chest. The first time she didn't feel anything but the pumping of her heart. The second time she discovered his beard. His beard had slid back and forth across her face like a brush.

And the third time? This is what Xu Yulan asked herself as she lay in bed in the quiet of night, her heart pounding as she imagined her father standing up to leave, walking out the front door, and turning the corner toward the public toilet. He Xiaoyong had jumped to his feet, toppling the stool on which he had been sitting, and pressed her against the wall for a third time.

Xu Yulan made a date to meet He Xiaoyong on the old wooden bridge. It was already dark. As soon as Xu Yulan caught sight of He Xiaoyong, she broke into plaintive sobs. She told He Xiaoyong that someone named Xu Sanguan had treated her to steamed dumplings, preserved plums, candied fruit, and half a watermelon, and how, when it was all over, she had found herself obliged to marry him.

He Xiaoyong, noticing that someone was crossing the bridge, said in an anxious whisper, "Hey, hey! Don't cry. Stop crying. If someone sees you crying, what'll they think? Where would that leave me?"

Xu Yulan said, "Go and give Xu Sanguan his eighty-three *fen* back. Then I won't owe him anything."

He Xiaoyong said, "We're not even married yet, and you want me to pay back *your* debts?"

"He Xiaoyong, you have to take my family name when we get married. Otherwise my dad's going to give me to Xu Sanguan."

"What the hell are you talking about? Do you think a man like me would actually agree to take on someone else's name? And let our sons be named Xu? Impossible."

"Then I have to marry Xu Sanguan."

Xu Sanguan married Xu Yulan one month later. She wanted a bright red *cheongsam* to wear at the wedding; Xu Sanguan bought one for her. She wanted two cotton-padded jackets, one bright red, one bright green, to wear during the winter; Xu Sanguan bought her a bolt of red fabric and a bolt of green fabric so that she could sew them for herself in her spare time. She said they should have a clock, a mirror, a bed, a table, and stools, plus a basin and a chamber pot for the house; Xu Sanguan told her he had already taken care of everything.

Xu Yulan began to think that Xu Sanguan wasn't necessarily any worse than He Xiaoyong. Xu Sanguan was even a little bit more handsome than He Xiaoyong. He certainly had a lot more money in his pockets. And from the looks of things, he was a lot stronger too. So now when she saw Xu Sanguan, she would break into a smile. "I'm very capable, you know. I can sew, and I'm a good cook. You're really pretty lucky, getting a wife like me."

Xu Sanguan sat on a stool, nodding and smiling.

"I'm pretty and I can work hard. In the future, I'll personally tailor all the clothes you wear, and I'll take care of all the housework too. Except for the heavy chores—like buying the rice and buying coal—you have to do those. But I won't let you do anything else, I'll take very good care of you. You're really very lucky to have me, don't you think? What's wrong? Why aren't you nodding?"

"I am. I've been nodding all along."

"Oh, and another thing," Xu Yulan remembered. "Listen carefully. When I'm on vacation, I can't do a thing, not even soak the rice or wash the vegetables. I'll need to rest for those few days, so you'll have to take care of all the housework. Understand? What's wrong now? Why aren't you nodding?"

Xu Sanguan duly nodded. "What kind of vacation do you mean? How long does it take?"

"Aiya!" Xu Yulan exclaimed. "You don't even know what kind of vacation I mean?"

Xu Sanguan shook his head. "I don't know."

"My period."

"Period?"

"Women get a period every month. Don't you know that?"

"I think I've heard something like that."

"What I'm saying is when I get my period, I can't do any work, I can't let myself get tired out, I can't touch any cold water, because as soon as I touch cold water or I get tired out, my stomach hurts and I get a fever."

CHAPTER FOUR

The obstetrician said, “You’re already bawling like a baby, and the hard part is still to come.”

Xu Yulan lay supine on the delivery table, legs splayed in the air, arms fastened to each side of the bed as the doctor stood to one side urging her to “push harder!” Furious with pain, she cursed with each contraction. “Xu Sanguan! You son of a bitch . . . Where are you hiding? . . . You turtle’s egg! . . . You ought to be shot! . . . Oh, you’re happy all right! . . . The pain is *killing* me, and you’re ecstatic! . . . Xu Sanguan, where are you? . . . Come help me push! . . . I can’t do it anymore . . . Get in here, Xu Sanguan! . . . Doctor, has the baby come out yet?”

“Push harder,” the doctor said. “You have a long way to go.”

“Oh mother! . . . Xu Sanguan . . . it’s all your fault . . . Men are all animals! . . . Only out for themselves . . . They have their fun and leave us with the dirty work . . . A woman’s fate is cruel . . . It hurts! . . . It’s killing me! . . . I’ve carried this thing around for nine months already . . . It hurts! . . . Where are you? . . . Xu Sanguan! . . . Doctor, has the baby come out yet?"

"Push harder," the doctor said. "The head's out."

"The head is out . . . I'm pushing, I'm pushing . . . I can't do it anymore . . . Xu Sanguan, help me! . . . Xu Sanguan, I'm going to die . . . I'm dying . . ."

THE OBSTETRICIAN SAID, "You're screaming and carrying on like it was the first time."

Xu Yulan was covered with sweat, gasping for air, shouting between each moan. "Aiya, aiya . . . It hurts . . . hurts! . . . Xu Sanguan . . . You've done it to me again . . . Aiya, aiya . . . I hate you! . . . It hurts . . . hurts! . . . If I make it through this . . . aiya . . . I'll never let you sleep with me again . . . even if it kills me! . . . Ouch . . . You think that's funny? . . . Even if you get down on your hands and knees and beg me! . . . I still won't let you do it . . . I won't even let you sleep . . . aiya . . . in the same bed! . . . aiya, aiya . . . It hurts . . . I'm pushing . . . harder."

THE OBSTETRICIAN SAID, "Harder, push harder."

Xu Yulan pushed as hard as she could, until her back arched up off the table, and she shouted, "Xu Sanguan! You con artist! You turtle's egg! You ought to be shot! . . . Xu Sanguan . . . black-hearted son of a bitch . . . I hope you get pockmarks all over your head!"

"Why are you screaming?" the nurse said. "It's all over."

"The baby's come out?" Xu Yulan propped herself up. "So soon?"

IN FIVE YEARS' TIME Xu Yulan gave birth to three sons. Xu Sanguan called his sons Yile (First Joy), Erle (Second Joy), and Sanle (Third Joy).

One day when Sanle was one year and three months old, Xu Yulan grabbed hold of Xu Sanguan's ear and asked, "When I was giving birth, you were standing outside and enjoying a good laugh, right?"

"I didn't laugh," Xu Sanguan said. "I was just chuckling, that's all. I never laughed aloud."

"Aiya!" Xu Yulan called out. "That's why you called the kids Yile, Erle, and Sanle. Because each of the three times I went through all that pain, you were outside enjoying yourself."

CHAPTER FIVE

People in town who knew Xu Sanguan noticed that Erle had Xu Sanguan's nose, and Sanle had Xu Sanguan's eyes, but Yile's face didn't look like Xu Sanguan's at all. They began to discuss their suspicions in private, saying among themselves that Yile didn't look like Xu Sanguan at all, that Yile's mouth looked a lot like Xu Yulan's mouth, but the rest of his face didn't look like hers either. They said to themselves, it seems that Xu Yulan is the child's mother, but is Xu Sanguan really his father? Who planted the seed? Could it have been He Xiaoyong? The shape of Yile's eyes, his nose, even those big ears of his made him look more and more like He Xiaoyong every day.

When these rumors reached Xu Sanguan's ears, he called Yile before him and began to carefully inspect his face. Yile was only nine years old at the time. After Xu Sanguan looked him over for several minutes, he was still unable to make up his mind, so he went to fetch the family mirror.

It was the mirror he had bought when they got married. Xu

Yulan had always kept it on the windowsill, and when she awoke in the morning, she would stand by the window, glance at the trees outside, and then gaze at herself in the mirror as she combed her hair and rubbed a layer of intensely fragrant Snowflower cream over her face. Later Yile had gotten taller, tall enough that he could reach up and grab the mirror on the sill. The mirror was still sitting on the sill when Sanle grew tall enough to reach up and knock it over. The biggest fragment was a triangle the size of an egg. Xu Yulan had picked this triangular piece off the floor and propped it right back on the windowsill.

Xu Sanguan held the triangular shard of mirror in his hand. He held it in front of his eyes and looked at himself. Then he looked at Yile's eyes. They didn't seem too different from his own. He held the mirror up to his own nose. Then he looked at Yile's nose. They didn't seem all that different either. Xu Sanguan thought to himself, *They say he doesn't look like me, but I think he looks a little like me.*

Yile watched his father staring woodenly toward him. "Dad, you keep looking at yourself and then looking at me. What are you looking at?"

Xu Sanguan said, "I'm trying to see if you look like me or not."

"I heard some people saying," Yile reported, "that I look like someone named He Xiaoyong who works at the machine tools factory."

Xu Sanguan said, "Yile, go get Erle and Sanle for me."

Xu Sanguan's three sons came inside. He asked them to sit in a row on the bed, then sat down on a stool opposite them. He scrutinized Yile's, Erle's, and Sanle's features in turn. This first inspection being inconclusive, he went back down the line, inspecting Sanle, Erle, and finally Yile.

The three brothers giggled, and when Xu Sanguan saw them laughing, he realized that they looked more alike that way. "Keep laughing," he said as his own body started to sway, "laugh as hard as you can."

When his sons saw the funny way he was rocking back and forth on the stool, they burst into loud guffaws. Xu Sanguan began to laugh along with them. "The more you kids laugh, the more you look alike."

Xu Sanguan said to himself, *They say Yile doesn't look like me, but Yile looks just like Erle and Sanle. If he can't look like me, at least he looks like his brothers. No one ever said Erle and Sanle don't look like my sons. Doesn't matter if Yile doesn't look like me, as long as he looks like his little brothers.*

Xu Sanguan said to his sons, "Yile has heard of He Xiaoyong over at the machine tools factory. How about you, Erle? Sanle? Don't worry about it if you haven't. He's the one Yile was talking about, lives on Old Post Office Lane on the west side, always wears a duck's bill cap. Now listen closely. His name is He Xiaoyong. Got it? Let me hear Erle and Sanle say it back to me. . . . Okay, good. Now listen to me again. He Xiaoyong is a bad man. Understand? Why is he a bad man? Let me tell you. A long time ago, before any of you were around, before your mother gave birth to you, He Xiaoyong was always hanging around your grandpa's place. And what was he doing there? He was drinking with your grandpa because back then your mom wasn't married to me yet. He'd go there every day, and every other day he'd bring a bottle of wine for your grandpa. But later on, after your mom had married me, he kept on going there almost every day. But he never brought any more wine for your grandpa. Instead, he ended up drinking more than ten bottles of your grandpa's wine. So one day, when your grandpa saw He Xiaoyong coming, he stood up and told him that he had stopped drinking. After that He Xiaoyong never dared to show his face at your grandpa's again."

XU SANGUAN heard the rumors over and over again. He thought to himself, *These people keep talking and talking, and once they get started, it never stops. Could it actually be true?* He approached Xu Yulan and asked, "Have you heard what they're saying?"

Xu Yulan knew exactly what he was talking about. She set down the clothes she had been washing, lifted her apron to wipe the soap suds from her hands, and stepped out the front door. Finally she sat squarely down on the doorstep and began to wail, "What did I do in my past life to deserve this?"

The sound of Xu Yulan weeping on the doorstep brought her sons running home. They gathered around her, looking on with fright as their mother's cries grew louder and louder.

Xu Yulan wiped a handful of tears from her face and flicked them down to the ground as if she had just wiped her nose. Then she rocked back and forth as she wailed, "What did I do in my past life to deserve this? They say my three sons have two different fathers. How can that be? I'm not a widow, I've only been married one time, and I've never fooled around with someone else's man. What did I do to deserve this? It's clear they just have one dad, but people keep saying there're two."

When Xu Sanguan realized Xu Yulan had gone to the doorstep to cry, his ears buzzed with anger and he shouted at her, "Get back in here! Don't sit on the doorstep. What the hell are you crying about? What are you saying? You're hopeless! What's the use of crying about it? What's the use of screaming like that? Get back inside!"

One by one their neighbors gathered around the doorstep. "Xu Yulan, why are you crying? Not enough grain coupons again? Has Xu Sanguan been bullying you?" "Hey, Xu Sanguan! Where's Xu Sanguan?" "I thought I heard him say something just a second ago." "Xu Yulan, what are you crying about? Did you lose something?" "You owe someone money?" "Did something happen to one of the boys?"

Erle said, "You've got it all wrong. My mom's crying because Yile looks like He Xiaoyong."

They said, "Oh, so that's what it's all about."

Yile said, "Erle, go back inside. Don't stand out here."

Erle said, "I'm not going anywhere."

Sanle said, "I'm not going either."

Yile said, "Mom, don't cry. Go on inside."

Xu Sanguan stood inside the door gnashing his teeth in frustration. *This woman,* he was thinking to himself, *is a stupid fool. You're not supposed to air your dirty laundry, and here she is sitting on the doorstep crying for the whole world to hear, and there's no telling what kind of idiocy she'll come up with next.* Xu Sanguan gnashed his teeth as he listened to Xu Yulan's tearful litany.

"What did I do in my past life to deserve this? I'm not a widow, I've never remarried, and I've never fooled around with another man. I've given birth to three sons. What did I do to deserve this? Why did I have to meet He Xiaoyong? Oh, *he's* just fine, it's not a problem for him, but what am I supposed to do? Yile looks more and more like him. There was only that one time, and I never let him do it again, but still Yile looks more and more like him."

What? Just that one time? Xu Sanguan's blood rushed to his head, and he kicked open the bedroom door and shouted to Xu Yulan on the doorstep, "Get the fuck back in here!"

Xu Sanguan's shout scared the living daylights out of everyone standing around outside, and Xu Yulan suddenly stopped crying and yelling and turned her head to look inside at Xu Sanguan.

Xu Sanguan advanced to the doorway and dragged Xu Yulan inside, shouting toward the neighbors as he turned, "Get out of here!" As he tried to shut the door, his sons clamored to come inside, so he shouted to them, "Get out of here!"

He shut the door, dragged Xu Yulan to the bedroom, closed the bedroom door, knocked her down onto the bed with a slap across the face, and screamed, "You let He Xiaoyong sleep with you?"

Xu Yulan, sobbing, rubbed her face with her hand.

Xu Sanguan screamed once again. "Tell me!"

Xu Yulan sobbed. "He slept with me."

"How many times?"

"Just once."

Xu Sanguan pulled Xu Yulan up from the bed and slapped her once again across the face. "You whore! I thought you said you've never fooled around with another man!"

"I've never fooled around with another man," Xu Yulan said. "He Xiaoyong did it. He pressed me up against the wall, then he dragged me into bed—"

"I've heard enough!" Xu Sanguan shouted, but immediately thought better of it. "So why didn't you push him away, bite him, kick him?"

"I pushed him, and I kicked him," Xu Yulan said. "He pressed me against the wall, and then he grabbed my tits—"

"That's enough!"

As he shouted, he slapped her again, first to the right and then to the left. But when he was finished slapping her, he still wanted to know more.

"So after he grabbed your tits, you just let him do it?"

Xu Yulan held her face in her hands and covered her eyes.

"Tell me!"

"I can't." Xu Yulan shook her head. "As soon as I say anything, you'll slap me again. You hit me so hard I can't see, and my teeth hurt, and my face feels like it's on fire."

"Tell me! After he grabbed your tits?"

"After he grabbed my tits, I didn't have any strength left in my body."

"So you got into bed with him?"

"I was completely worn out. He carried me over to the bed—"

"Enough!" As he shouted, he aimed a kick at her thigh. Xu Yulan was left speechless with pain. Xu Sanguan said, "Was it at our house? On our bed?"

After a moment Xu Yulan replied, "It was at my dad's place."

Xu Sanguan suddenly felt tired. He sat down on a stool and was overcome by sadness. "Nine years. I was happy for nine years, but Yile isn't really my son. I was happy for no reason. I've wasted nine years raising that boy, and it turns out that after all he really belongs to someone else."

Something else occurred to Xu Sanguan, so he sprang up from the stool and shouted, "He Xiaoyong was your first?"

"No," Xu Yulan said. "You were the first man I ever slept with."

"No, I remember now. He Xiaoyong must have been your first. I wanted to turn on the lamp, but you wouldn't let me. Now I know it was because you were afraid I'd find out that you'd already slept with He Xiaoyong."

"I didn't let you turn on the lamp," Xu Yulan cried, "because I was too embarrassed."

"He Xiaoyong must have been first. If he wasn't first, why doesn't Erle look like him? Why doesn't Sanle look like him? No, it's Yile who looks like that bastard, and he was our first child. My woman did it for the very first time with another man. And that's why my first son belongs to someone else. How can I go on living? I'm ruined. I'll never be able to hold up my head again."

"Xu Sanguan, think about it," Xu Yulan said. "Didn't you see some blood on our first night?"

"So what if I did? You whore. You were 'on vacation' that day."

"Oh, for the love of heaven."

CHAPTER SIX

Xu Sanguan sat back in a rattan chair, his feet resting on a stool.

Xu Yulan approached him and said, "Xu Sanguan, we're running out of rice. There's just enough for tonight. Here are the grain coupons, the money, and the rice sack. Go down to the store and buy some rice."

Xu Sanguan said, "I'm not going to buy the rice. I'm not going to do anything around here anymore. As soon as I come home, all I'm going to do is sit back and enjoy myself. You know what that means? I'm going to sit in this chair, with my feet up on the stool, just like I'm doing now. You know why I'm going to sit back and enjoy myself? To punish you. You made a serious mistake. You slept with that bastard He Xiaoyong behind my back. What's even worse is that he knocked you up with Yile. It makes me angry just to think about it. You want me to go buy you rice? Dream on."

Xu Yulan said, "I can't lift one hundred pounds of rice by myself."

Xu Sanguan said, "Then get fifty."

"I can't handle fifty pounds either."

"Try twenty-five."

XU YULAN said, "Xu Sanguan, I'm going to wash the sheets. Will you help me move the trunk? I can't move it by myself."

Xu Sanguan said, "Nothing doing. I'm sitting back in my chair and enjoying myself."

XU YULAN said, "Xu Sanguan, time to eat."

Xu Sanguan replied, "Bring me my bowl. I'll sit in my chair and eat."

XU YULAN asked, "Xu Sanguan, are you done enjoying yourself yet? I can't keep my eyes open much longer, so when you're finished enjoying yourself, get your ass out of that chair and come to bed."

Xu Sanguan said, "I'll be right there."

CHAPTER SEVEN

One good thing about working at the silk factory was that Xu Sanguan was given a new pair of white work gloves every month. When the women on the factory floor saw them, they would always ask with envy in their voices, "Xu Sanguan, how many more years until you decide to switch to a new pair of gloves?"

Xu Sanguan lifted up his hands to show them his tattered old gloves. When he waved his hands, loose threads swung back and forth like so many pendulums from the places where they'd already worn through. "I've worn this pair for three years now."

They said, "You call those things gloves? We can see your fingers sticking out from all the way across the factory floor."

Xu Sanguan said, "They're new the first year, and old for the next two years. After two years I'll mend them. That way I'll be able to use this pair for at least three more years."

They said, "Xu Sanguan, if you wear the same pair of gloves for six years and the factory gives you a new pair every month, what does that get you? Six years of gloves comes to seventy-two pairs. What are you going to do with the seventy-one pairs that you *don't* wear? What's the point of hoarding that many gloves? Why don't you give some of them to us? We only get a new pair every six months."

Xu Sanguan carefully folded his new gloves, placed them in his pocket, and smilingly made his way home. When he arrived, he took the gloves from his pocket and presented them to Xu Yulan. Xu Yulan took them and immediately walked over to the window, lifting the gloves to the light to see if they were sewn of coarse or fine cotton thread.

"Aiya!"

Her exclamations always scared Xu Sanguan into thinking she had discovered that this month's gloves were moth-eaten.

"They're the good kind."

There were two days every month when Xu Yulan would stick out her hands and say to Xu Sanguan as he got home from work, "Hand it over." The first day was payday and the other was when the factory distributed new gloves.

Xu Yulan stored the gloves at the bottom of the trunk. When she saved up four pairs of gloves, she could use them to make a sweater for Sanle. With six pairs she could make one for Erle. Once she had eight or nine, she could sew a sweater for Yile.

But it would take more than twenty pairs to make Xu Sanguan a new sweater, which gave her pause. She would often say to Xu Sanguan, "Your arms are getting bigger, there's more meat around your waist, and you're putting a little weight on your stomach. Now even twenty pairs of gloves won't be enough."

Xu Sanguan said, "Then why don't you just make something for yourself?"

Xu Yulan said, "I'll wait and see."

Xu Yulan didn't sew anything for herself until she had collected seventeen or eighteen pairs of the finer quality gloves. And Xu Sanguan only brought home three or four pairs of the fine cotton gloves every year. After nine years of marriage she decided to use seven years of gloves to make herself a good sweater.

Xu Yulan finished sewing the sweater just as spring came and the weather began to warm. She washed her hair by the well, sat on the doorstep holding the as-yet-unbroken mirror in her hand, and issued directions to Xu Sanguan as he stood behind her, trimming her hair. When he was finished, she sat in the sun to dry her hair. Then she smeared a thick layer of Snowflower cream across her face and, redolent with its fragrance, donned her newly crocheted sweater. Finally, she pulled her only silk scarf from out of the trunk, tied it around her neck, and stepped out the door.

Before she took another step, she turned and addressed Xu Sanguan. "You sift and wash the rice, okay? You're cooking. I'm on vacation today. No housework for me today. I'm going out for a walk now."

Xu Sanguan said, "What? You had your 'vacation' just last week! How come you're on vacation again today?"

"I'm not having my period. Can't you see I'm wearing my new sweater?"

She wore the sweater for two years. She washed it five times and mended it once, using the fine thread of one pair of the better quality gloves to make a patch. Xu Yulan wanted Xu Sanguan to bring more of the better gloves home from the factory, because that way "I can have a new sweater."

Whenever Xu Yulan was deciding whether to use up another glove, she would stick her head out the window to see if the stars were shining. When she saw the moon shining brightly in the night sky and the stars shimmering next to it, she knew the sun would be bright the next day and she could go ahead and unravel a glove.

Unraveling a glove was a job for two people. First, she needed to find the ends of the thread. Once she had pulled them out, it was merely a question of continuing to unravel the thread while at the same time spooling the cotton around two outstretched arms in order to pull it taut. The thread from the just-unraveled gloves was usually too crooked for sewing, so she would have to soak it in water for two or three hours. After removing the thread from the water, she would suspend it from a bamboo pole to dry in the sun, letting the weight of the water pull the cotton threads straight.

Xu Yulan was about to unravel a glove. In need of two outstretched arms, she called, "Yile, Yile!"

Yile ran into the house from outside. "Did you call me, Mom?"

Xu Yulan said, "Yile, help me unravel this glove."

Yile shook his head. "I don't want to."

When he had gone, Xu Yulan called, "Erle, Erle!"

When Erle came home and saw that she wanted him to help her unravel a glove, he sat happily down on the stool and immediately stuck out his arms so that she could spool the thread around them.

Sanle came over to join them, standing next to Erle and sticking out his arms in imitation of his big brother. When Xu Yulan saw him trying to usurp his big brother's role, she said, "Sanle, get out of here. Your hands are covered with snot."

Whenever Xu Yulan and Erle sat together, they would always talk for what seemed like forever. She was a thirty-year-old woman, and he an eight-year-old boy, but their conversations sounded either like the gossip exchanged by a pair of thirty-year-old women, or the banter of two eight-year-old boys. They would talk at every opportunity—as they ate, before they went to sleep, as they walked together down the street—and their conversations became more and more animated as they continued.

Xu Yulan might say, "I saw the Zhangs' daughter the other day. The Zhangs who live on the south side. That girl's getting prettier and prettier."

Erle said, "Do you mean the Zhang girl whose braids come down to her rear end?"

Xu Yulan said, "That's the one. She's the girl who gave you a handful of watermelon seeds that time. Don't you think she's getting better looking all the time?"

Erle said, "I heard some people calling her Big Boobs Zhang."

Xu Yulan said, "I saw Lin Fenfang over at the silk factory wearing some white sneakers over red nylon socks. I've seen red nylon socks before, Lin Pingping around the corner wore them a few days back. But it was first time I've ever seen women's sneakers that come in white."

Erle said, "I've seen those before. There was a pair on display at the counter in the department store."

Xu Yulan said, "I've seen plenty of men's sneakers in white. Lin Pingping's brother has a pair. And Wang Defu on our street."

Erle said, "That lady who always goes over to Wang Defu's house wears white sneakers too . . ."

Xu Yulan said. Erle said. And so on.

But Yile and Xu Yulan had very little to say to each other. Yile never wanted to hang around Xu Yulan or do anything with her. If Xu Yulan was going to buy vegetables at the market, she would call to him, "Yile, help me carry the shopping basket."

Yile would say, "I don't want to."

"Yile, help me thread this needle."

"I don't want to."

"Yile, fold the laundry."

"I don't want to."

"Yile . . ."

"I don't want to."

Then Xu Yulan's temper flared, and she would shout, "What *do* you want to do?"

Xu Sanguan paced back and forth across the room, looking up at the rays of sunlight filtering down into the house through the ceiling. Then he said, "I'm going up on the roof to fix the tiles. Otherwise, when the rainy season comes and it's pouring outside, it'll be drizzling in here too."

Yile quickly said to Xu Sanguan, "Dad, let me go borrow a ladder."

Xu Sanguan said, "You're still too little to carry a ladder."

"Dad, will you let me ask for it? Then you can carry it home yourself."

When Xu Sanguan got the ladder home and was about to climb up to the roof, Yile said, "Dad, I'll hold the ladder steady for you as you climb up."

Xu Sanguan mounted the roof, the tiles below squeaking and straining under his weight. As soon as he reached the roof, Yile was off like a shot. He ran to get Xu Sanguan's teapot and set it down next to the bottom of the ladder. Then he ran to get a washbasin, filled it with water, and folded a washcloth neatly over the rim.

Finally, teapot in hand, he shouted up to the roof, "Dad, come down and take a break. I brought you some tea."

Xu Sanguan, standing on the roof, replied, "I don't want any tea. I just got up here."

Yile wrung out the towel, draped it over his arm, and called up to the roof, "Dad, come down and take a break. I brought you a washcloth."

Xu Sanguan, squatting atop the roof tiles, replied, "I'm not sweaty."

Sanle wobbled toward them. As soon as Yile saw him coming, he waved him off. "Sanle, go away. This is none of your business."

But Sanle didn't want to leave. He walked under the ladder and held it steady.

Yile said, "We don't need you to hold the ladder now."

So Sanle sat down on the first rung of the ladder.

Yile, at his wit's end, looked up and shouted, "Dad, Sanle won't go away."

Xu Sanguan shouted at Sanle from the rooftop, "Sanle, go away. What if one of these tiles were to fall and hit your head?"

Yile often said to Xu Sanguan, "Dad, I don't like to be with mom and the rest of them. All they do is go on and on about which girls are pretty and who has the nicest clothes. I like to spend time with the men. Men talk about more interesting stuff."

Xu Sanguan, wooden bucket in hand, went to the well to get water. The rope attached to the handle of the bucket had been soaked a hundred times and dried in the sun just as many times. This time, when Xu Sanguan attempted to draw the bucket out of the well, all that emerged was a piece of broken rope. The bucket had been swallowed up by the water and sunk to the bottom of the well.

Xu Sanguan went home and fetched a long bamboo pole that they usually used for hanging the wash out to dry. Then he brought a stool over to the side of the well, sat down, and working with a pair of pliers, fashioned a slender hook out of a piece of wire. With another piece of wire, he fastened the hook to the end of the pole.

When Yile saw him, he walked over and asked, "Dad, did the bucket fall into the well again?"

Xu Sanguan nodded. "Help me make a knot."

Yile sat down on the ground next to him and held the long pole steady while Xu Sanguan fastened the hook onto its tip. Then Yile took one end of the pole over his shoulder and Xu Sanguan took the other end. Father and son carried the pole over to the well.

Usually it only took Xu Sanguan less than an hour or so to find the bucket. He would reach down into the well with the pole and feel around the bottom. After thirty minutes or an hour he was able to hook the handle of the wooden bucket and bring it back up to the surface.

But this time he grappled with the pole for almost an hour and a half, all to no avail. Wiping the sweat from his brow, he said, "It's not on top, and it isn't to the left or the right. It just seems like it's nowhere to be found. Must be that it landed handle side down. This time it's bad. This time we're in real trouble." He slid the pole from out of the water and laid it across the top of the well, scratching his head in bewilderment.

Yile bent over the edge of the well and gazed down at the water for a moment. Then he said, "Dad, look how hot and sweaty I am."

Xu Sanguan grunted absently.

"Hey, Dad, you still remember the time I put my face in the washbasin and held my breath? I was under water for one minute and twenty-three seconds."

Xu Sanguan said, "If the handle's on the bottom, what the hell are we going to do?"

Yile said, "Dad, the well's too deep. I'm too scared to jump. Dad, the well's too deep, and I'm scared I wouldn't be able to get back out. Dad, get some rope to tie to my waist. Let me down little by little, and then I'll dive in. I can dive for one minute and twenty-three seconds. I'll find the bucket, and then you can pull me up."

Xu Sanguan, slowly coming to the realization that Yile's plan might actually work, ran home to grab a length of brand-new rope. He was afraid that if he fastened him with a piece of old rope, Yile might disappear down the well just like the bucket. That would really be the end.

Xu Sanguan wound the two ends of the rope around Yile's thighs and then fastened the rope to his own belt. Just as he began to let Yile slide slowly down into the well, Sanle came wobbling over toward them. As soon as he approached, Xu Sanguan warned him, "Sanle, go away! You might fall down the well."

Sanle stood quietly to one side as the rope, and Yile along with it, slid deeper and deeper into the well. Soon the rope went taut and tugged sharply at Xu Sanguan's belt.

Xu Sanguan began to slowly and softly count the seconds to himself as Sanle, mouth agape, looked on. "Ten seconds . . . twenty seconds . . . thirty seconds . . . forty seconds . . ." Xu Sanguan paused to take a deep breath and continued, "Fifty seconds . . . sixty seconds . . . one minute and ten seconds . . ."

There was a sudden sharp tug on his belt that dragged Xu

Sanguan a step closer to the mouth of the well. He braced his feet against the stone steps and began to pull with all his might on the rope. Sanle took up the count where his father had left off, sounding out the seconds as Xu Sanguan panted with the effort of pulling the rope up from the depths: "One minute and eleven seconds . . . one minute and fifteen seconds . . . one minute and twenty seconds . . ." Xu Sanguan heard what sounded like the distant echo of a heavy stone falling into the water, and then a gasp and a splutter as Yile emerged above the surface of the water.

Dripping wet, he clambered the last few steps out of the well and shouted through pale blue lips, "Dad, I found the bucket! Dad, I almost couldn't hold my breath long enough! Dad, the bucket was caught under a ledge! Dad, how long was I down in the well?"

Sanle ran eagerly forward to announce the total but was quickly and dismissively waved away by Xu Sanguan, who was stroking the water from Yile's forehead with his other hand.

"Sanle, didn't I already tell you to get out of here?"

XU SANGUAN said things like that to "the little brat" all the time.

So did Xu Yulan.

Even Yile and Erle told him to go away sometimes.

And when they told him to go away, he really would go away, walking through the streets, salivating as he stood for what seemed like hours outside the candy shop, squatting alone by the river looking at the little fish and the little shrimps in the shallows, pasting himself against electrical poles to listen to the sound of the electricity rushing across the wires above, falling asleep in somebody else's house with his arms wrapped around his knees. He would always walk and walk until he didn't know where he was, then ask for directions until he found his way home.

Xu Sanguan always said to Xu Yulan, "Yile's like me and Erle takes after you. But I have no idea who that little brat takes after."

When Xu Sanguan said such things, what he really meant was that of the three children, he liked Yile best of all. But it was also Yile who had become someone else's son. Sometimes Xu Sanguan would sit back in the rattan chair thinking about Yile and start to cry.

As Xu Sanguan cried, Sanle approached, and seeing his father cry, he too burst into tears without knowing why. His father's sadness was catching, like a yawn.

When Xu Sanguan discovered that someone was crying even more brokenheartedly than himself, he turned his head to discover "the little brat" standing by his side. He would dismiss him with a wave of his hand. "Sanle, go away."

Sanle could only turn and leave. By this time Sanle was already seven years old. He carried a little slingshot in one hand, and his pockets were stuffed full of little stones. He would pace back and forth, and when he caught sight of a magpie moving along the eaves of a house or stirring among some tree branches, he would aim the slingshot and fire. Even if he didn't succeed in actually hitting the bird, he could usually send it packing, twittering as it flew into the distance. Then he would shout, "Come back, you! Come back!"

Sanle's slingshot was often aimed at street lamps, at cats, chickens, and ducks. He would aim for clothes hanging from bamboo poles to dry, at bundles of dried fish hanging from the eaves of houses, at bottles, baskets, and vegetables floating in the river. One time he even hit another boy on the head with a rock.

The boy was about the same age as Sanle himself. He was walking down the street when the rock hit his head. At first his body rocked back and forth with the unexpectedness of the blow. Then he reached out his hand to rub the spot that had been hit. Finally, he burst into tears. Still crying, he turned to see Sanle holding the slingshot and grinning in his direction. He walked over toward Sanle and extended one arm to slap him. Rather than landing on Sanle's face, the slap somehow landed on the back of his head. Sanle, in turn, reached out and slapped the other boy. Then they traded blows, the sound of their slaps ringing out like an ovation. But the sound of their crying was even louder, because by now Sanle too was sobbing with anger and pain.

The other boy said, "I'm gonna go get my brother. I have two big brothers. My brothers will beat you up."

Sanle said, "So what? I have two big brothers too. My brothers'll beat up your brothers."

The two children stopped slapping each other and negotiated. They agreed that they would each fetch their brothers and meet at the same place an hour later.

When Sanle arrived home, he saw Erle sitting drowsily inside. "Erle, I had a fight with another kid. Come out and help me."

Erle asked, "Who was it?"

Sanle said, "I don't know his name."

Erle asked, "How big is he?"

Sanle said, "The same as me."

As soon as Erle learned that the kid was only as big as his little brother, he slapped the table and shouted, "Goddamn! Trying to bully my little brother, is he? I'll show him a thing or two."

By the time Sanle led Erle back to the street where the slapping match had taken place, the other boy had arrived with his own brother in tow. The other boy was taller than Erle by a head.

Chills ran down Erle's spine, and he turned and said to Sanle, "Stand behind me, and don't say a word."

When the other boy's big brother saw Erle and Sanle approach, he gestured at them with a dismissive air of nonchalance. "Is that them?" Then he approached, arms swinging expectantly back and forth, glaring balefully in Erle's direction. "Which one of you hit my brother?"

Erle spread out his hands, palms up, and smiled placatingly. "It wasn't me." As he spoke, he lifted his index finger over his shoulder to point at Sanle standing behind him. "It was my little brother who did it."

"Then I'll beat up your little brother."

"Let's be reasonable and talk this thing out," Erle said to the other boy's brother. "If we can't work things out, then I won't stand in your way, even if you have to hit him."

"So what if you did stand in the way?" He shoved Erle, sending him reeling several yards back. "I *want* you to stand in the way. I'm dying to beat the shit out of both of you."

"I'm definitely not going to get involved." Erle waved his hands for emphasis. "I'm the kind of person who likes to talk things out, to be reasonable."

"Talk all you goddamn want." He took a step forward and punched Erle in the nose. "First I'll beat the shit out of you, and then I'll beat the shit out of your little brother."

Erle began to retreat, one step at a time, asking the smaller child as he went, "Who is this guy to you? What's his problem? Why's he so unreasonable?"

"He's my oldest brother," the child replied, not without a certain elation. "And I have another big brother too."

As soon as Erle heard this, he shouted, "Hold everything." He pointed at the two younger children. "This is no fair. My little brother called his second oldest brother, but your little brother went and got his oldest brother. That's not fair. If you had any guts, you'd let my little brother go get our oldest brother too. You think you have the guts to take on our big brother?"

The other boy waved his hand through the air. "I'm not scared of anyone or anything. Go get your big brother then. I'll beat the shit out of all three of you."

Erle and Sanle ran home to fetch Yile. Yile came but was quick to realize as he arrived on the scene that the other boy was almost half a head taller than himself. He said to Erle and Sanle, "I want to take a piss first."

As he spoke, he turned and walked down a lane. When he emerged, his hands were held behind his back. In his hands he held a sharp triangular rock. He approached the bigger boy with his eyes fixed firmly to the ground.

"*This* is your big brother? Too scared to even look at me?"

Yile looked up long enough to determine just where the bigger boy's head was located. Then he lifted the rock and brought it down on top of it. The bigger boy cried out once. Yile brought the rock down on his head three more times. The bigger boy tumbled to the ground, blood trickling onto the pavement around his head.

When Yile was sure the boy wouldn't be able to get up again, he threw away the rock, wiped the dirt from his hands, and gestured toward his silent and frightened little brothers.

"Let's go home."

CHAPTER EIGHT

People said, "Blacksmith Fang's son was beaten so badly by Xu Sanguan's son that he broke his head right open. I heard his skull is cracked open, like a watermelon that's been dropped on the ground and broken into bits and pieces." "I heard he used a cleaver, cut almost an inch into the skull, so you could see his brains oozing out. The nurse at the hospital said his brains looked like stewed tofu, and steam was coming out from between the cracks in his head." "Dr. Chen had to sew up his head with almost a hundred stitches." "How can you sew through something as hard as a skull?" "I don't know how he did it." "He used steel needles, they're about so thick, a few times thicker than the ones you use to stitch the soles of your shoes." "Even those wouldn't work. I heard he had to use a little hammer to hammer in the steel needles." "But first you have to pull out all his hair." "What do you mean, pull out his hair? How do you do that?" "I mean shave his head clean. It's not as easy as pulling up a patch of weeds, with the skull all broken to pieces like that. If you pulled too hard, pieces of his skull might come away along with the hair." "That's called 'clearing the area.' Before an operation you have to clear away all the hair. When I had my appendix removed last year, they shaved off all my pubic hair."

XU SANGUAN said to Xu Yulan, "Have you heard what people are saying?"

PEOPLE SAID, "Dr. Chen saved Blacksmith Fang's son's life. He was operating on him for over ten hours." "Blacksmith Fang's son's head is completely wrapped in gauze bandages, all you can see are his eyes, his nose, and a little bit of his mouth." "After the kid got out of the operation he didn't move for almost twenty hours. Wasn't till yesterday morning that he finally opened his eyes." "Blacksmith Fang's son can eat a little gruel now, but as soon as he takes a sip, he brings it all up again. Vomits everything. He even threw up some of his own shit."

XU SANGUAN said to Xu Yulan, "Have you heard what people are saying?"

PEOPLE SAID, "As long as he's in the hospital, Blacksmith Fang's son is going to need medicine, and shots, and an IV bottle too. It costs a fortune. Who's going to pay for all that? Xu Sanguan? Or He Xiaoyong? Anyway, Xu Yulan's the one who's really on the hook, because no matter who the dad might be, we all know that she's his mom." "Is Xu Sanguan going to pay? He's been going around saying that He Xiaoyong should take Yile back." "He Xiaoyong really should pay. After all, Xu Sanguan has raised his son for nine years now for nothing." "Xu Sanguan's slept with Yile's mom for nine years for nothing too. If I'd spent nine years with a woman for nothing and her son got himself in trouble, I sure would stand to one side." "You're right there." "What's so right about that? Spending nine years with a woman as pretty as Xu Yulan doesn't seem so bad to me. If her son got into trouble, I think it would only be natural to do what you can to help out. And Xu Sanguan spent good money to get her for his own. So no matter what you think, they're still a married couple. That's hardly what you could call 'spending nine years together for nothing.'" "You think Xu Sanguan will pay up?" "No way." "No way." "Xu Sanguan's been a cuckold for nine years now. But he didn't know what was going on before. I guess it wouldn't matter if he was still in the dark. But now that he knows, wouldn't paying up just add insult to his injury?"

XU SANGUAN said to Xu Yulan, "Have you heard what people are saying? Even if you haven't heard all of it, you must have heard some. Blacksmith Fang has already come by a few times to ask you to bring the money to the hospital. So tell me, how much have you and He Xiaoyong been able to come up with? What are you crying about? What's the use of crying? Don't come begging to me. If it had been Erle or Sanle who'd gotten into trouble, I'd do everything in my power. Hell, I would willingly wipe Blacksmith Fang's ass for him. But Yile isn't my son, I raised him for nine years, and for what? All for nothing. How much of my own money have I spent on him? I've been kind enough not to demand that He Xiaoyong pay me for what he owes. Haven't you heard what they're saying? They're saying that I'm a good man, that I'm generous, that if it was someone else in my position, He Xiaoyong would already have been beaten within an inch of his life, not once but several times over. So don't ask me to talk it over, because this has nothing whatsoever to do with me. This is a He family affair. Haven't you heard what they're saying? Wouldn't paying up just add insult to injury? . . . All right already, stop crying, it's driving me crazy, the way you're always crying. All right, I give up. Forget it. Go see He Xiaoyong. You can tell him that we've been together almost ten years. You can tell him that Yile's thought of me as his dad for almost as long. That's why I'm allowing him to stay here. And why I'll agree to be responsible for raising him from now on. But *only* if he pays what he owes this one time. Just this once. He has to pay up, if only just this once. Otherwise I'll have no face left at all. Why am I letting that bastard off so damn easy?"

CHAPTER NINE

Xu Yulan announced to Xu Sanguan that she was on her way to see He Xiaoyong.

Xu Sanguan was sitting inside, knotting some rags to make a mop. When he heard what Xu Yulan said, he stuck out his hand to rub his nose, wiped his mouth, and wordlessly continued to work on the mop.

Xu Yulan continued, "I'm going to see He Xiaoyong, but only because you asked me to. I swore long ago that I would never see him again." She asked Xu Sanguan, "Should I dress up before I go over there, or is it better if I go as I am?"

Xu Sanguan thought to himself, *She wants to dress up to see He Xiaoyong? Does that mean she's going to comb her hair in the mirror, moisten it with hair oil, rub Snowflower cream on her face, put on her best sweater, pat the dust from her shoes, and wear that silk scarf around her neck? And then cheerfully saunter off to see the man who made me a cuckold these nine years?* Xu Sanguan threw the mop to one side and bounded up from his seat.

"You still want He Xiaoyong to squeeze your fucking tits? You still want to have your fun with him? You want to look nice for him? You're going just as you are. Better yet, rub your face with ashes from the stove."

Xu Yulan said, "But if I go with stove ash on my face and my hair all a mess, don't you think He Xiaoyong might say, 'Hey everyone! Come look! *This* is what Xu Sanguan's woman looks like!'"

Xu Sanguan had to agree that she was right. He was not about to let that bastard He Xiaoyong have a good laugh at his expense. "Then you better dress up before you go."

So Xu Yulan put on her finely woven sweater, over which she wore a dark blue khaki jacket with a turned-down collar. She adjusted the collar so as to show as much as possible of the sweater underneath, then went to get the silk scarf from her trunk. She tied and knotted it around her neck, but after a glance in the mirror revealed that it covered the sweater, she shifted the knot to the side and tucked it under her collar. After another glance in the mirror, she tugged the two ends of the knot out from underneath and let them rest atop her collar.

Xu Yulan walked over to He Xiaoyong's house enveloped in a cloud of fragrance emitted by the Snowflower cream on her face. The ends of her scarf fluttered in the breeze like a pair of chicks flapping their wings. She passed two intersections, turned down a small lane, and came to He Xiaoyong's door.

Xu Yulan saw a thirty-year-old woman sitting by his door scrubbing clothes on a washing board. This, she knew, was He Xiaoyong's woman. He Xiaoyong's woman was as skinny as a bamboo pole. She had been just as skinny ten years before, when she had walked through the streets with He Xiaoyong in tow, letting out a little snort of derision whenever they happened to run into Xu Yulan and bursting into giggles after they had passed her by. At the time Xu Yulan had thought to herself, *He Xiaoyong's gone and married a woman without any tits or ass.*

Now she saw that the woman still didn't have any tits and that her ass was sitting squarely atop a stool.

Xu Yulan shouted into the open front door, "He Xiaoyong! He Xiaoyong!"

"Who is it?"

He Xiaoyong stuck his head from out of the second-floor window. But when he realized to his dismay that it was Xu Yulan standing outside, he immediately recoiled. After a moment his head reappeared, and his eyes looked down in her direction. He looked at this woman standing downstairs who was prettier than his own wife, this woman with whom he had made love; this woman who never talked to him anymore when they ran into each other in the street; this was the woman who was smiling in his direction. He spluttered, "What do you want?"

Xu Yulan said, "He Xiaoyong, I haven't seen you for a long time. You've gained weight. You even have a double chin now."

He Xiaoyong heard the sound of his wife spitting in disgust. "What do you want?"

Xu Yulan said, "Come down here. We can talk after you come downstairs."

He Xiaoyong, eyes on his woman, said, "I'm not coming down. I'm just fine up here. Why should I come down?"

Xu Yulan said, "Come downstairs. It'll be easier to talk if you're down here."

"I'm staying up here."

Xu Yulan glanced at He Xiaoyong's woman, then smiled up at He Xiaoyong. "He Xiaoyong, could it be that you're actually afraid to come down and talk to me?"

He Xiaoyong looked over toward his wife, then said in a low, diffident voice, "I'm not afraid of anything."

At this point his wife could no longer remain silent. She got to her feet, looked up at the window, and said, "He Xiaoyong, come down here. What can she do to you? She's not going to eat you, for heaven's sake."

He Xiaoyong came down the stairs and walked over to where Xu Yulan was standing. "Say whatever it is you have to say, and make it quick. I don't have time for this shit."

Xu Yulan smiled nicely and said, "I came to tell you the good news. It's Xu Sanguan. He says he's not going to come and settle his debt with you, so you can put your mind at rest on that score. At first he was planning to chop you into pieces with a cleaver, because you knocked up his woman and forced him to take care of your own son for nine years. That's why he was going to chop you to bits with a cleaver. And if he had, no one would have blamed him for it either. Xu Sanguan says he's not going to ask you to pay back the money he's spent on Yile. And he's not going to send him back to live with you. He Xiaoyong, you're getting off pretty easy, having someone else raise your son for you and never having to lift a finger to help. You get to be a dad for nothing. But Xu Sanguan has had himself a raw deal, from the very start. After Yile was born, he never got any sleep. He'd hold the baby and walk back and forth across the room all night so he wouldn't cry. Xu Sanguan washed all of Yile's diapers, and every year he made him a new set of clothes. Not to mention that he always provided him food to eat and water to drink, day in and day out. And Yile eats more than I do. He Xiaoyong, Xu Sanguan says he's not going to settle his accounts with you. And he says all you have to do in return is give the money to Blacksmith Fang."

He Xiaoyong said, "What does Blacksmith Fang's son being in the hospital have to do with me?"

"Your son smashed his head in with a rock."

"I don't have a son," He Xiaoyong said. "Since when do I have a son? All I have is two daughters. One's called He Xiaoying and the other's He Xiaohong."

"You really have no conscience, do you?" Xu Yulan jabbed her finger toward him. "I suppose you've forgotten that summer when you took advantage of my dad's going to the public toilet and pulled me onto the bed. You're a heartless bastard. What did

I do in my past life to deserve this? What did I do to deserve your bastard seed finding its way into my belly?"

He Xiaoyong brushed away her finger with his hand. "Do you think I would waste my precious seed on a bitch like you? That kid is Xu Sanguan's bastard, and there's two more where he came from."

"Oh, for heaven's sake." Xu Yulan's tears began to come. "Everyone who sees Yile says so. They all say he's the spitting image of He Xiaoyong. Don't think you can deny it. Even if your face was scarred by fire or scalded by coals, you wouldn't be able to deny it. Because he looks more and more like you every day."

When she saw that a group of spectators had begun to gather around and watch, He Xiaoyong's woman chimed in, "Take a good look. She's a shameless bitch, this one. Trying to steal my man in broad daylight."

Xu Yulan swung around to look at her. "If I was going to steal anyone, it sure as hell wouldn't be He Xiaoyong. He Xiaoyong! Back then I was as pretty as a flower. Everybody called me the Fried Dough Queen. He Xiaoyong was nothing to me. I threw He Xiaoyong out like a piece of trash, and you stooped down to collect him like he was some kind of treasure."

He Xiaoyong's woman straightened and slapped Xu Yulan across the face. Xu Yulan slapped her right back. In an instant their arms were flailing through the air, and each had grasped hold of the other's hair and was tugging with all her might. As she pulled at Xu Yulan's hair, He Xiaoyong's woman called out to her husband, "He Xiaoyong! He Xiaoyong!"

He Xiaoyong stepped forward, grabbed hold of Xu Yulan's arms, and squeezed them so hard that she was forced to let go of her opponent with an anguished "Aiya!" He let fly with a slap to her face that sent her tumbling to the ground.

Xu Yulan, rubbing her own face, burst into tears. "He Xiaoyong, you ought to be cut to pieces with a thousand knives! You're a bastard, a son of a bitch, your conscience must have been eaten by a pack of dogs." She stood up from the pavement and pointed an accusing finger at him. "Just you wait, He Xiaoyong! You won't live to see another day. I'll send Xu Sanguan after you with a cleaver. He'll chop you to pieces. You won't live to see another day."

But Xu Sanguan didn't support the death sentence Xu Yulan had pronounced so summarily for He Xiaoyong. When Xu Yulan got home, Xu Sanguan was still working on his mop. Xu Yulan sat down exhaustedly across from him, her face streaked with tears, and gazed in his direction. After a while her tears began to fall again.

When Xu Sanguan saw that she was crying, he knew she hadn't succeeded in getting any money from He Xiaoyong. "I knew you'd come back empty-handed."

Xu Yulan said, "Xu Sanguan, go chop him to pieces."

Xu Sanguan said, "You fell to fucking pieces as soon as you saw him, didn't you? You went soft, right? Couldn't bear to ask for the money after all?"

Xu Yulan said, "Xu Sanguan, go chop him to pieces."

Xu Sanguan said, "I'm telling you, if you don't get the money today, Blacksmith Fang is going to come tomorrow and confiscate all our things. He's going to take your bed, your table, your clothes, your Snowflower cream, your silk scarf. He's gonna fucking take it all away."

Xu Yulan began to weep. "I asked them for the money. They wouldn't give it to me. And they pulled my hair, and he slapped me right across my face. Xu Sanguan, are you actually going to let someone get away with treating your woman that way? Xu Sanguan, I'm begging you to go chop him to pieces. There's a cleaver in the kitchen. I sharpened it just yesterday. Go cut him to pieces."

Xu Sanguan said, "What do you think would happen to me if I chopped him to pieces? If I went over there with a cleaver, I'd end up in jail, that's what. I'd be executed, and you'd be a fucking widow, that's what would happen."

When Xu Yulan had heard him out, she stood, walked out of the room, and took a seat on the doorstep. When Xu Sanguan saw her sit down on the doorstep, he knew what was coming. Xu Yulan, flicking the handkerchief she had just been using to wipe her tears back and forth through the air, began her tearful litany.

"What did I do in my past life to deserve this? He Xiaoyong took advantage of me. And if that wasn't enough, he got me pregnant. Not only did he knock me up, but I even gave birth to Yile. If giving birth to Yile wasn't enough, he had to go and get himself into trouble."

Xu Sanguan growled at her, "Goddamnit, get back in here! Do you have to let everyone on the fucking street know that I'm a cuckold?"

Xu Yulan sobbed, "And if Yile getting into trouble wasn't bad enough, Xu Sanguan said he couldn't help him out of it. Xu Sanguan won't do anything, and neither will He Xiaoyong. He Xiaoyong not only refused to pay up but even pulled my hair and slapped my face. He Xiaoyong's a crime against nature. He Xiaoyong will not die a happy death. But what am I supposed to do when Blacksmith Fang comes for the money tomorrow? What am I supposed to do? What am I going to do?"

Yile, Erle, and Sanle heard their mother's sobs and ran to her side.

Yile said, "Mom, don't cry, go inside."

Erle said, "Mom, don't cry. Why are you crying?"

Sanle said, "Mom, don't cry. Who's He Xiaoyong?"

The neighbors came to her as well. The neighbors said, "Xu Yulan, don't cry, you'll strain yourself." "Xu Yulan, why are you crying?" "What are you crying for?"

Erle said to the neighbors, "It's like this. My mom is crying because Yile—"

Yile cut in, "Erle, do me a favor and shut up."

Erle said, "I will not shut up. It's like this: Yile isn't my dad's kid."

Yile said, "Erle, if you don't shut up, I'll kill you."

Erle continued, "Yile is He Xiaoyong and my mom's kid—"

Yile slapped Erle on the face, and Erle broke into loud sobs as well.

Xu Sanguan heard what was happening from inside the room and thought to himself, *So that little bastard Yile thinks he can get away with hitting one of my sons?* He catapulted out the door and slapped Yile's face. Then he pinned him against the wall and shouted, "Little bastard! Just because your dad messes with me, you think you can bully my son too?"

Yile, dazed by Xu Sanguan's sudden attack, stood in silence, rubbing his hand against the wall.

Xu Yulan pointed in their direction and once again sobbed, "My fate is bitter. But that child's fate is even worse. Xu Sanguan doesn't want him. He Xiaoyong doesn't want him either. The child has no father, no one to call his own."

One of the neighbors said, "Xu Yulan, why don't you have Yile go over to He Xiaoyong's place? Who wouldn't be moved by seeing their own flesh and blood? He Xiaoyong doesn't have a son yet, just two daughters. Who knows? Maybe he'll even start to cry when he finally sees his own son."

Xu Yulan immediately stopped crying and turned toward Yile, who was still standing against the wall, biting his lip. "Yile, didn't you hear what the man said? Go on. Go find He Xiaoyong. Go over there and call him your dad."

Yile backed himself against the wall and shook his head. "I'm not going."

Xu Yulan said, "Yile, listen to what your mother's telling you. Go on. Quick. Go call He Xiaoyong your dad. If he doesn't listen to you, just try again."

Yile shook his head. "I'm not going over there."

Xu Sanguan pointed at him. "You're not going, huh? If you don't go over there right now, I'll beat the shit out of you."

As he spoke, Xu Sanguan approached Yile, grabbed him with one hand, pulled him away from the wall, and then pushed him a few steps forward. But as soon as Xu Sanguan had released him, Yile backed himself once more against the wall.

When Xu Sanguan turned and saw Yile pressed flat to the wall, he lifted his hand menacingly in the air. But just as he was about to slap him, he thought better of it. *Damn. Yile isn't even my own son. I have no right to hit someone else's child.*

As Xu Sanguan began to walk away, Yile's voice rang out, "I'm not going. He Xiaoyong's not my dad. My dad is Xu Sanguan."

"Bullshit," Xu Sanguan commented to the neighbors. "Look at this little bastard. He thinks he can implicate me, but I had nothing to do with him."

At this point Xu Yulan once again burst into sobs. "What did I do in my past life to deserve this?"

By now Xu Yulan's litany had lost much of its interest for the spectators. She went through the changes several more times, but her voice had begun to weaken with fatigue and, lacking its original bite and elasticity, became dry and gravelly. She waved her handkerchief back and forth with less and less force, and the gasps she took for air between sentences became lower, heavier, and slower. Her neighbors picked up and left, like theater patrons after a show. Even her husband left. Xu Sanguan had long ago become accustomed to her litanies on the doorstep. She might as well be sitting there knitting a sweater, for all he cared.

Only Yile was left standing there, glued against the wall, with hands behind his back scraping up against the whitewash. When everyone else had left, Yile approached his mother.

Xu Yulan's body was propped against the door frame. She was no longer waving the handkerchief in the air. Her chin was cupped in her palm. When she saw Yile approach, the tears that had already ebbed once again began to flow.

Yile said to her, "Mom, don't cry anymore. I'll go over and call He Xiaoyong my dad."

When Yile arrived at He Xiaoyong's door, he saw two girls a little younger than himself playing with rubber bands. As they stretched out their hands and hopped back and forth, their braids bobbed back and forth behind them. "You're He Xiaoyong's daughters, right?" he asked. "That means you're my little sisters."

The two girls stopped jumping up and down. One of them sat on the doorstep, and the other sat down next to her sister, and together they stared in Yile's direction.

When Yile saw He Xiaoyong and his skinny wife emerge from inside, he called to him, "Dad."

He Xiaoyong's woman said to He Xiaoyong, "Your wild oat is here. What are you going to do about him?"

Yile called out again, "Dad."

He Xiaoyong said, "I'm not your dad. Why don't you go home now? And don't come around here again."

Yile called out once again, "Dad."

He Xiaoyong's woman said to He Xiaoyong, "Why don't you just get rid of him?"

Yile called out once more, "Dad."

He Xiaoyong said, "Who's your dad? Get out of here!"

Yile stuck out his hand to wipe the snot from his nose. "My mom said so. My mom said if I called you my dad and you didn't answer me, then I should say it a few more times. I've called you my dad four times now, but instead of answering me, you just told me to go away. I'll be going home now."

CHAPTER TEN

Blacksmith Fang came to Xu Sanguan and demanded that he bring the money to the hospital immediately. "If you don't bring the money," he said, "they won't give him any more medicine."

Xu Sanguan said to Blacksmith Fang, "I'm not Yile's dad. You've got the wrong man. You ought to go after He Xiaoyong."

Blacksmith Fang asked, "When did you stop being Yile's dad? Before Yile injured my son? Or just after?"

"Of course it was before," Xu Sanguan said. "Think it over. I've been cuckolded for nine years now. And I've taken care of his son for nine years despite all that. If I were to pay the hospital bill for your son in addition to everything else, then I'd really be the king of cuckolds."

Blacksmith Fang could not help but concur with Xu Sanguan's point of view. So he went to He Xiaoyong and said to him, "Because of you, Xu Sanguan's been cuckolded for nine years. And he's raised your son for nine years despite all that. The saying goes that one ought to repay a drop of water with a flood. For the sake of those nine years, you could at least pay my son's hospital bill."

He Xiaoyong said, "How do you know Yile is my son? You think he's mine just because he looks like me? That doesn't prove a thing. Lots of people look alike."

When he finished, he went inside, opened up a trunk, and took out his official residence permits to show to Blacksmith Fang.

"Take a good look. Do you see Yile written anywhere on this permit? Do you or don't you? Whoever has Yile's name on their residence permit should be the one who has to pay for your son's hospital bill."

Since neither Xu Sanguan nor He Xiaoyong was willing to pay, Blacksmith Fang was forced to call on Xu Yulan. "Xu Sanguan says Yile isn't his son, and He Xiaoyong says he isn't his son either. Since neither of them will admit that they're Yile's dad, you're the only one left to ask for money. Thank heaven Yile only has one mom."

When Xu Yulan heard what Blacksmith Fang had to say, she wrapped her face in her hands and began to sob.

Blacksmith Fang stood patiently by her side, and when it seemed that she had cried her fill, he added, "If you don't pay up, I'm going to have to bring some men over to go through your things and take whatever's worth any money. And you better believe that I'll go through with it. I'm not the kind of man who talks big but doesn't follow through."

Two days later Blacksmith Fang arrived with two three-wheeled carts and six men to help with the job. His entourage filled almost the entire lane.

It was around noon, and Xu Sanguan was just about to go out the door and back to work when he saw Blacksmith Fang arrive. He knew that this was the day everything in his home would be confiscated. He turned to Xu Yulan and said, "Get seven glasses ready and boil a kettle of water. Any tea left in that canister? We have company. Seven men in all."

Xu Yulan, wondering who all these people might be, walked to the door to see. When she saw that it was Blacksmith Fang, her face went white and she said to her husband, "They've come to confiscate our things."

Xu Sanguan said, "That doesn't matter. They're still our guests. Get the tea ready."

Blacksmith Fang and his men arrived at the house, parked the carts, and stood by the door. Blacksmith Fang began, "There's nothing I can do about this. We've known each other more than twenty years now, and we've always been on the level with each other. But there's nothing else I can do. My son's waiting for me in the hospital, and if I don't pay up, they won't give him any more medicine. After your Yile smashed my son's head, did I come to your house and make a scene? No. I've sat with my son in the hospital the whole time, waiting for the money. But it's been more than two weeks, and I really can't wait any longer."

At this point Xu Yulan sat down in the middle of the doorstep and stuck out her arms as if to block their entrance. "Don't come into my house and take my things. This house is my life. I've struggled for ten years. I've scrimped and saved for ten years. Please, I'm begging you, don't come in."

Xu Sanguan said to Xu Yulan, "Come on now. They're already here, and they've even brought the bicycle carts along. It's not like they would turn around and go home with just a few words from you. Why don't you get up and make a kettle of tea?"

Xu Yulan stood up, wiped the tears from her face, and went inside to boil the water.

After she had gone, Xu Sanguan said to Blacksmith Fang and his men, "Come on in. Take everything you can move. Just don't take any of my things. This problem with Yile has nothing to do with me, so you can't take any of my things."

Xu Yulan, standing by the stove making tea, saw them come into the house through the door by the kitchen. She watched them rifle through the trunks and remove the table. Two of the men took their stools and set them atop one of the carts. The two trunks she had brought with her to the house as dowry were carried out and piled on a cart, as were the two silk dresses that had also been part of her dowry. She had never been able to bear the thought of actually wearing them; now they were draped across trunks that sat atop a cart.

Xu Yulan watched them take her house apart piece by piece. By the time she had boiled the water and prepared seven cups of tea, there was no table to put them on. Xu Sanguan was helping them haul away the little table where they shared their meals, where their children wrote their homework assignments. They loaded it onto one of the carts. Xu Sanguan, panting from his exertions, straightened and wiped the sweat from his brow.

Xu Yulan's tears continued to flow. "Can you believe it? Not only is he helping you confiscate our things, but it looks like he's even working even harder than you too."

Finally Blacksmith Fang and his men began to remove the bed where Xu Sanguan and Xu Yulan slept. When Xu Sanguan saw what was happening, he hastily interjected, "Wait! You can't take that bed. Half of that bed belongs to me."

Blacksmith Fang replied, "This is just about the only thing in this house that's worth any money."

Xu Sanguan said, "You took our kitchen table. Half of that table was mine too. You took the table, so why don't you leave me the bed?"

Blacksmith Fang looked around the emptied room and nodded. "All right. Leave them the bed. Otherwise they won't have anywhere to sleep tonight."

As soon as Blacksmith Fang had secured the table and the trunks and all their other household items to the carts with strong rope, his men began to pull them down the lane. Blacksmith Fang said, "We'll be on our way then."

Xu Sanguan smiled and nodded toward them.

Xu Yulan, tears streaming down her face, said, "Why don't you have a cup of tea before you go?"

Blacksmith Fang shook his head. "No, thank you."

Xu Yulan persisted, "But I've already made you a kettle of tea. It's on the floor by the stove. Have some tea before you go. I made it especially for you."

Blacksmith Fang looked toward Xu Yulan. "In that case, I suppose we will have a cup of tea before we go."

They went into the kitchen to drink the tea. Xu Yulan stood by the doorstep. When they were finished, she watched them step past the threshold and out of the house. She watched as they began to pull the carts down the lane. And only then did she begin to cry in earnest.

"I don't want to live anymore. I've had enough of this life. It would be better if I was dead. If I was dead, I wouldn't have to worry so much. If I was dead, I wouldn't have to cook and clean for the husband and kids. I wouldn't be so tired, and I wouldn't be so sad. If I was dead, I would be happy. I would be even happier than I was before I got married."

Blacksmith Fang and his men were still pushing the carts down the lane. When Blacksmith Fang heard her lament, he pushed one of the carts to a side of the lane, turned around, and said to Xu Yulan and Xu Sanguan, "Listen, I'm not going to sell these things right away. I'll keep them at my house for a few days. Even four days would be all right with me. I'll give you three or four days. If you can come up with the money in time, I will personally bring every single one of your things back and see to it that they're put exactly where they came from."

Xu Sanguan said to Blacksmith Fang, "Listen. She knows just as well as I do that you had no choice in the matter. It's just that she's a little upset right now."

Then Xu Sanguan knelt down beside Xu Yulan and said, "Blacksmith Fang had no choice. The fact is that your son smashed his son's head open with a rock. Blacksmith Fang has done his best to be kind to us. If it had been someone else, they'd have smashed all our things long ago."

Xu Yulan covered her face with her hands and began a fresh bout of weeping.

Xu Sanguan hurriedly waved in Blacksmith Fang's direction. "Go on, you go on now."

Xu Sanguan looked on as his home of ten years, piled precariously atop two carts, clattered and wobbled down the lane. When the carts disappeared around the corner, he too began to cry. He bent over toward Xu Yulan, slumped down wearily beside her on the doorstep, and together they wept for the home they had lost.

CHAPTER ELEVEN

The next day Xu Sanguan called Erle and Sanle to his side. "You two sons are all I have left now. I want you to remember who it was who brought us this low. We don't even have a stool left to call our own. There was once a table where the two of you are standing now, and a trunk where I'm standing. Now everything's gone. Our house was full of things before, and now it's empty. Sleeping in my own house is like sleeping out in the open country. I want you to remember who brought us to this pass."

His two sons said, "It was Blacksmith Fang."

"It most definitely was not Blacksmith Fang," Xu Sanguan said. "It was He Xiaoyong. Why do I say it was He Xiaoyong? Because He Xiaoyong knocked up your mom behind my back to make Yile, and then Yile broke Blacksmith Fang's son's head open with a rock. Don't you think it was He Xiaoyong's fault?"

His two sons nodded their heads.

"So"—Xu Sanguan paused for a mouthful of water—"when you two grow up, I want you to take revenge on He Xiaoyong for me. You know who He Xiaoyong's daughters are, don't you? You do. Do you know what their names are? No? Doesn't matter, as long as you recognize them. Remember, when you're all grown up, I want you to rape He Xiaoyong's daughters for me."

After one night's sleep in his newly cavernous home, Xu Sanguan felt that he couldn't go on like this, that he must get his things back from Blacksmith Fang no matter the cost. And it was thus that he thought once again of selling blood, because if he hadn't gone to sell blood with Ah Fang and Genlong ten years earlier, he would never have had this home in the first place. Now he needed to sell blood once more. With the money he would earn selling blood, he could buy back his table, his trunks, and all his stools. But that would be letting He Xiaoyong off too easily. He had raised He Xiaoyong's son for nine years. Would he now have to pay back his son's debts for him as well? His heart began to sink, and his throat felt constricted. So he once again called Erle and Sanle to his side and told them that He Xiaoyong had two daughters, that taking proper revenge required patience, and that ten years was by no means too long to wait. What did patience mean? Patience meant that in ten years time he wanted Erle and Sanle to rape He Xiaoyong's daughters.

When Xu Sanguan's two sons listened again to his instruction that they should rape He Xiaoyong's daughters, they began to giggle. Xu Sanguan quizzed them: "So what are you going to do after you grow up?"

The two sons replied, "Rape He Xiaoyong's daughters."

Xu Sanguan broke into roars of laughter. He felt better now. He felt good enough to go sell some of his blood. He walked out of the house and to the hospital. This was the decision he had made that morning: to go to the hospital, to look up the blood chief he hadn't seen in many years, to let them tie a cord around his arm until the veins stuck out and the fattest needle the hospital had to offer slid into his thickest vein, sucking out his blood through a tube until it filled a big glass bottle. He had seen his own blood before. It was so thick that it looked black, with a bubbly whitish froth that rose to the top of the bottle.

Xu Sanguan, holding a pound of white sugar in one hand, pushed open the door to the blood donation room at the hospital. Blood Chief Li was sitting behind his desk, wearing a filthy white smock, and holding a newspaper that had been used to wrap some fried dough. The paper looked as if it had been soaked in oil, because it was almost transparent in the light that shone through the window and into the room.

Blood Chief Li set down his newspaper and watched as Xu Sanguan advanced toward him. Xu Sanguan placed the packet of sugar in front of him on the desk. Blood Chief Li reached out a hand to squeeze the parcel, then turned his attention back to Xu Sanguan.

Xu Sanguan smilingly took a seat across from the blood chief, noticing at the same time that Blood Chief Li had a lot less hair and a lot more flesh around his face than the last time he had seen him. He smiled and said, "It's been quite a few years since you've come by the factory."

Blood Chief Li nodded. "You're from the factory?"

Xu Sanguan nodded. "I've come here before, with Ah Fang and Genlong. We met once a long time ago. You live over by the South Gate Bridge, right? How's your family doing? You still remember me?"

Blood Chief Li shook his head. "I can't remember now. A lot of people come to see me. They usually know who I am, but I don't always know who they are. But I do know Ah Fang and Genlong. They came by just three months ago. When did you come here with them?"

"Ten years ago."

"Ten years?" Blood Chief Li spat a gob of phlegm onto the floor. "How do you expect me to remember someone who came through here ten years ago? Even a god wouldn't be able to remember as far back as all that." He lifted his feet onto the chair in front of him and rested his arms on his knees. "You came in today to sell blood?"

Xu Sanguan replied, "Yes."

Blood Chief Li pointed at the parcel on the table. "Is this for me?"

Xu Sanguan replied, "Yes."

"I can't take it." Blood Chief Li drummed on the tabletop with his fingers. "If you'd come six months ago, I would take it, but now I really can't accept any gifts. Last time Ah Fang and Genlong came they brought me two dozen fresh eggs, but I didn't even keep one of them. I'm a Communist Party member now, know what I mean? Now I can't even take 'so much as a needle and thread from the masses.'"

Xu Sanguan nodded. "I have five in my family, so we get enough coupons for a pound of white sugar every year. I spent all of this year's coupons just to show my respect for you."

"It's refined sugar?" Blood Chief Li lifted up the parcel, opened it, and peered at the shiny white crystals inside. "White sugar's actually quite valuable. Just now I thought it was salt." As he spoke, he poured a little sugar in his palm and gazed down at the crystals. "This white sugar's nice and soft and fine, just like a young girl's skin. Don't you think so?"

Blood Chief Li bent his head to his hand, stuck out his tongue, and licked the sugar out of his own palm. He savored the sweetness for a moment, eyelids dropping shut with pleasure. Then he carefully wrapped up the parcel and handed it back to Xu Sanguan.

Xu Sanguan pushed it back across the table. "Keep it."

"I can't keep it," Blood Chief Li said. "I can't even take 'so much as a needle and thread from the masses' anymore."

"I bought it just to show my respect for you. If you won't take it, who else would I give it to?"

"Keep it for yourself."

"I wouldn't waste such good stuff on myself. Refined sugar's for giving away."

"You're right there," said Blood Chief Li, edging the packet toward his side of the table. "It really would be a shame to use such good sugar yourself. Let me have another taste of the stuff."

Blood Chief Li poured another spoonful of sugar into his palm, stuck out his tongue, and licked. As he savored the sugar, he once again pushed the parcel back to Xu Sanguan.

Xu Sanguan promptly slid it back over toward Blood Chief Li. "Take it. If I don't say anything, no one will ever know."

Blood Chief Li was clearly displeased by this last offer. His smile instantly disappeared, and he said, "I was just having a taste to make you feel better. If I give you a yard, don't think you can take a mile."

Xu Sanguan could only reach out and take the sugar. "Then I'll keep it for myself."

The blood chief watched as Xu Sanguan put the parcel back into his pocket. Then he tapped the tabletop with his finger and asked, "What's your name?"

"Xu Sanguan."

"Xu Sanguan?" He drummed on the table. "That sounds familiar."

"I came once before."

"No, that's not why." Blood Chief Li waved his hand. "Xu Sanguan, Xu Sanguan."

Suddenly the blood chief let out a hoot and then a guffaw. "I remember now. So you're Xu Sanguan? You're the famous cuckold."

CHAPTER TWELVE

After Xu Sanguan sold blood, he didn't hand the money directly over to Blacksmith Fang. Instead, he went to the Victory Restaurant and sat down at a table by the window.

Recalling to memory the first time he had come here after selling blood with Ah Fang and Genlong ten years before, he scratched his head and remembered the way they had slapped the table for emphasis as they ordered their food. So he reached out and slapped the tabletop as he shouted to the waiter. "A plate of fried pork livers and two shots of yellow rice wine."

The waiter took his order and was turning to go when Xu Sanguan realized that something was missing. He signaled for the waiter to stay where he was. The waiter stood waiting by his side, wiping the already immaculate table with a washcloth. "What else would you like?"

Xu Sanguan, hand still poised in midair, thought for a moment but couldn't remember what it was. Finally, he said to the waiter, "I'll let you know when I remember."

The waiter nodded his assent.

Just as he moved away across the room, Xu Sanguan remembered the phrase for which he had been searching and shouted across the restaurant, "I remember now!"

The waiter immediately walked back toward his table. "So what is it?"

Xu Sanguan slapped the tabletop for emphasis. "Warm up that wine for me!"

AS SOON AS Xu Sanguan came with the money, Blacksmith Fang sent for three of the six men and one of the carts he had used the day before and returned their things. Blacksmith Fang said, "Actually, all your things fit on just one cart. Yesterday I brought one cart and three men too many for the job."

One of the three men pulled the cart through the street, while the other two stood to the sides propping up the pile of furniture and household items on top. They soon arrived at Xu Sanguan's door.

"Xu Sanguan, if you had just given us the money yesterday, we wouldn't have had to haul all this stuff back and forth," they said.

"But things never work out that way," Xu Sanguan replied as he unloaded one of the stools. "Necessity is the mother of invention. It's only when you're at the end of your tether that you finally figure out how to solve a problem. If I wasn't at the end of my tether, I might have figured out a way to get out of this mess, but I wouldn't have known whether I could actually go through with it. If the people at the hospital hadn't told you they were going to stop giving your son his medicine, you would never have come here to confiscate my things, right? What do you think, Blacksmith Fang?"

Before Blacksmith Fang even began to nod his agreement, Xu Sanguan suddenly let out a yelp: "I'm done for!"

Startled, the blacksmith and his men looked on as Xu Sanguan repeatedly slapped the sides of his own head. They watched in silence, unsure as to whether Xu Sanguan actually intended to do himself bodily harm.

Then Xu Sanguan gazed mournfully over toward Blacksmith Fang. "I forgot to drink water." Xu Sanguan had only just remembered that he hadn't drunk any water before he went to sell blood. "I forgot to drink water."

"Water?" Blacksmith Fang and his men were mystified. "What water?"

"Any water would do."

Xu Sanguan picked up the stool he had just unloaded, set it down by the wall, and sat down. He lifted up his arm, flexed his muscles so that the veins began to protrude, rolled down his sleeve, and gazed at the reddish puncture mark on the skin underneath.

"I sold two bowls. But those two bowls were thick enough for three. If only I hadn't forgotten to drink water. It just seems like nothing's going right for me these days."

Blacksmith Fang and his men asked, "Two bowls of what?"

XU YULAN was at her father's place, sitting in the rattan chair where he usually took his afternoon nap, wiping the tears from her face. Her father sat across from her, and his eyes were red around the rims from crying. Xu Yulan told him about how Blacksmith Fang and his men had come to take their things. She provided her father with an inventory of what they had taken, ticking off each item with her fingers.

Then she added a list of what remained. When she was finished, she added, "It took them two hours to take away ten years of hard work. They even took those two silk robes, the ones you gave me for my wedding dowry. I'd never even used them."

Just as she was ticking off her household on her fingers, Blacksmith Fang and his men were busy putting each item back into its original place. By the time she got home, the job was finished. She stood at the door gazing wide-eyed into the house.

Her ten years of hard work were once again laid out neatly inside the room. Her eyes shifted back and forth from the table to the trunks and over to the stools. She looked everything over, then went to look for the man with whom she'd worked together for those ten years to make a home. Xu Sanguan was sitting by the table inside the house.

CHAPTER THIRTEEN

Xu Yulan asked Xu Sanguan, "So who did you borrow the money from?"

As she spoke, Xu Yulan reached out her hand and pressed her fingers to the tip of Xu Sanguan's nose, rocking it back and forth until it started to ache. Xu Sanguan pulled her hand away, but she simply replaced it with the other hand.

"You've paid Blacksmith Fang back," she continued, "but now we're in debt to someone else. That's just taking bricks from the east wall to repair the west wall. What are you going to do about the holes in the east wall? Who's going to lend you more money to pay back the debt?"

Xu Sanguan rolled up his sleeve to show her the puncture mark on his arm. "See that? See the red spot? The spot where it looks like I got bitten by a fly? That's from the thickest needle they've got at the hospital." Then Xu Sanguan rolled his sleeve back down. "I sold blood! I sold my own blood to pay back He

Xiaoyong's debt. I sold my own blood so I could keep on being a cuckold."

When Xu Yulan understood what he was saying, she erupted, "Aiya! You sold your blood and didn't even ask me about it first? Why didn't you say something? We're through, we're finished. This family is ruined! What will people think if they find out that someone in the family's been selling blood? They'll say that Xu Sanguan's been selling blood, Xu Sanguan's all washed up, Xu Sanguan's gone and sold his own blood."

Xu Sanguan said, "Can you be a little quieter? If you didn't shout like that, no one would ever know."

Xu Yulan continued every bit as loudly as before. "My dad used to tell me when I was little that your blood is passed down from your ancestors. You can sell fried dough, sell a house, sell off your land, but you can never ever sell your blood. Better to sell your body than sell your blood! At least your body belongs to you. But selling your blood is like selling your ancestors. Xu Sanguan, you've sold your ancestors!"

Xu Sanguan said, "Keep quiet. What are you trying to say anyway?"

A tear rolled down Xu Yulan's face. "I would never have imagined you'd sell your blood. You can sell anything you like, as long as it isn't blood. Sell the bed, sell the house, sell whatever you like. But why did you have to go and sell your blood?"

Xu Sanguan said, "Keep quiet. Why did I sell my blood? I sold my blood so I could keep on playing the cuckold."

Xu Yulan sobbed. "I heard what you just said. I know what you mean. I know you're mocking me. I know deep down you really hate me. Why else would you say something like that?" She weepingly made her way to the door.

Xu Sanguan growled from behind her, "Come back here, you bitch. You're going to the doorstep again. You're gonna start screaming and yelling and making a scene again."

But instead of sitting down on the doorstep, Xu Yulan walked right past the threshold, turned, and made her way down the lane and onto the street. She walked all the way down to the end of the street, veered down another lane, and arrived at He Xiaoyong's doorstep.

Standing in front of He Xiaoyong's open front door, she patted down her clothes, combed out her hair with her fingers, and raised her voice loud enough for the whole neighborhood to hear.

"You're all neighbors of He Xiaoyong. All of you know He Xiaoyong. You all know that he's a rotten, black-hearted son of a bitch. You all know that he won't take in his only son. You all know that because I sinned in my past life, He Xiaoyong screwed me over in this one. You've heard the story already, so I don't have to tell it to you again today. I came today to tell you about something else. What you don't know and what I just found out today is that I must have burned a lot of incense in my past life too. That's why I got to marry Xu Sanguan. What you don't know is just how good a man Xu Sanguan really is. I could talk for days on end about how good Xu Sanguan is, but I won't. What I will tell you is that Xu Sanguan sold his own blood. He did it for Yile, for our family. He went to the hospital today to sell his own blood. Think about it. You can die from selling blood. And even if you don't die, you'll still get dizzy, your vision will blur, and you'll feel weak from head to toe. But Xu Sanguan didn't care about all of that. He risked his life for me, for Yile, for our whole family."

He Xiaoyong's skinny wife appeared at the door and sneered, "If Xu Sanguan's so great, how come you want to steal my man?"

When Xu Yulan saw He Xiaoyong's woman, she sneered, "Now here's a woman who must have done a lot of bad things in her last life. She's being paid back for it in this life, let me tell you, and the punishment is that she can't bear any sons, only daughters. Once her daughters are grown up, they'll belong to other people's families, and her own family line will be broken."

He Xiaoyong's woman strode out from the door and slapped her thighs for emphasis as she railed at her nemesis, "And here's a woman who's so shameless that she'll even boast about stealing someone else's seed!"

Xu Yulan countered, "Of course I do! Any woman who's had three sons in a row has a right to brag!"

He Xiaoyong's woman shouted, "Three sons by two different dads! Do you want to brag about that too?"

"Whether your daughters really have the same dad remains to be seen."

"Only someone like you! Only a slut like you could have had so many men."

"So you're not a slut? You know what's inside your pants? A department store, that's what! Anybody can go inside!"

"If I've got a department store in my pants, you have a public toilet!"

SOMEONE CAME to Xu Sanguan and said, "Xu Sanguan, quick! Go bring your woman home. She's arguing with He Xiaoyong's woman, and the more they argue, the raunchier it gets. You better go quick, or you'll have no face left at all by the time they're through."

Another person rushed in the door. "Xu Sanguan! Your woman's fighting with He Xiaoyong's woman. They're pulling each other's hair and spitting and even biting."

The last person to come through the door was Blacksmith Fang. Blacksmith Fang said, "Xu Sanguan, I was just walking by He Xiaoyong's place. There's a big crowd there, thirty people at the very least, and they're all laughing at your woman. Your woman and He Xiaoyong's woman are screaming and cursing and fighting, and believe me it's not pretty. Everyone's laughing and enjoying the show, and I even heard some of them saying that Xu Sanguan's been selling blood just so he can keep getting cuckolded."

Xu Sanguan said, "Do I care? Let her do what she wants."

As he spoke, he sat down on the stool by the table, then glanced up toward Blacksmith Fang standing at the threshold.

"She's like a broken pot that's not afraid of shattering, and I'm a dead pig who no longer minds that the water's coming to a boil."

CHAPTER FOURTEEN

Xu Sanguan was thinking of Lin Fenfang. Lin Fenfang, whose braids had once reached to her waist, had married a man who wore glasses, given birth to a boy and a girl, and proceeded to get fat. She grew fatter and fatter with each passing year, and in the end she cut her braids and wore her hair in a bob that was level with her ears.

Xu Sanguan had watched as her neck got shorter and shorter, seen her shoulders thicken, looked on as the contours of her waistline softened and swelled, observed her fingers grow stubby with excess flesh. Yet he still held all the best silk cocoons in reserve for her even now.

These days Lin Fenfang was usually to be seen walking through town carrying a shopping basket. Sometimes it was full of oil, salt, soy sauce, and vinegar. Sometimes it was loaded with fresh vegetables. Sometimes you might see a chunk of fatty pork or a pair of dead carp sticking out from amid the vegetables. When her basket was full of dirty clothes, she would head over to the riverbank, a little wooden stool dangling from one hand because she had grown too heavy to squat, and if she squatted by the riverbank her legs would eventually start to tremble under her weight. She would sit on the stool by the river, remove her shoes and socks, roll up her pants legs, and finally bring her plump feet to rest in the water. Only then would she take the clothes out from the basket and begin to do her wash.

When Lin Fenfang walked down the street with her basket, her body swayed with each step because of her weight, and even the slowest pedestrians were always able to pass her by. She always walked cheerfully behind the rest, and everybody else knew that she was Lin Fenfang from the silk factory, the fattest woman in town, the woman who would gain weight even if she only ate rice, who could put on pounds just by drinking water.

Xu Yulan usually saw Lin Fenfang when she went to buy vegetables in the morning. She would see her carrying her basket and moving from stall to stall, bargaining with each of the vendors, then slowly bending down and carefully sorting through the produce to select the best greens, cabbage, celery, or whatever else. Xu Yulan sometimes said to Yile, Erle, or Sanle, "You know Lin Fenfang at the silk factory? She uses fabric for two just for one new dress for herself."

Lin Fenfang knew all about Xu Yulan too. She knew that she was Xu Sanguan's woman, that she had given him three sons, but that after having given birth three times, she hadn't put on any weight at all, except perhaps a little bit around the stomach. When she talked with the vegetable sellers, her voice was loud and commanding, and she knew how to use it to press them for bargains. When she bought produce, she didn't squeeze in with everybody else and pick out her vegetables one at a time. Instead, she would put all the vegetables in her own basket and then throw the ones she didn't want back onto the pile. She never selected her produce along with everybody else; she let everyone else go through her leavings. Lin Fenfang often stood next to her. When she knelt down and her clothes pulled flush to her body, she could see that her waist hadn't thickened at all over the years. Her hands flew nimbly back and forth from the basket to the produce, while her eyes appeared to be gazing at something in the distance.

Lin Fenfang said to Xu Sanguan, "I know who your woman is. She's called Xu Yulan. She's the Fried Dough Queen of Nantang Street. She's given you three sons, but she's still as pretty as a young girl. Not like me, always putting on weight. Your woman's pretty and smart, and she moves quickly. When she goes shopping—well, I've never seen such a bossy woman."

Xu Sanguan said to Lin Fenfang, "She's no good. As soon as she gets mad about anything, she sits on the doorstep and cries and carries on, and it's because of her that I've been a cuckold for nine years."

Lin Fenfang burst into laughter.

Xu Sanguan looked toward her and continued, "Now when I think about it, I feel really terrible. If I had married you instead of her back then, then I wouldn't have been a cuckold. Lin Fenfang, I think you're better than Xu Yulan in every way. Even your name sounds nicer, and it looks pretty when you write it down. When you talk, it's always nice and soft. Xu Yulan's yelling and shouting all day long, and she snores at night too. When you get home after work, you shut the door and keep your business to yourself. All these years I've never once heard anything bad about your man, but Xu Yulan, well, if three days go by and she hasn't gone out to the doorstep to cry and carry on, she starts to feel uncomfortable, just like she hadn't taken a shit for a week. But the worst of it is that I've been a cuckold for nine years, and I didn't even know it. And if Yile hadn't started to look like that fucking He Xiaoyong, I would have been in the dark my whole goddamn life."

When Lin Fenfang saw that Xu Sanguan had broken into a sweat, she shifted the fan in her hand in his direction. "Your Xu Yulan is prettier than I am."

"She isn't even as pretty as you," Xu Sanguan said. "You used to be prettier than her."

"I used to be good looking, but now I'm fat. Now I can't compare to Xu Yulan."

Xu Sanguan suddenly asked, "If I had asked you to marry me back then, would you have agreed?"

Lin Fenfang looked over at Xu Sanguan and giggled. "I can't remember anymore."

Xu Sanguan asked, "What do you mean, you can't remember?"

Lin Fenfang said, "I really can't remember. It's been ten years now."

THIS CONVERSATION took place as Lin Fenfang lay on her bed and Xu Sanguan sat on a chair at the foot of the bed. Her bespectacled husband looked down on them from a picture frame on the wall. Lin Fenfang had broken her right leg slipping on the stone steps that led down to the riverbank. She had just put her freshly washed clothes into her basket and stepped up onto the steps when her left foot alighted on a watermelon rind. Before she could even call out, she had tumbled over and broken her right leg.

When Xu Sanguan pushed his cart onto the factory floor that day and noticed that Lin Fenfang wasn't there, he stood for a moment next to her spinning machine, then continued on his way around the workshop. After he had made small talk for a few moments with one of the other spinning girls, and she still hadn't shown up, he thought she must have gone to the bathroom.

"You think Lin Fenfang fell into the privy or something? How come she's been gone for so long?"

The other girls said, "How could Lin Fenfang fall into the privy? She's too fat. Her backside would never fit. One of *us* maybe, but not her."

Xu Sanguan asked, "Then where did she go?"

They replied, "Didn't you notice that her spinning machine's been turned off? She fell and broke her leg. She's at home with a cast. She slipped on a watermelon rind with her left foot, but somehow her right leg broke instead. That's what she told us. We all went to visit her already. Why don't you go too?"

Xu Sanguan thought to himself that he would go pay her a visit that very day.

It was that same afternoon that Xu Sanguan sat down in the chair by her bed. Lin Fenfang lay in bed, clad in brightly colored undershorts, and holding a fan in one hand. Her right leg was wrapped in bandages, and her left leg was splayed out whitely across the woven rattan mat spread across the bed. When she saw Xu Sanguan come in, she reached for a blanket to cover up her legs.

Xu Sanguan looked at her corpulent body lying supine on the bed. Her body looked like the ruins of a collapsed house strewn across the expanse of the bed. Her enormous chest bulged over her shoulders and tumbled to either side. The blanket lay over her legs, but Xu Sanguan was still able to make out the contours of her ample thighs. Xu Sanguan asked, "Which leg is it that's broken?"

Lin Fenfang pointed to her right leg. "This one."

Xu Sanguan put his hand on her right leg. "The right leg?"

Lin Fenfang nodded.

Xu Sanguan's hand, sitting atop her leg, squeezed. "I can feel the cast." His hand rested on her thigh for a moment. Then he said, "Your leg's sweating."

Lin Fenfang smiled.

Xu Sanguan continued, "Must be hot under that blanket."

As he spoke, Xu Sanguan pulled the blanket from Lin Fenfang's body and looked at her legs. One of them was wrapped in a cast, and the other one was white and bare. Xu Sanguan had never seen such enormous legs in his life. Her powdery white flesh spread out across the mat, and the way her legs protruded from her undershorts left Xu Sanguan breathless.

He looked up at her and saw that she was still smiling. He

grinned and said, "I never thought your legs would be so soft and white. They're even whiter than fatty pork."

Lin Fenfang said, "Xu Yulan's are soft and white too."

Xu Sanguan replied, "Xu Yulan's face is about as pale as yours, but not the rest of her." He squeezed her knee and asked, "Is this where it's broken?"

Lin Fenfang said, "A little below the knee."

Xu Sanguan squeezed her leg a little below the knee. "Does it hurt?"

"A little bit."

"So this is where the bone is broken?"

"A little bit farther down."

"Then it must be here."

"Right. That spot's very tender."

Xu Sanguan's hand returned to her knee. He gave it another squeeze and asked Lin Fenfang, "Does it hurt here?"

Lin Fenfang said, "No."

Xu Sanguan's hand shifted above her knee and squeezed. "How about here?"

"No."

Xu Sanguan gazed at the spot where Lin Fenfang's thighs emerged from her undershorts and then squeezed her there too. "Does your thigh hurt?"

Lin Fenfang said, "No, it doesn't hurt."

Before she even finished her sentence, Xu Sanguan bolted toward her, and his hands came to rest on top of her enormous breasts.

CHAPTER FIFTEEN

When Xu Sanguan emerged from Lin Fenfang's house, he felt as drained as a man who has just come from the steam room of a public bathhouse. He moved down the sun-drenched summer street bathed in sweat. Just as he was about to turn down another street, he caught sight of two peasants from out of the corner of his eye. Waving their arms despite the empty carrying poles suspended from their shoulders, they shouted across the street, "Aren't you Xu Sanguan?"

Xu Sanguan said, "Yeah, I'm Xu Sanguan."

It was only then that Xu Sanguan recognized them. They had come from the village where his grandpa, who had died a few years before, had lived.

Pointing his arm back in their direction, he called, "I know you all right! You're Ah Fang, and you're Genlong. I know what you're doing in town too. You came in today to sell blood. And I know why you're both carrying empty mugs. You used to have bowls, but I guess you've switched to mugs. How much water have you drunk this time?"

"How much *have* we drunk?" Genlong asked Ah Fang.

Genlong and Ah Fang crossed the street toward Xu Sanguan. Ah Fang said, "Truth be told, we don't really know how much we've drunk."

Xu Sanguan suddenly recalled something Blood Chief Li had told them ten years before. "Do you still remember? Blood Chief Li was saying your bellies, I mean your bladders, were bigger than a pregnant lady. Actually, what he said was your bladders. *Bladder*'s the scientific word for it."

They stood laughing in the street. Xu Sanguan had seen them only twice since they had sold blood together ten years before. On both occasions he had gone down to the countryside for a funeral. The first funeral had been for his grandpa, and the second had been for his fourth uncle. Ah Fang said, "Xu Sanguan, it's been seven or eight years since you last came to see us."

Xu Sanguan said, "My grandpa died and then my fourth uncle died too. They were my only family in the country, so I don't have as much reason to come anymore."

In the seven or eight years in between, it seemed to Xu Sanguan that Ah Fang had grown old. His hair was going gray, and when he smiled, his face creased into a whorl of wrinkles like the waves that fan out across the surface of a pond after a rock has hit the water. Xu Sanguan said to Ah Fang, "You've aged."

Ah Fang nodded. "Well, I'm already forty-five."

Genlong added, "We country folks show our age. A forty-five-year-old in town looks about thirty to us."

Xu Sanguan glanced at Genlong. Genlong, wearing a sleeveless undershirt, looked much sturdier than he had before, and his chest and arms were braided with solid clumps of muscle. Xu Sanguan said to him, "Genlong, you're getting stronger and stronger. Look at those muscles. Every time you move, it looks like a little squirrel's running back and forth across your chest. Did you ever get together with Guihua, the girl with the big behind? You still hadn't gotten married when my fourth uncle died."

Genlong said, "She's given me two sons."

Ah Fang asked Xu Sanguan, "How many sons has your woman given you?"

At first Xu Sanguan wanted to say three, but he quickly changed his mind. Yile, after all, was He Xiaoyong's child.

"Just the same as Genlong's woman. Two sons." Xu Sanguan thought to himself, *If Ah Fang had asked me the same question two months ago, I would have said I have three sons. They don't know that I've been a cuckold for nine years now. And what they don't know, I'm not going to tell them.* He continued, "I don't know why, but as soon as I saw you two on your way to sell blood, I started to feel a little itch to sell some blood myself."

Ah Fang and Genlong said, "That little itch means you have too much blood in you. It can be awfully uncomfortable, having too much blood. Your whole body starts to itch and swell and all that. You better come with us and sell some blood too."

Xu Sanguan thought for a moment, then decided to walk with them over to the hospital. As he walked, he thought about Lin Fenfang. He couldn't help feeling she had been very good to him. When he wanted to rub her feet, she let him. When he wanted to touch her thigh, she let him. When he had jumped up to squeeze her breasts, she had let him squeeze. She had let him do whatever he wanted to do. She had let him do whatever he liked despite the fact that her leg was broken. When he had bumped painfully against her leg, she had merely let out a little grunt. Xu Sanguan was thinking that he really ought to give her ten pounds of soup bones and five pounds of yellow beans. The doctors in the hospital were always telling people with broken bones, "You ought to eat a lot of yellow beans stewed with soup bones."

But merely giving her soup bones and yellow beans somehow didn't seem sufficient. He thought he should give her some mung beans as well, because mung beans were cooling. Lin Fenfang was lying inside all day, and the weather was so hot lately. She would certainly feel cooler after eating some mung beans. And he ought to give her a pound of dried chrysanthemums too. Chrysanthemum tea had cooling properties as well. He would go sell blood with Ah Fang and Genlong so he could earn enough to buy her the soup bones, yellow beans, mung beans, and chrysanthemums. That way he could pay her back for her kindness.

He could earn thirty-five *yuan* selling blood. After he bought the things for Lin Fenfang, he would still have a little more than thirty left over. He would put away what was left to spend on himself, on Erle, and on Sanle. He might even spend some on Xu Yulan from time to time. Anything he liked—as long as he didn't spend any on Yile.

Xu Sanguan followed Ah Fang and Genlong to the hospital. When they got there, they didn't go right in, because Xu Sanguan had yet to have any water. They went instead to the well near the hospital. Genlong picked up the wooden bucket and drew some water from the well. At the same time Ah Fang handed Xu Sanguan his ceramic mug. Xu Sanguan knelt down next to the well, mug in hand, and drank mug after mug of the cold water. Ah Fang stood over him counting. By the time Xu Sanguan had finished six mugs of water, he said he couldn't drink any more. Ah Fang told him he had to drink at least ten mugs, and Genlong said Ah Fang was right. Xu Sanguan started in on his seventh cup. But after a few sips, he began to gasp for air. When he reached the ninth mug, he stood up and told them he really couldn't take any more. If he drank any more, he said, he might die, and besides, he had pins and needles from squatting by the side of the well. Ah Fang said if his legs had fallen asleep, he should drink the water standing up. Genlong told him to drink another mugful. Xu Sanguan shook his head and told them he simply could not swallow any more.

His blood was already swollen, he added, and if he were to drink any more, he might burst. With that, Ah Fang suggested that they set out for the hospital. And so they walked through the hospital gate.

AFTER THEY SOLD their blood to Blood Chief Li and he handed them their money, they made their way to the Victory Restaurant and sat down at a table by the window. Xu Sanguan, beating Ah Fang and Genlong to the punch, pounded on the table and called to the waiter, "A plate of fried pork livers and two shots of yellow rice wine. And warm the wine up for me."

Then he sat back and watched contentedly as Ah Fang and Genlong each pounded the table, calling out to the waiter in turn:

"A plate of fried pork livers and two shots of yellow rice wine."

"A plate of fried pork livers and two shots of yellow rice wine."

When Xu Sanguan noticed that they had forgotten to add the part about warming up the wine, he waved the departing waiter back to the table, pointed at Ah Fang and Genlong, and added, "Warm up the wine for them."

The waiter said, "In all my forty-three years in this business, I've never once seen anyone ask for warm wine on a hot summer day."

Xu Sanguan glanced over at Ah Fang and Genlong. The bemused smiles lighting up their faces told him that he had made a fool of himself. He laughed along with them.

After a good long chuckle, Ah Fang said to Xu Sanguan, "Now remember. You shouldn't sleep with a woman for at least ten days after you sell blood."

Xu Sanguan asked, "Why do you say that?"

Ah Fang said, "Eating a bowl of rice will get you no more than a few drops of blood. And you need a whole bowl of blood just to produce some seed. Well, anyway, that's what we country folk call it, though I guess Blood Chief Li would call it sperm."

Xu Sanguan felt a sudden jolt of alarm. After all, he had just finished his business with Lin Fenfang moments before. He might end up crippled if he went on like this. He asked Ah Fang, "What if you slept with someone just before you went to sell blood?"

Ah Fang said, "You'd be a dead man."

CHAPTER SIXTEEN

A sweaty, bespectacled man carrying ten pounds of soup bones, five pounds of yellow beans, two pounds of mung beans, and one pound of chrysanthemum flowers appeared at Xu Yulan's door. She watched as this stranger set his things down on their table, picked up a glass of boiled water that she had left out to cool, and gulped it down.

When he finished drinking, he said to Xu Yulan, "You're Xu Yulan, I know who you are. You're the lady everybody calls the Fried Dough Queen. Your man is Xu Sanguan. I know who he is too. Do you know who I am? I'm Lin Fenfang's man. The Lin Fenfang who works at the silk factory with your husband. They're on the same shop floor. My woman went to wash clothes by the river and fell and broke her right leg—"

Xu Yulan interrupted, "How did she do that?"

"She slipped on a watermelon rind." The bespectacled man asked Xu Yulan, "Is Xu Sanguan here?"

"He's not home," Xu Yulan said. "He's still at work over at the factory. Should be back any minute now." She looked down at the soup bones and beans and everything else on the table. "You've never come to visit before, and Xu Sanguan's never mentioned you to me either. When you came in, I was wondering who you were. So how come you're giving us so much stuff? There's barely enough room on the table for it all."

The bespectacled man said, "I'm not giving you these things. Xu Sanguan gave all these things to my woman, Lin Fenfang."

Xu Yulan said, "Gave them to your woman? Who's your woman?"

"I just told you, my woman's called Lin Fenfang."

"Oh, I know," Xu Yulan said. "You mean Fatty Lin over at the silk factory."

The bespectacled man said nothing more. Instead, he sat down next to the door to quietly wait for Xu Sanguan, as unruffled as a tree on a windless day. Xu Yulan was left to stand by the table, looking down at the soup bones and beans and flowers and feeling increasingly befuddled.

Xu Yulan said, half to the man and half to herself, "Why would Xu Sanguan give all these things to your woman? They almost fill up the whole table. That's nearly ten pounds of soup bones, four or five pounds of yellow beans, and I'd say there's at least two pounds of mung beans, and a pound of chrysanthemum flowers too. Why would Xu Sanguan give so much stuff to your woman?"

Suddenly, she understood. "Xu Sanguan must have slept with your wife!"

Xu Yulan began to shout, "Xu Sanguan, you home-wrecker! You're always so goddamn stingy. Every time I buy a little strip of fabric, it takes you six months to get over the shock. But when it comes to giving gifts to someone else's wife, then it's different, then there's more stuff than we can afford, more than I can count on my fingers."

Xu Sanguan arrived home from work soon afterward. When he saw the bespectacled man sitting in his doorway and realized that he was Lin Fenfang's husband, he heard two alarms go off in his head. When he stepped into the house and saw the table laden with things, his head buzzed twice more. When he looked over at Xu Yulan and saw that she was screaming, he thought to himself that he was a dead man.

The bespectacled man stood up from the doorstep, stepped out into the lane, and addressed Xu Sanguan's neighbors. "Come over here, I have something I want to tell all of you. Come on over. Bring your kids too. Come and listen to what I'm going to tell you."

The bespectacled man pointed inside at the table and said to Xu Sanguan's neighbors, "Do you see all those soup bones, yellow beans, and mung beans on the table? There's a pound of chrysanthemum flowers too, but they're hidden behind the soup bones. Xu Sanguan gave those things to my woman. My woman's name is Lin Fenfang. Lots of people in town know who she is, and I bet some of you know her too. I see a few of you are nodding your heads. My woman and your Xu Sanguan both work at the silk factory. They work on the same shop floor. My woman slipped and broke her leg when she was washing clothes by the river. Xu Sanguan came to visit my woman. Now, when other people came by for a visit, they would sit by the bed, make some small talk, and then take their leave. Not your Xu Sanguan. When he came for a bedside visit, he ended up *in* bed with the patient. That's right. He raped my woman. Think about it now. A woman with a broken leg—"

Xu Sanguan protested, "But it wasn't rape at all."

"That's exactly what it was." The bespectacled man stated categorically. "What do you people think? You think she would have had the strength to push him away with a broken leg? The slightest move left her in pain for hours. You think my woman could have pushed him away? This Xu Sanguan—this Xu Sanguan wouldn't even spare a woman with a broken leg! What do you say to that? Is he any better than a beast?"

The neighbors didn't bother to answer his query. Instead, they gazed curiously at Xu Sanguan.

Only Xu Yulan emerged to give her assent, grasping hold of Xu Sanguan's ear with one hand and screaming, "You're no better than a beast! You've ruined me! How can I ever hold my head up again?"

The bespectacled man continued, "After this Xu Sanguan raped my wife, he went out and bought these soup bones and yellow beans for her. And it worked. He got her to shut up about the whole thing. If I hadn't noticed all these things in the house, I wouldn't have known someone else had slept with my wife. But when I saw all these things, I knew something was going on. If I hadn't shouted and pounded on the table, she wouldn't even have told me what happened."

At this point in his speech he walked over to the table, picked up the soup bones and yellow beans, and slung them over his back. Then he told Xu Sanguan's neighbors, "I brought these things over here today for your benefit. I thought I should let you know what kind of man Xu Sanguan really is. In the future, you'd best be on your guard. The man's a pervert. Whoever has women in the family had better watch out."

With that, the bespectacled man strode off with the ten pounds of soup bones, five pounds of yellow beans, two pounds of mung beans, and one pound of chrysanthemum flowers on his back.

Xu Yulan, wholly occupied with pulling and scratching at Xu Sanguan's face as she berated him, failed to notice at first what exactly the bespectacled man was doing. When she finally turned to look, he had vanished, and the tabletop was empty. She immediately gave chase, shouting as she went, "Come back here! How dare you take our things?"

The bespectacled man ignored her shouts and continued down the lane without so much as turning to glance in her direction.

Xu Yulan pointed at his retreating figure and shouted to her neighbors, "I've never seen anyone so shameless! He steals your things and still struts away like he's done you a good turn."

She continued to curse in the direction of the bespectacled man until he disappeared into the distance. Then she turned and caught sight of Xu Sanguan. As soon as she saw him, she fell heavily on the doorstep and began to cry.

"It's all over for us. With other folks the old saying holds true: 'As goes the nation so goes the family.' But it's different for us. The country's just fine, but we're ruined. First Blacksmith Fang came to take away all our things. Not one month later, and we've been betrayed by one of our own. That Xu Sanguan is no better than a beast. Usually, he's famously stingy! If I buy a yard of fabric, he feels sick to his stomach for a whole month! But as soon as that Fatty Lin comes on the scene, things change. As soon as that bitch shows up, he's handing out ten pounds of soup bones, four, even five pounds of yellow beans, and no less than two pounds of mung beans! Not to mention the chrysanthemum flowers! I wonder how much all of that stuff cost?"

At this point Xu Yulan appeared to have thought of something else, because she interrupted her harangue to shout toward Xu Sanguan, "You stole my money! You must have stolen the money I hid inside my trunk. I saved that money one or two *fen* at a time. I worked for ten years to save that money! Ten years of blood, sweat, and tears! And you gave it all away to that fat bitch!"

Xu Yulan darted over to her trunk, opened the lid, and rifled through the contents. Soon she fell silent; she had found her savings intact.

Having securely refastened the lid of the trunk, she looked up to see that Xu Sanguan had closed the front door, shutting the neighbors outside. He smiled ingratiatingly toward her with thirty *yuan* in his hand, the three ten-*yuan* notes fanned out from his fingers like a poker hand. Xu Yulan sidled over to where he was standing, took the money from his hand, and asked in a low voice, "Where did this money come from?"

Xu Sanguan also lowered his voice. "I earned it selling blood."

"You sold blood again?"

Xu Yulan gave a low moan and, after a moment of silence, began to cry. Between her sobs, she said, "Why did I marry you? I've suffered and I've struggled for ten years now, and I've given you three sons. When did you ever sell blood for my sake? I never knew until now what a heartless son of a bitch you are. I can't believe you sold your blood just to give that fat bitch some soup bones."

Xu Sanguan tapped her on the shoulder. "Since when have you given me three sons? Is Yile my son? And when I sold blood to pay Blacksmith Fang, who do you think I was doing it for?"

Xu Yulan fell silent. Then she gazed at Xu Sanguan for a moment. "Tell me. What exactly happened between you and that Fatty Lin? Did you really want a woman as fat as all that?"

Xu Sanguan stroked his face thoughtfully. "She broke her leg, so I went to see her. It was just common courtesy."

"And was it just common courtesy to hop in bed with her? Go on."

Xu Sanguan said, "I reached out my hand to squeeze her leg and asked her where it hurt."

"On her thigh? Or her calf?"

"At first it was the calf, but then I somehow got to her thigh."

"You're shameless." Xu Yulan jabbed a finger at his face. "Then what happened? What did you do next?"

"What happened next?" Xu Sanguan hesitated for a moment. "What happened next was I grabbed her tits."

"Aiya!" Xu Yulan cried out. "You worthless son of a bitch! Since when did you start taking tricks from that bastard He Xiaoyong's book?"

CHAPTER SEVENTEEN

Xu Yulan spent twenty-one and a half of the thirty *yuan* that she had captured from Xu Sanguan's outstretched fingers to make new clothes. She made herself a new pair of gray cotton pants and a light blue cotton-padded jacket embroidered with dark blue flowers. Yile, Erle, and Sanle each got a new cotton-padded jacket as well. Xu Sanguan was the only one in the family who didn't get any new clothes, because every time Xu Yulan thought of the incident with Lin Fenfang, she was too angry.

Soon winter came. When Xu Sanguan saw that Xu Yulan, Yile, Erle, and Sanle all had new padded jackets, he said to Xu Yulan, "If you spend the money I earned selling blood on yourself or on Erle and Sanle, that's fine with me. But I can't stand for you to spend it on Yile."

"Would you feel any better if I spent it on Fatty Lin?"

Xu Sanguan, hurt by this outburst, lowered his head and continued quietly, "Yile's not my son. I've raised him for nine years already, and it looks like there'll be many more years to come.

I've already accepted that. And I'm perfectly willing to spend the money I make sweating over at the factory on him. But it just doesn't feel right to spend any more of my blood money on him."

Xu Yulan took the remaining eight and a half *yuan*, supplemented the sum with two *yuan* of her own, and used it to make Xu Sanguan a navy blue Mao jacket. She told Xu Sanguan, "This jacket was made with the money you earned selling blood. And I contributed two *yuan* of my own. Do you feel any better now?"

Xu Sanguan remained silent. Xu Yulan had something on him now, and he couldn't afford to ride as high as he once had. In the past Xu Yulan had taken care of all the household chores while Xu Sanguan worked at the factory. After the affair with Lin Fenfang came out into the open, it was Xu Yulan's turn to ride high. She took to wearing her finely woven sweater and strolling around with a handful of melon seeds, leisurely ducking in and out of the neighbors' places for a chat. And once they had gotten started, she and her friends might prattle on for two, even three hours. Xu Sanguan, meanwhile, would be in the kitchen cooking rice and stir-frying some dishes, bathed in sweat. His neighbors would often poke their heads inside the door and, catching sight of Xu Sanguan busy with his cookery, laugh and say:

"Xu Sanguan, cooking again tonight?"

"Xu Sanguan, go a little easier. Chopping vegetables isn't like chopping firewood, you know."

"Xu Sanguan, since when did you get become so hardworking?"

Xu Sanguan would say to them, "There's nothing I can do. Xu Yulan's got something on me. It's like the old saying goes: 'A moment of pleasure leads to a lifetime of regret.' "

For her part, Xu Yulan was wont to tell the others, "I think I've finally got things straight. It used to be that I was always looking out for my man and doing everything for the sake of the kids. Just as long as they got enough to eat, I was perfectly happy to go hungry. As long as they were comfortable, I was willing to put up with any kind of discomfort. But I've finally got things straight. In the future, I'm going to look after myself. If I don't care about my own welfare, no one else will. You just can't trust men. Even if they have a beauty at home, they still think they can play around with other women. You can't count on the kids either."

Xu Sanguan realized how stupid he had been. The affair itself was one thing, but buying Lin Fenfang a heap of soup bones and yellow beans had been stupid. Even an idiot would have started to suspect something was going on when he found all those things on his wife's table.

But the more he thought about it, the more he felt that the affair with Lin Fenfang hadn't done much harm. After all, he hadn't knocked her up. That was more than he could say for He Xiaoyong and Xu Yulan. They had produced Yile, and he was still responsible for the boy.

The more he thought about it, the angrier he became. So he called Xu Yulan over and told her, "From this day on, I'm not doing the housework anymore." He said to Xu Yulan, "You did it one time with He Xiaoyong, and I did it once with Lin Fenfang. You and He Xiaoyong ended up with Yile. Did Lin Fenfang and I make a 'Four-le'? We did not. We've both made serious mistakes, but yours was much more serious than mine."

Xu Yulan burst into howls of protest and jabbed both hands toward his face. "You're really no better than a beast. I'd already forgotten about your affair with that bitch. Now you insist on reminding me. What did I do in my past life to deserve this? Whatever it was, it's coming back to haunt me."

As she shouted, she edged toward her place on the doorstep.

Xu Sanguan rushed to block her way, saying as he held her fast, "Okay, okay, okay then, I'll never bring it up again, all right?"

CHAPTER EIGHTEEN

Xu Sanguan said to Xu Yulan, "This year is 1958. We've had People's Communes, the Great Leap Forward, Backyard Steel Furnaces, and what else? They took back my grandpa's and my fourth uncle's land down in the countryside. From now on it looks like no one will have their own land anymore. All the land belongs to the state. If you want to plant crops, you'll have to rent the land from them, and when you harvest the crop, you have to give some grain to the state too. The state is just like the landlords before. Of course, you can't say that the state is a landlord. You should call it the People's Commune instead. And our silk factory's started to smelt steel too. We made eight little furnaces. Me and four other people are responsible for looking after one of them. So now I'm not the man who distributes the silkworm cocoons anymore. I'm a steel smelter now. You know why we have to smelt so much steel? Because steel is like grain, grain for the state. It's like rice, wheat, meat, and fish for the state. That's why smelting steel is just like planting rice in the paddies."

Xu Sanguan said to Xu Yulan, "I was out taking a walk today, and I saw lots of people in red armbands going from house to house confiscating people's woks, and their bowls, and their rice, and all their oil, salt, soy, and vinegar. I'll bet they'll show up at our place too in a couple of days. They say no one's allowed to cook at home anymore. If you want to eat, you have to go to the canteen. You know how many canteens there will be in town? I counted three on the way home. There's one at the silk factory, one at Heavenrest Temple, and they turned the old Buddhist monastery into a canteen too. All the monks have to wear white hats and aprons, so they look like real chefs now. And then there's the theater around the block. That's a canteen now too. You know where the kitchen is? Right on the stage. All the singing clowns from the Yue Opera Company are up onstage rinsing vegetables. I hear the leading man's the deputy of the canteen, and the guy who always played the villains is the vice deputy."

Xu Sanguan said to Xu Yulan, "I took you to the canteen at the silk factory the day before yesterday, and we went to Heavenrest Temple canteen yesterday. I'll take you to the canteen at the theater again to eat today. There's not enough meat in the dishes at the Heavenrest Temple canteen. The monks who do the cooking all used to be vegetarians, so they don't use much meat. When we had the green pepper fried pork yesterday, didn't you hear everyone joking that it was 'green pepper minus the pork'? Now that we've tried three of the canteens, it looks like you and the kids like the one at the theater the best, but I still like the big canteen at the silk factory. The dishes at the theater aren't bad, but they don't have big enough portions. Over at the factory they give you more of everything, including meat, and you can eat as much as you want. I didn't burp once after I ate at Heavenrest Temple canteen, and I didn't burp after eating at the canteen at the theater either. But when I ate at the silk factory, I was burping all night long. Tomorrow I'll take you to the big canteen at City Hall. They have the best food in town. That's what Blacksmith Fang told me. He said the chefs over there are all from the Victory Restaurant, and those chefs definitely know how to cook the best dishes in town. You know what their specialty is? It's fried pork livers."

Xu Sanguan said to Xu Yulan, "Let's not go to the City Hall canteen tomorrow. It's so exhausting to eat over there. At least a quarter of the people in town go there for dinner. It's more like getting in a big fight than having a meal. Besides, the kids almost got squashed to death over there, it was so crowded. My undershirt was wet through with sweat. And with so many people farting and stinking up the place, it's hard to have much of an appetite. Let's go to the silk factory tomorrow, okay? I know you want to go to the theater, but they've already shut down the canteen there, and I hear the one at Heavenrest Temple has been closed for a few days too. But the silk factory's canteen is still open. But we'd better go early or else there won't be anything left to eat."

Xu Sanguan said to Xu Yulan, "They shut down all the canteens in town. Looks like the good times are over. No one's going to take care of our meals anymore. Does that mean we have to cook for ourselves again? But what are we going to cook?"

Xu Yulan said, "There's two crocks of rice underneath the bed. When they first came by to take the wok, the rice, the oil, salt, soy, and vinegar, I couldn't bear to give them those two crocks of rice. That's the rice I saved over the years by shortchanging all of you, so I just couldn't bear to let them take it away."

CHAPTER NINETEEN

Xu Yulan had been married to Xu Sanguan for more than ten years now, and she had spent those years scrimping and saving and carefully calculating just to get by. The two crocks of rice she had under the bed were originally used for ladling; there was a slightly larger crock in the kitchen. Every day when she cooked rice, Xu Yulan removed the wooden lid from the rice crock in the kitchen and ladled just enough for the whole family's daily consumption into the pot. Then she removed one handful of rice from the pot and placed it in one of the crocks under the bed. As she explained to Xu Sanguan, "None of you would have especially noticed an extra mouthful of rice anyway, and you won't really miss a mouthful either."

What this signified was that Xu Sanguan had eaten two less mouthfuls of rice than he was due every day. After Yile, Erle, and Sanle came along, they too were made to miss out on two mouthfuls a day. As for Xu Yulan, she cheated herself of even more rice. The rice that was saved by way of these measures ended up in a small crock underneath the bed. When the first crock was full, she got another empty rice crock and proceeded to fill that one up as well.

But Xu Sanguan disagreed. "It's not as if we're planning to open a rice shop or something. What's the point of keeping so much rice around? If we don't eat it by the summer, the bugs will get into it."

Xu Yulan agreed, and she stopped putting away any more rice after she filled up the second crock.

If the rice was kept in storage for too long, the bugs would start to infest the crock. The bugs lived, ate, shat, and slept in the rice, turning grain after grain into powder. Their excrement looked a bit like flour, and it was difficult to tell the two apart—the only difference was that their shit was slightly yellow. As soon as the two crocks were full, then Xu Yulan would dump the contents into the bigger crock in the kitchen.

She would sit on the bed measuring how much rice there had been in the two small crocks and, based on its weight, how much money the rice had been worth. She would proceed to fold an equivalent sum into a neat packet and place it on the bottom of her trunk. This money was not to be spent.

She told Xu Sanguan, "This money was snatched bit by bit from out of your mouths. And you didn't even notice the difference, did you?" She added, "We can't use this money for anything ordinary. Something really important has to come up before we can spend it."

Xu Sanguan took exception to this entire procedure. "This makes about as much sense as taking off your pants to fart. It's all completely unnecessary."

Xu Yulan said, "I really can't agree with you. No one can get through life without ever getting sick or having some kind of disaster happen to them. Everyone has their ups and downs. And when hard times come, it's better to be prepared than not. Smart folks always prepare some way out of a jam before it happens. And anyway, this is how I save a little money for all of us."

Xu Yulan would often say, "Hard times are going to come. No one can go through their life without running into hard times once or twice. You just can't escape."

When Sanle was eight, Erle was ten, and Yile was eleven, the whole town was flooded. The floodwaters reached one meter at their deepest, and even the shallows came up to the knees. That June Xu Sanguan's house lay in a pool of water for seven days. The water lapped back and forth across the floor, and when they slept at night, they could hear the sound of the rippling waves.

After the flood came famine. At first Xu Sanguan and Xu Yulan did not realize what was happening. They heard that most of the rice in the countryside was rotting in the paddies. Xu Sanguan thought of his grandpa and his fourth uncle and reassured himself that it was a good thing they were already gone—otherwise, how could they make it through the year? His other three uncles were still alive, but they almost never occurred to him, because they had never been good to him or paid him any mind.

It wasn't until a constant stream of destitute people begging for food began to arrive in town that Xu Sanguan and Xu Yulan truly understood that famine was at hand. Every morning when they opened the front door, they would see beggars sleeping in the lane in front of their house. There were new faces every day, but they all grew more and more wasted and sallow as time went by.

The rice shop was open on occasion and sometimes closed. Every time it reopened, the price of rice would double or even triple. After a short while the money that used to buy ten pounds of rice would get you only two pounds of sweet potatoes. The silk factory stopped work, because there were no more silkworms. Xu Yulan no longer needed to go fry dough in the morning because there was no flour and no cooking oil. The schools shut down, and most of the shops in town closed their doors. Of the twenty or so restaurants that used to be in operation, only one—the Victory Restaurant—remained open.

Xu Sanguan said to Xu Yulan, "This famine has come at the

worst possible time. If it had been a few years back, we would have been able to squeak through just fine. But we were already running low on supplies.

"Think about it. First they took away our wok and bowls, and then the rice, oil, soy, and vinegar. Then they dismantled the stove. I thought we'd be eating at those big canteens for the rest of our lives. I never thought that after only a year we'd be responsible for ourselves again. And it costs money to build another stove. It costs money to buy a new wok, new bowls, new spoons, and new plates again. It costs money to replace the oil, salt, soy, and vinegar. And all of a sudden we've had to spend most of that money you had saved, one *fen* at a time, over the years.

"It's not that I mind spending the money—if we had had a couple of peaceful years, we would have been able to get back to speed after a while. But have we had any peace of mind the last couple years? First it was Yile. Yile's not even my own son, and that in itself was a real shock. But what was worse was that he got us into so much trouble and I had to give Blacksmith Fang thirty-five *yuan.* It's already been a tough couple of years, and *now* we've got a famine on our hands. Lucky we've still got two crocks of rice under the bed."

Xu Yulan said, "We can't eat the rice under the bed yet. There's still some left in the kitchen crock. And we can't eat plain rice anymore either. I've already figured everything out. The famine will last another six months, at least until the new crops start to come up next spring. We only have enough rice for another month, and even if we eat rice gruel instead, we still only have enough for a little more than four months. That leaves more than a month and a half without anything to eat. You can't go without food for a month and a half. We're going to have to eat even less in the first four months just to save some food for that last month and a half. And before winter comes, we'd better go out into the fields and gather all the wild vegetables we can find. Once the rice in the kitchen is done, we can fill the crock with wild vegetables, then cover them with salt so that they don't go bad. They should last at least four or five months. We still have some extra money. I sewed it into the quilt. I never told you before, but I save the money from marketing as well. All told, there's still nineteen *yuan*, sixty-seven *fen* left. We should take thirteen of that and buy corn. I think we can still get about a hundred pounds for the money. Then we can strip the kernels and grind them into corn flour. That should make about thirty pounds of corn flour. If we add the corn flour to the rice gruel, it'll get nice and thick, and our stomachs won't feel quite so empty."

XU SANGUAN said to his sons, "All we've been eating for a month now is corn flour gruel. We've had so much of the stuff that you kids have lost your color, and you're getting skinnier and skinnier, and you don't have any energy at all. All you know how to say these days is 'I'm hungry, I'm hungry, I'm hungry.' It's a good thing that all you little ones are still alive and well. But everyone in town is in the same boat. Go over to the neighbors' places or your classmates' houses, and you'll see that we're doing better than most. At least you get a bowl of corn flour gruel every day. You say you're sick of eating wild vegetables and corn flour gruel? Well, that's all you're going to get, because these hard times won't be over for a long time yet. I know you want to eat some plain rice or some rice gruel without the corn flour, and I've talked it over with your mom. We're going to make you some, but we can't do it yet.

"For now you're going to have to keep eating the wild vegetables and the corn flour gruel. You complain that even the corn flour gruel is getting thinner and thinner, and that's true, because we're not out of the woods yet, and it might be a long, long time before it's all over. So all your mom and I can do is protect you little ones and make sure you get through this alive.

What they say is true: 'You have to have a mountain before you can gather some wood.' That means we have to get through these tough times now, so we'll live to see better days. So you have to keep on eating corn flour gruel, even if it gets thinner and thinner, even if you say that the gruel's all gone as soon as you take a piss.

"Which one of you said that? Must have been Yile. I know it was you. Little brat. You're going on all day long about how hungry you are, but you kids are still small, and you get to eat as much corn flour gruel as I do every day. You go on all day long about how hungry you are, but you know why you're so hungry? Because you're out running around all day. As soon as you eat your gruel, you're running out to play, and when I tell you to come back inside, you never listen. Sanle was even screaming and hollering out in the street today. Little brat. How can you carry on like that in times like these? In times like these you've got to speak softly and conserve your energy. Your stomach's grumbling, you're running on empty, and you still manage to run and shout and carry on? It's no goddamn wonder you're so hungry! You're digesting all the gruel as soon as you've eaten it.

"From today on, Yile, Erle, and yes, you too, Sanle, are going to lie down after you've eaten your gruel. No more moving around. As soon as you start to move around too much, you get hungry. So do me a favor and just lie down and be quiet. Your mom and I are going to be lying there with you. I can't say anymore. I'm so hungry I don't have the energy to speak. The gruel we had just now is already gone."

From that day on Xu Sanguan's family ate corn flour gruel twice a day, once in the morning and once in the evening. The rest of the time they lay on the bed without moving or even speaking. As soon as they moved or started to speak, their stomachs would start to rumble, and the hunger would come. And lying quiet and motionless in bed all day long, they would naturally fall asleep. And so Xu Sanguan's family began to sleep all day and every day, from morning to evening. And after they awoke for their gruel, they would sleep from the evening until the next morning. They slept until December 7.

On the night of December 7 Xu Yulan cooked an extra bowl of corn flour gruel and made it much thicker than usual. Then she roused Xu Sanguan and their sons from bed and smilingly told them, "We'll have something good to eat tonight."

Xu Sanguan, Yile, Erle, and Sanle sat at the table craning their necks to see just what Xu Yulan was going to bring to the table. But what she brought to the table was the same corn flour gruel that they had eaten day after day.

Yile was the first to voice his disappointment. "It's just the same old corn flour gruel."

Erle and Sanle, just as disappointed, echoed, "Just the same old gruel."

Xu Yulan said to them, "Take a closer look. This stuff is a lot thicker than what we ate yesterday or the day before yesterday or any day for a long time now. You'll know what's special about it as soon as you take a sip."

After each of the three sons took a sip, their eyes rolled in their sockets. Something *was* different about the gruel, but they were unable to place what exactly the difference was. Xu Sanguan also took a sip. Xu Yulan asked, "Now do you know what I put in there?"

The three sons shook their heads, picked up their bowls, and began to hurriedly slurp down the gruel.

Xu Sanguan said to them, "You kids have lost your minds. Can't you tell that something is sweet when you taste it?"

Yile, coming to a sudden realization, cried, "It's sugar! You put some sugar in the gruel."

Erle and Sanle nodded enthusiastically as they continued to slurp noisily from their bowls, breaking into happy giggles as they swallowed. Xu Sanguan laughed as he slurped just as noisily and enthusiastically as the children.

Xu Yulan explained to Xu Sanguan, "I took out the sugar that was left over from Spring Festival and made the gruel nice and thick and sticky today. And I made you an extra bowl too. Do you want to know why? Because today's your birthday."

Xu Sanguan had already finished his first bowl of gruel. He slapped his head and exclaimed, "Today's the day my mama gave birth to me!" Then he continued, "So you put some sugar in the gruel and made it thicker than usual and cooked an extra bowl for me, all because it's my birthday. I get to eat a little more today."

But before he could reach for the extra bowl, Yile, Erle, and Sanle had extended their empty bowls entreatingly toward him.

"Let's give the extra bowl to them." He gestured toward his sons.

"You can't give it to them. I made it especially for you."

Xu Sanguan said, "It doesn't matter who eats it in the end. It'll turn into shit no matter who eats it. Let the kids shit a little extra. Let's give it to them."

Xu Sanguan watched the children lift their bowls to their mouths and suck down the sweetened corn flour gruel. He said to them, "When you're finished eating, each of you has to wish me a happy birthday with a kowtow."

As soon as he had said it, though, he began to feel uneasy. *When is this ever going to end? It's been so hard on the little brats. They don't even remember what it's like to eat sweets, and when they finally got something sweet, they didn't even recognize the taste of sugar anymore.*

That night, as the family lay in bed, Xu Sanguan said to them, "I know what you kids want most badly of all. To eat, right? You want white rice, and dishes stir-fried with oil, and you want to eat fish and meat and everything nice. Today was my birthday, and you kids got to enjoy it along with me. You even got to eat some sugar. But I know that in your hearts you still want to eat even more. The question is, what exactly do you want to eat? Since it's my birthday, I'm going to do something special for you kids. I'm going to cook a meal for each of you with my mouth, and you can eat it with your ears. You won't be able to eat it with your mouth because there's nothing to eat, but prick up your ears, because I'm going to start cooking any moment now. You can order whatever you feel like eating. You can take turns. Sanle goes first. Sanle, what do you feel like eating?"

Sanle said very softly, "I don't want to eat gruel anymore. I want white rice."

"We've got plenty of white rice," Xu Sanguan said. "Unlimited supply. As much as you could possibly want. But I want to know what dishes you feel like eating."

Sanle said, "I want to eat meat."

"Sanle wants to eat meat," Xu Sanguan announced. "I'll make him some red-braised pork. There's lean pork and fatty pork, but when you're making red-braised pork, it's best to use a little of both, and it's even better if you throw in some skin as well. All right then. I'll start chopping the pork into slices about as thick as a finger and as long as half your palm. Here's three slices of meat for Sanle."

Sanle said, "Dad, I want four pieces."

"Then I'll cut four pieces for Sanle."

Sanle said, "Dad, I want five pieces."

Xu Sanguan said, "You'll be able to eat four pieces at the very most. You're still little. If you had five, you'd be much too stuffed when you were done. Now listen to me cook. First I'll blanch the four pieces in boiling water. Only for a minute, though, because I don't want the meat to get tough. When it's done, I'll remove it from the pot and let it dry. When it's dry, I'll throw it into the wok with some bubbling hot oil. Then I'll add some soy sauce, a pinch of five-spice powder, some yellow rice wine, and a little water to cover. I'll braise it slowly over gentle heat, covered, for about two hours, and when the liquid has finally cooked down, your red-braised pork will be ready."

Xu Sanguan heard the sound of saliva being swallowed.

"I'll take the cover off the wok, and the aroma of meat will fill the room. You'll lift up your chopsticks, spear a piece of meat, put it in your mouth, and start to chew."

Xu Sanguan heard the sound of swallowed saliva grow louder and louder. "Is that Sanle swallowing, or are the other two swallowing too? By the sound of it, you're all swallowing. How about you, Xu Yulan? Listen to me carefully. This meal is for Sanle and Sanle alone. Sanle's the only one who's allowed to swallow. Every time one of you swallows, it's just like you're stealing some of Sanle's red-braised pork. Your meals are coming up next. But we have to let Sanle eat to his heart's content first, and then I'll make something for each of you as well.

"All right Sanle, prick up your ears. You'll pick up that piece of meat with your chopsticks, put it in your mouth, and start to chew. And the flavor—let me tell you about the flavor. The fatty meat's rich but not too rich, and the lean meat's still nice and juicy. You know why I braised it over low heat for so long? So the flavor would all be absorbed into the meat. Sanle, take your time, and enjoy the meal.

"Erle's next. What do *you* feel like eating, Erle?"

Erle said, "I want red-braised pork too. I want five slices."

"Okay, first I'll slice five pieces for Erle, half fatty and half lean. Then I'll blanch it in some boiling water, and when it's ready, I'll take it out and set it aside to dry. Next, I'll go ahead and—"

Erle cut in, "Dad, Yile and Sanle are swallowing."

"Yile," Xu Sanguan scolded, "it's not your turn to swallow yet." He continued, "Erle gets five pieces of meat. I'll throw the meat into the wok and brown it in oil, and then add some soy sauce, a pinch of five-spice powder—"

Erle said, "Dad, Sanle's still swallowing."

Xu Sanguan said, "Sanle's swallowing because he's still eating his meat, not yours. Yours isn't ready yet."

When Xu Sanguan had finished making Erle's red-braised pork, he turned to Yile. "Yile, what are you going to have?"

Yile said, "Red-braised pork."

Xu Sanguan, slightly annoyed, said, "If all three of you brats want red-braised pork, why didn't you say so in the first place? If you had told me before, I could have made it all at the same time. I'll slice five pieces for Yile—"

Yile said, "I want six pieces."

"I'll slice six pieces for Yile, half fatty and half lean—"

Yile said, "I don't want lean meat. I just want the fatty meat."

Xu Sanguan said, "It tastes best if you use some of both."

Yile said, "I want fatty meat. There shouldn't be any lean meat at all."

Erle and Sanle joined in. "We want fatty meat too."

When Xu Sanguan finished making the fatty red-braised pork for Yile, he proceeded to clear-braise a carp for Xu Yulan. He secreted a few slices of ham inside the fish's belly, added a couple slices of ginger and some dried mushrooms, rubbed its scales with a coat of salt, drizzled the dish with yellow rice wine, and sprinkled chopped spring onions over the top. Then he braised it for an hour in the wok. When the fish finally emerged from under the lid, its delicate scent filled the room.

Xu Sanguan's vividly depicted clear-braised carp made another wave of swallowing sounds resonate through the room. Xu Sanguan scolded his sons, "I made this fish for your mom, not for you. What are you salivating for? You ate so much meat already. I think it's time for you to go to bed."

Finally Xu Sanguan made himself something to eat. His meal consisted of fried pork livers. He said, "First I'll cut the livers into slices, very fine slices, then I'll put them all in a bowl and sprinkle them with salt and a little cornstarch. The cornstarch helps keep the liver nice and tender. Next I'll pour in a half cup of yellow rice wine for flavor and sprinkle little slices of spring onion over the top. When the oil in the wok starts to smoke, I'll pour the livers into the oil, stir once, stir twice, stir three times. . . ."

"Stir four times, stir five times, stir six times," Yile, Erle, and Sanle continued his sentence for him, each taking one turn at the wok.

But Xu Sanguan corrected them. "No, you only need to stir it three times. After four turns it would be overdone, after five it would start to get tough, and after six turns you wouldn't even be able to bite through the liver. After the third turn, I'll take the livers out of the wok. But I'll take my time before I start to eat. First I'll pour myself two shots of yellow rice wine and take a sip. I'll let the wine roll slowly down my throat and warm up my insides. It feels just like washing your face with a hot towel. The wine just cleans out your belly. Then I'll pick up a pair of chopsticks and lift a slice of liver up to my mouth. This is the life, this is the moment of paradise."

The sound of saliva once again resonated throughout the room. Xu Sanguan said, "The fried pork livers are my dish. Yile, Erle, Sanle, and you too, Xu Yulan—you're all swallowing. You're stealing my dish."

Xu Sanguan burst into loud and happy laughter.

"It's my birthday. I want all of you to have some of my fried pork livers."

CHAPTER TWENTY

The day after his birthday Xu Sanguan counted on his fingers the number of days that his family had eaten corn flour gruel: fifty-seven days in a row. And then he said to himself, *I've got to sell some blood so they can eat a square meal.*

It was thus that Xu Sanguan arrived at the hospital and found himself facing Blood Chief Li. And he thought to himself, *Everyone in town is gray with hunger, but Blood Chief Li still has ruddy cheeks. Everyone in town has lost weight, but Blood Chief Li's face is as fleshy as ever. Everyone in town is always scowling, but Blood Chief Li has a big smile on his face.*

Blood Chief Li gave Xu Sanguan a welcoming grin. "I know you. You've come to sell blood before. Last time you brought some things for me. How come you don't have anything today?"

Xu Sanguan said, "My family's been eating corn flour gruel for fifty-seven days in a row. All I have left is my blood. I'm coming empty-handed to beg you to let me sell two bowls of blood. If I can bring some money home, my family will finally be able to eat a square meal. If you can help me out now, I'll find a way to pay you back later."

Blood Chief Li asked, "How are you planning to pay me back?"

Xu Sanguan said, "I don't have anything I can call my own right now. But in the past I've given you eggs, meat, and even a pound of sugar. You didn't want the sugar. Not only did you not want it, you even scolded me for bringing it. You said you were a Communist Party member and that you wouldn't take 'so much as a needle and thread from the masses.' I didn't know that you'd be willing to accept things again now, so I didn't come prepared, and I don't know how I should repay you."

Blood Chief Li said, "These days I don't have any choice in the matter. With times as hard as these, the town blood chief might end up starving to death if he didn't accept a little something to eat and drink now and again. When things get a little better, I'll go back to the old policy of not taking 'so much as a needle and thread from the masses.' Just forget that I'm a party member for the time being. Look at me as your benefactor. They say that you should repay a drop of kindness with a flood. But I don't want a flood. All I want is a drop in return. Why don't you just give me a few *yuan* from out of what you make selling blood? You can give me the change and pocket the rest."

After Xu Sanguan sold his blood, he gave five *yuan* to Blood Chief Li and took thirty home. He handed the money to Xu Yulan and told her he had earned it selling blood and that he had "flooded" Blood Chief Li with the remaining five *yuan*. Then he told her that the family had eaten corn flour gruel for fifty-seven days in a row and they couldn't go on eating the stuff forever. Now they had enough money to add a little something different to their diet every few days, and when they ran out of money, he would go sell blood again because his blood was like a well—the level would stay about the same no matter if you drew water every day or never at all.

Finally he added, "Let's not eat corn flour gruel tonight. Let's go to the Victory Restaurant and eat a square meal." He said, "I feel really weak right now. I can't even talk too loud. Can't you tell? Listen to me. After I sold blood today, I didn't drink two shots of yellow rice wine or eat a plate of fried pork livers. That's why I don't have any energy left. It's not that I didn't want to eat some. I went over to the Victory Restaurant, but all they have is plain soup noodles. They're in the same boat as everyone else, what with the famine. Used to be they'd make their soup noodles with meat broth, but now they use boiled water and throw in a little soy sauce. They don't even have any spring onions. That's the way it is. And they're asking one *yuan* seventy *fen* a bowl. Before it was just nine *fen* a bowl. I'm totally exhausted. I didn't eat any fried pork livers. I'm running on empty. They say that if you don't have enough to eat, you should supplement your diet with sleep. I'm going to sleep now."

As he spoke, Xu Sanguan lay down in bed, stretched out his arms and legs, and shut his eyes.

"I'm seeing spots," he continued, "and my heart is thumping like it's all worn out, and my stomach's convulsing. I feel like I need to throw something up. I'm going to bed now. If I sleep for four or five hours, don't worry about it. But if I sleep for seven or eight hours and still don't wake up, then you'd better call someone to help take me over to the hospital."

After Xu Sanguan fell asleep, Xu Yulan sat on the doorstep squeezing the thirty *yuan* between her fingers. She gazed at the deserted street and watched the wind blow eddies of dust across the ground.

Staring at the dull, gray wall across the lane, she said to herself, *When Yile broke open Blacksmith Fang's son's head, he went to sell blood. And when Fatty Lin broke her leg, he went to sell blood again. I still can't believe he was willing to sell his own blood for a fat slut like that. It's not like it's mere sweat. It's blood, after all. Now that the family's eaten corn flour gruel for fifty-*

seven days in a row, he goes to sell blood once again. And then he says he'll do it again because otherwise we're not going to make it through these hard times. When are these hard times ever going to end?

Tears fell down her face as she spoke. She folded the money into a neat bundle, slid it into her inside pocket, and raised a hand to her face to wipe away the tears. She wiped the tears across her cheek with her palm, and then wiped the tears from her eyes with her fingertips.

CHAPTER TWENTY-ONE

That evening Xu Sanguan and his family were going to the Victory Restaurant for a good meal. Xu Sanguan said, "We should act like today is Spring Festival."

That was why he asked Xu Yulan to wear her finely woven sweater and khaki pants, as well as the light blue cotton-padded jacket embroidered with dark blue flowers. Xu Yulan put them on for him. Xu Sanguan also asked her to wear the silk scarf around her neck, so she got it out of the trunk and put it on. Xu Sanguan asked her to wash her face. When she was finished, he asked her to put on some Snowflower cream. She rubbed her face with the fragrant cream.

But when Xu Sanguan asked her to go down the street to Wang Erhu's little grocery store to buy Yile some sweet potatoes, Xu Yulan stood her ground. "I know what you're thinking," she said. "You don't want to take Yile to the Victory Restaurant to eat a good meal. You don't want to spend your blood money on Yile, because he's not your son. I know he's not your son, and I know no one wants to spend their money on outsiders, so I won't argue with you about all that. But Fatty Lin wasn't your woman either, was she? She's never given you a child, washed up for you, cooked you any meals, and yet you were perfectly willing to spend your blood money on her."

Since Xu Yulan couldn't bear to pacify Yile with a meal of sweet potatoes, Xu Sanguan had no choice but to speak with the child himself. He called for Yile to come to him, took off his cotton-padded jacket, and showed him the red puncture mark on his arm.

"Do you know what this is?"

Yile said, "You bled there."

Xu Sanguan nodded. "You're right. That's where they put the needle. I went to sell my blood this morning. You know why I went to sell blood? So you all could eat a square meal. Your mom and I and Erle and Sanle are going to the Victory Restaurant tonight to eat noodles. And you're going to take this fifty *fen* and go buy yourself some sweet potatoes over at Wang Erhu's store."

Yile reached out and took the fifty-*fen* note. "Dad, I heard what you and Mom were saying just now. You want me to go get fifty *fen* worth of sweet potatoes, while everyone else gets noodles that cost one *yuan* and seventy *fen.* Dad, I know I'm not your own son, and Erle and Sanle are. So they get to eat better than I do. Dad, do you think you could pretend for a little while that I'm your own son so I can eat some noodles too?"

Xu Sanguan shook his head. "Yile, I almost never treat you any worse than them. If Erle and Sanle get something good to eat, you get some too. But the money I made today came from selling blood. This money is special. This money's harder to come by than other kinds of money. I put my life at risk to get this money. So if I let you eat noodles too, I'd be doing that bastard He Xiaoyong a favor."

Yile nodded as if he had understood what Xu Sanguan had said. Holding the fifty-*fen* note in his hand, he moved toward the front door. Just as he got to the doorstep, though, he turned back to ask, "Dad, if I was your own son, you would bring me to eat noodles too, right?"

Xu Sanguan pointed toward him. "If you were my own son, you would be my favorite son of all."

With these words, Yile beamed. Still grinning, he made his way over to Wang Erhu's shop.

Wang Erhu stood at the charcoal grill roasting the sweet potatoes. A few sweet potatoes were cooling on a bamboo tray. Wang Erhu, his wife, and four children were arrayed around the grill eating gruel, and when Yile came in, he heard the sound of six mouths noisily slurping gruel.

Yile handed the fifty *fen* to Wang Erhu and then pointed at the biggest sweet potato on the tray. "Give me that one."

Wang Erhu took his money and handed him one of the smaller potatoes.

Yile shook his head. "I'll still be hungry after I eat this one."

Wang Erhu pressed the sweet potato into his hands, saying, "The big ones are for adults. The little ones are for little kids like you."

Yile looked down at the sweet potato in his hand. "This one isn't even as big as my hand. I'll still be hungry after I eat this one."

Wang Erhu replied, "How will you know until you've eaten it?"

Yile, convinced by this logic, nodded and took the sweet potato home. By the time he got home, Xu Sanguan and the rest of the family had already set out for the restaurant. He sat down alone at the table, put the still-warm sweet potato down in front of him, and began to slowly and carefully peel the skin. The mass of flesh inside the sweet potato was orange, like sunlight. He could smell its intense fragrance and its sweetness. He took a bite, and the fragrance and the sweetness filled his mouth.

But before he had even taken his fourth bite, the sweet potato was gone. He sat at the table rolling his tongue back and forth inside his mouth, drinking in what was left of the taste of sweet potato until all that remained was saliva. He knew the sweet potato was all gone, but he wanted more. He looked at the sweet potato skin he had only just peeled off and put a piece in his mouth. There was still some sweetness in the skin despite the blackened parts that tasted of charcoal. He ate the entire sweet potato peel.

When he finished the peel, he still wanted to eat more. That meant he wasn't full. He stood up from the table and went out the door, arriving once again at Wang Erhu's little shop. By this time Wang and his family had just finished their gruel, and all six of them were in the process of licking their bowls clean with their tongues.

Yile watched them wide-eyed and then told Wang Erhu, "I'm not full yet. Give me another sweet potato."

Wang Erhu said, "How do you know you're not full yet?"

Yile said, "Because I finished it, but I still want to eat some more."

Wang Erhu asked, "Was the sweet potato good?"

Yile nodded. "It was good."

"Was it really good? Or just medium good?"

"Really good."

"That explains it," Wang Erhu said. "If something's really good, of course you're going to want to have some more."

Yile thought he was right, so he nodded.

Wang Erhu continued, "Go on home now. You're full."

Yile went back home, sat by the table, and looked across the empty tabletop. He still wanted to eat. He thought about Xu Sanguan and the rest of them. They would be sitting around a table right now, eating huge bowls of steaming hot noodles. And all he had gotten was a sweet potato that wasn't even as big as his hand. He began to cry. At first the tears ran silently down his face. Then he threw his head down on the table and began to sob.

After he cried for a while, he thought once more of Xu Sanguan and the others sitting at the restaurant eating big steaming bowls full of noodles. He immediately stopped crying. He felt that he really ought to go to the restaurant to find them. He really ought to be eating a big steaming bowl of noodles, too. He went out the front door.

It was already dark outside, and because of the lack of electric power, the street lamps were as weak as candles. He walked rapidly down the street, panting to himself as he went: faster, faster, faster. He didn't dare run, because both Xu Sanguan and Xu Yulan had told him that if he ran right after he ate, he'd burn up all the food in his stomach. So he told himself as he went, *Don't run, don't run, whatever you do, don't run.* He stared at his feet as he walked along the road toward West First Street. There was a restaurant called the Liberation on the west side of the intersection. During the evening the Liberation Restaurant was always the brightest place on the street.

He propelled himself forward with his eyes to the ground and passed the intersection, not noticing his mistake until the road dead-ended into a small lane. Here he stopped, gazed around for a moment, and realized that he must have passed the Liberation Restaurant. He turned and started to retrace his steps, this time taking care not to look down at the pavement as he went. Instead, his eyes roved up and down the street until he had regained the intersection. When he saw that the doors were locked, the windows shuttered, and the lights out, he thought the restaurant must have closed already and that Xu Sanguan and the others had already finished their noodles. He leaned against a concrete electrical pole and burst into sobs.

Soon a couple of pedestrians came up to him. "Whose kid is that crying?"

Yile answered, "Xu Sanguan's kid is crying."

They asked, "Who's Xu Sanguan?"

He said, "Xu Sanguan from the silk factory."

"It's too late for a kid like you to be out in the streets. Why don't you go home?"

"I'm looking for my mom and dad. They went out to eat noodles at a restaurant."

"Your mom and dad went out to eat?" they asked. "Then you better look for them over at the Victory Restaurant. The Liberation has been closed for almost two months now."

Yile immediately began to walk down the street that led north from the intersection. He knew that the Victory Restaurant was right next to the Victory Bridge. He lowered his eyes to the pavement once again, because that way he would be able to walk faster. When he came to the end of the street, he swerved down a little lane and followed it until he had emerged into another avenue. When he caught sight of the river that ran through town, he began to walk alongside the water until he reached the Victory Bridge.

The lights of the Victory Restaurant glittered across the darkness. The bright lights made Yile happy. A surge of joy welled up in his heart, as if he were already eating the noodles. He broke into a gallop. But when he ran across the bridge and arrived at the front door of the restaurant, he did not find Xu Sanguan, Xu Yulan, Erle, or Sanle sitting inside. Instead, there were only two waiters sweeping the floor with big brooms. They had already swept everything but the area by the front door.

As Yile stood by the front door, they swept the refuse onto his shoes. He asked them, "Did Xu Sanguan and the others come here to eat noodles?"

They said, "Move."

Yile hurriedly shifted to the side and repeated, "Did Xu Sanguan and the others eat noodles here tonight? I mean the Xu Sanguan from the silk factory."

They said, "They left a long time ago. Everyone who came to eat noodles left a long time ago."

Yile hung his head and walked over to the trees by the side of the road. He stood by the tree for a while looking at the ground. Then he sat down on the ground, circled his arms around his knees, and began to cry. He made himself cry harder and harder, louder and louder, until he couldn't hear any of the nocturnal sounds around him. The sound of the wind blowing disappeared, and the sound of the trees rustling came to a stop, as did the sound of stools being moved around inside the restaurant behind him. The only sound left was that of his own sobs floating through the night.

After a while he grew tired of crying and stopped to wipe the tears from his eyes. He heard the waiters closing up the restaurant.

They shut the door, saw Yile sitting across from them, and said to him, "Aren't you going home?"

Yile said, "I want to go home."

They said, "If you want to go home, what are you waiting for? Don't just sit there."

"I'm sitting here because I need to rest. I walked a long way. I'm really tired now. I need to rest."

They left, and Yile watched them walk together down the street until they reached the next corner. One of them turned down a side street, and the other continued straight down the street until Yile couldn't see him anymore.

Then he stood up and began to walk home. He walked down the streets and through the lanes, listening to the sound of his own footsteps, feeling hungrier and hungrier as he went along. He felt like he had never eaten the sweet potato at all. He began to feel weaker and weaker.

When he arrived home, the whole family was laid out on the bed asleep. He heard the rumbling of Xu Sanguan's snores. He heard Erle roll over and mumble something in his sleep. Only Xu Yulan had heard him push open the front door and come inside.

Xu Yulan said to him, "Yile."

Yile said, "I'm hungry."

Yile stood by the door for another moment before Xu Yulan asked, "Where did you go?"

Yile said, "I'm hungry."

After another moment Xu Yulan said, "Come to bed. You won't feel hungry if you go to sleep."

Yile continued to stand by the door for a long while. But Xu Yulan didn't say anything more, and when Yile realized she had fallen asleep and wouldn't be saying anything else, he fumbled his way through the dark to the foot of the bed, took off his clothes, and lay down.

He did not fall asleep right away. He stared into the darkness, listening to Xu Sanguan's snores, and said to himself, *This man, this man who's snoring in his sleep, is the one who wouldn't let me go to the restaurant to eat noodles. And this man is also the one who's responsible for my having to go to bed with an empty stomach. And he is also the same man who is always saying I'm not his own son.* And finally, he replied to Xu Sanguan's snores with a declaration: *If I'm not really your son, then you're not my dad either.*

CHAPTER TWENTY-TWO

After Yile finished his gruel the next morning, he got up and walked out the door. Xu Sanguan and Xu Yulan were still in the bedroom, and Erle and Sanle were sitting on the doorstep. Erle and Sanle watched as Yile's legs stepped over their shoulders and moved outside the door.

Erle gazed at Yile as he moved down the street without so much as a parting look, and called out, "Yile, where are you going?"

Yile said, "To find my dad."

When Erle heard his reply, he glanced inside the house to see Xu Sanguan licking his bowl clean with his tongue. This seemed funny to him, so he burst into giggles, saying to Sanle, "Dad's inside, but Yile's going out to look for him."

Sanle too giggled. "He must not have seen him."

That morning Yile walked in the direction of He Xiaoyong's house. He was on his way to find his real father. He was going to tell his real father, He Xiaoyong, that he was never going back to

Xu Sanguan's house again. He wouldn't go back even if Xu Sanguan took him to the Victory Restaurant to eat noodles every day. He was going to take up residence at He Xiaoyong's house. He wouldn't have two little brothers anymore. He would have two little sisters instead. One was called Xiaoying and the other was Xiaohong. And he wouldn't be called Xu Yile anymore either. He would become He Yile. What it all amounted to was this. From now on, whenever he saw He Xiaoyong, he would call to him: Dad, Dad, Dad.

The doorstep at He Xiaoyong's house was just like the doorstep Yile had just left at Xu Sanguan's. There the doorway had been occupied by Erle and Sanle. Here He Xiaoying and He Xiaohong were sitting on the doorstep. When they saw Yile approach, they turned to look inside.

Yile announced, "Your big brother's here."

They swiveled their heads back in his direction.

Yile saw He Xiaoyong standing inside the door and called out to him, "Dad, I'm home."

He Xiaoyong emerged from the house, pointed at Yile, and barked, "Who are you calling Dad?" Then he waved Yile away. "Get out of here."

Yile stood his ground. "Dad, this time it's different. Last time Mom made me come see you. I didn't want to come. This time I came on my own. Mom doesn't even know I'm here. Xu Sanguan doesn't know either. Dad, now that I'm here, I'm not going back again. Dad, I'm moving in with you."

He Xiaoyong repeated, "Who are you calling Dad?"

Yile answered, "You're my dad."

"Bullshit," He Xiaoyong said. "Xu Sanguan is your dad."

"Xu Sanguan isn't my real dad. You're my real dad."

He Xiaoyong told Yile, "If you call me your dad one more time, I'm going to kick you with my feet and beat you with my fists."

Yile shook his head. "You wouldn't do that to your own son."

The neighbors were gathering around the door. A few of them stepped forward and said, "He Xiaoyong, even if he's not your son, you really shouldn't treat him like that."

Yile told them, "I *am* his son."

He Xiaoyong's woman emerged from the house and, gesturing toward Yile, told the onlookers, "It's that Xu Yulan woman again. That bitch must have sent him here. One day she's screwing around with some jerk, and the next day it's some other jerk, and then what does she do? She sends her little bastards to other people's houses to beg for money. She wants other people to feed, clothe, and house her bastard kids. It's really too much. Most people can't even take care of their own these days. Our family hasn't eaten anything in days, we've been hungry for a month, and there's almost nothing left between our bellies and our backsides by now."

Yile waited for He Xiaoyong's woman to finish. Then he turned to He Xiaoyong and said, "Dad, you're my real dad. Take me to the Victory Restaurant for a bowl of noodles."

"Did all of you hear what he said?" He Xiaoyong's woman shouted to her neighbors, "He wants to eat noodles. Our family's been eating chaff and weeds for two months now, but he's coming over here asking for noodles. And he wants to have them at the Victory Restaurant no less."

"Dad, I know you don't have any money now. Why don't you go over to the hospital and sell blood? You'll have plenty of money if you sell some blood, and then you can take me to eat noodles."

"Aiya!" He Xiaoyong's woman began to scream. "And now he wants He Xiaoyong to go to the hospital to sell blood! He wants to kill our He Xiaoyong! He wants to murder him! He Xiaoyong, can't you just get this kid out of here?"

He Xiaoyong took a step toward Yile. "Get the hell out of here."

Yile didn't move. "Dad, I'm never leaving you again."

He Xiaoyong reached out, picked Yile up by his collar, and hauled him a few steps backward. Unable to hold him off the ground any longer, he put Yile back down and began to drag him down the lane. Yile's hands grabbed frantically for his own collar, and his face contorted as he gasped for air. He Xiaoyong pulled him to the end of the lane, pushed him against a wall, and brandished a finger in front of his face. "If you ever come by here again, I'll slaughter you."

With this warning he turned and left. Yile stood with his back against the wall and watched him retreat down the lane to his house. Then he stepped away from the wall and walked into the street. After looking to his left and to his right to orient himself, he began to head west, head bent and eyes lowered to the ground.

A few people who were acquainted with Xu Sanguan saw an eleven- or twelve-year-old boy walking to the west with his head down and his eyes to the ground. They saw that his eyes were streaming with tears and that his tears sometimes fell onto his shoes. They wondered whose family he belonged to, and why he was crying as if his heart were broken. When they moved in for a closer look at the child, they realized that he was Xu Sanguan's Yile.

The first one to approach him was Blacksmith Fang. Blacksmith Fang said, "Yile! Yile, why are you crying?"

Yile said, "Xu Sanguan isn't my real dad. He Xiaoyong isn't my real dad either. I don't have a dad. That's why I'm crying."

Blacksmith Fang said, "Yile, why are you heading west? Your house is to the east."

Yile said, "I'm not going home."

Blacksmith Fang said, "Yile, you'd better go home now."

Yile said, "Blacksmith Fang, why don't you buy me a bowl of noodles? Then you can be my real dad."

Blacksmith Fang said, "Yile, what sort of nonsense is that? Even if I bought you ten bowls of noodles, I would never be your real dad."

Farther along the road, others came up to talk to him.

"You're Xu Sanguan's Yile, right? Why are you crying like that? Why are you walking west all on your own? Your house is on the east side. Why don't you go on home?"

Yile said, "I'm not going home. Go tell Xu Sanguan that I'm never coming home again."

They said, "If you're not going home, then where do you think you're going?"

Yile said, "I don't know where I'm going. All I know is that I'm not going home."

Yile added, "If any of you will buy me a bowl of noodles, I'll be your son. Do any of you want to buy me some noodles?"

THEY WENT to tell Xu Sanguan.

"Xu Sanguan, your Yile is bawling his head off and walking toward the west side."

"Xu Sanguan, your kid doesn't want you to be his dad anymore."

"Xu Sanguan, your Yile is saying that anyone who's willing to buy him a bowl of noodles can be his dad."

"Xu Sanguan, your Yile is going around everywhere asking people to be his dad, just like a beggar, and you're still sitting with your feet up in that chair of yours? Why don't you go get him home?"

Xu Sanguan stood up from his rattan chair. "That little brat's getting worse and worse. If he wants to find his real dad, he should go look for He Xiaoyong. What does he think he's doing, asking everyone else to be his dad? If He Xiaoyong isn't his real dad, who the hell is? What's he doing going west? That's the opposite direction from his real dad's house."

When he was finished speaking, he sat back down in his rattan chair. The others said, "How come you're sitting back down? Go and bring him home!"

Xu Sanguan said, "If he wants to look for his real dad, who am I to stand in his way?"

They could not very well argue the point, so one by one they went on their way. But a little later a few others arrived at the door.

"Xu Sanguan, have you heard? This morning Yile went over to He Xiaoyong's house looking for his real dad. It was really awful! The poor kid. He Xiaoyong's woman cursed him to his face, and then she cursed Xu Yulan, and it wasn't pretty, what she said, let me tell you. Poor Yile. He Xiaoyong dragged him all the way down the lane and into the street."

Xu Sanguan asked them, "Did He Xiaoyong's woman curse at me too?"

They said, "No, you were the only one she didn't talk about."

Xu Sanguan said, "Then it's none of my business."

When afternoon arrived and Yile still hadn't come home, Xu Yulan started to get nervous. She said to Xu Sanguan, "Everyone who's seen Yile says he's heading west. Everyone said the same thing. But if he's heading west, where do you think he'll end up going? If he gets all the way out to the countryside, he might forget the way home. He's only eleven after all, Xu Sanguan. Can't you please go and find him?"

Xu Sanguan said, "I'm not going. I feed him. I give him the clothes on his back. I send him to school. I've been very good to that little brat, and he still goes behind my back looking for his real dad. That bastard He Xiaoyong yells and screams and hits him, even drags him down the lane, and Yile still wants to look for his real dad. It's crystal clear to me now. If a kid really isn't your own flesh and blood, there's no way he'll ever become your own, no matter how well you raise him."

Xu Yulan was forced to go off in search of Yile alone. "You may not be Yile's real dad, but I'm his mom, and I'm going to go find him and bring him home."

Xu Yulan was away the whole afternoon. When she finally got back, it was already dusk. As soon as she came through the door, she asked, "Is he back yet?"

Xu Sanguan said, "No, I've been sitting here all afternoon watching the door. Erle and Sanle have been in and out, but Yile hasn't come back yet."

Xu Yulan began to cry. Then she told Xu Sanguan, "I kept heading west, and I asked everyone I saw if they'd seen him. They all said they'd seen him walk by. When I got into the fields, I asked around, but no one had seen him out there. I walked in the country for a while, but there wasn't anybody around to ask, so I didn't know where to look." She swung around and immediately went out again in search of Yile.

Xu Sanguan began to feel uncomfortable sitting in his chair. He rose, stood on the doorstep, and watched as night fell around him. *Yile still hasn't come home,* he thought to himself. *Maybe that means something's happened to him.* Xu Sanguan began to feel anxious. As he watched the sky grow darker and darker, he said to Erle and Sanle, "You two stay at home and don't go away. If Yile comes home, you tell him that your mom and I are out looking for him."

Xu Sanguan shut the front door and moved off toward the west side of town. But before he had gone more than a few steps, he heard sobs somewhere by his feet. When he bent over to look, he saw Yile crouching next to a neighboring doorstep. Yile trembled as he gazed up at Xu Sanguan.

Xu Sanguan quickly stooped down beside him. "Yile, it's you, isn't it?" When he was sure that it was indeed Yile, he shouted, "Goddamnit, you scared your mom half to death, and you scared the hell out of me too, but you're just fine, aren't you? You were just sitting next door the whole time we were worrying."

Yile said, "Dad, I'm hungry. I'm so hungry I'm weak."

Xu Sanguan said, "It's your own damn fault. Even if you starved to death, it would still be your own fault. No one made you run away from home. And I thought you said you weren't coming back."

Yile lifted one hand to smear away his tears. As he rubbed his eyes, he said, "I didn't want to come back. You wouldn't take me as your real son, so I went to find He Xiaoyong. He Xiaoyong wouldn't take me either. I didn't want to come back—"

Xu Sanguan cut him off in midsentence. "So what are you doing here? Go on. It's not too late. Get out of here. It would be better if you never came back."

Yile cried even harder. "I'm hungry, I'm sleepy, I want something to eat, I want to go to sleep. And even if you won't have me as your real son, I thought you loved me more than He Xiaoyong . . . so I came back."

Yile stuck out one hand, gripped the wall, and pulled himself to a standing position. Then, still holding on to the wall, he began to walk down the lane toward the west.

"Stop right there, you little brat. Where do you think you're going?"

Yile stopped walking. Shoulders bent and head to the ground, he began to cry so violently that his body shook with his sobs.

Xu Sanguan knelt down by his side. "Climb onto my back."

Yile clambered onto Xu Sanguan's back, and Xu Sanguan carried him eastward down the lane. They passed by their own door, walked to the end of the lane, then walked down another lane until they reached the main street. They walked down the street until they had crossed the river that ran through town.

As they walked, Xu Sanguan kept up an incessant stream of curses directed at Yile. "You little brat. You little bastard. You little jerk. You're gonna drive me to my grave one of these days, you make me so mad. If you want to run away, fine. Go ahead. Run away. Do you have to tell everyone in town about it too? The whole damn town thinks I abuse you now. They must think that your stepdad beats you up every day, curses you every day. I've taken care of you for eleven years now, and all I am is your stepdad. That bastard He Xiaoyong hasn't spent one *fen* on your behalf, and he's your real dad. So who's the unlucky one? And I sure as hell don't want to be your dad in my next life either. No way. Next time around, I want you to try being *my* stepdad. You just wait. I'll drive you crazy. I'll make you so mad, you won't know whether you want to live or die."

Yile caught sight of the gleaming lights of the Victory Restaurant. Timidly, he asked Xu Sanguan, "Dad, are you taking me to eat noodles?"

Xu Sanguan stopped cursing Yile. His voice suddenly grew gentle. "That's right."

CHAPTER TWENTY-THREE

One day two years later, as He Xiaoyong was walking down the street, he was hit by a truck from Shanghai. He was thrown so hard against a neighboring house that the closed front door was knocked open by the impact, and he came to a stop only on the floor inside.

When the news that He Xiaoyong had been hit by a truck spread through town, Xu Sanguan gloated for a day. It was a hot summer night, and Xu Sanguan, clad in shorts and a sleeveless T-shirt, made the rounds of his neighbors' houses, saying as he went, "This is what is meant by karma. You get what you deserve. You do something bad and try to pretend that you didn't do it, but Old Man Heaven always knows exactly what's going on. And if Old Man Heaven wants to punish you for what you've done, don't think you'll get away. You might be hit by a truck. You could be walking down the street minding your own business one day when a roof tile falls on your head. Or say you're crossing the bridge: the bridge might suddenly collapse into the water. Old Man Heaven will find a way. Look at me, for instance.

I'm strong, I'm energetic, and my color is good. I've lived the life of a poor man and I've been through hard times, but I'm healthy. And health is the most important thing of all. Looks like Old Man Heaven's rewarding me for being good."

As he spoke, he flexed his arms and legs to show his neighbors his muscles. Then he continued.

"And sure, I've been a cuckold for thirteen years, but look at Yile. He and I are very close, even closer than Erle and Sanle. If there's something good to eat, he always asks me, 'Dad, do you want some?' When those brats Erle and Sanle get something good to eat, they never offer me any. You know why Yile is so good to me? It's because Old Man Heaven's rewarding me for being good."

Xu Sanguan concluded, "So people ought to try their best to do good and stay away from doing bad. If you do something bad and don't change your ways, you'll end up like He Xiaoyong and be punished by Old Man Heaven. And let me tell you, when Old Man Heaven punishes somebody, he shows no mercy. He'll take your very life if he feels like it. Look at He Xiaoyong. He's laid up in the hospital right now, and no one knows if he'll live or die.

"People like me, who always do good, well, Old Man Heaven remembers us, and every once in a while he'll throw something nice our way. Take my blood selling, for instance. You all know that I sell blood. Most people in town think selling blood is something to be ashamed of, but in my grandpa's village they believe that the men who sell blood are stronger than the ones who don't. Now look at me. I've sold blood. Am I the weaker for it? No, of course not. And why not? Because Old Man Heaven's rewarding me. I'd continue to survive even if I sold blood every day. Blood for me is like a money tree. All I've got to do is give myself a little shake, and Old Man Heaven's bounty rains down on me."

Xu Yulan was not as happy as her husband to hear that He Xiaoyong had been hit by a truck. She merely acted as if nothing had happened. When it was time to fry dough, she went to fry dough. When it was time to go home and cook dinner, she went home to cook dinner. When it was time to do the laundry, she piled Xu Sanguan and the children's dirty clothes in a wooden basin and went down to the river. When she heard what had happened to He Xiaoyong, her eyes went wide and her chin gaped open with surprise, but she didn't smile.

Xu Sanguan was annoyed by her reaction, so she explained, "What's in it for us if He Xiaoyong gets hit by a truck? If we got a stack of money every time he got hit by a truck, there might be some reason to feel good about it. But we haven't gotten a single thing. What's the point of gloating?"

And as Xu Yulan watched Xu Sanguan dart in and out of the neighbors' places in his sleeveless T-shirt, dispensing his karmic platitudes, she grew annoyed. "If you have something to say about him, go on and say it. But don't go on and on about it. You were saying the same things yesterday, and you're repeating them again today, and I suppose you'll be going on and on about it again tomorrow too. But no matter how bad He Xiaoyong may be, he's still lying half dead in a hospital bed right now. If you keep going on like this, Old Man Heaven's going to punish you too."

This last sentence was a splash of cold water. She was right. If he spent his days taking delight in someone else's misfortune, Old Man Heaven just might take offense. Xu Sanguan furled in his sails, and from that day on was never again to be seen darting in and out of doors to chat with the neighbors.

HE XIAOYONG was laid up in the hospital for a total of seven days. He was unconscious for the first three days. On the fourth day he opened his eyes, looked around for a moment, and then suddenly lapsed into a coma that lasted for another three days.

The truck had broken his right leg and his left arm. The doctor said the broken bones were the least of his worries. Worse was that he had no way to stem the tide of He Xiaoyong's internal bleeding. Every day He Xiaoyong's blood pressure slid up and down the dial. In the morning, after a transfusion, his blood pressure would shoot up to normal. But by evening he would lose more blood, and the mercury would once again plummet down toward the bottom of the dial.

He Xiaoyong's friends said among themselves, "He Xiaoyong's blood pressure is shooting up and down every day. It climbs up in the morning and falls back down in the evening. He might survive three or four days of that, but we're afraid that if this goes on any longer, there will come a time when it refuses to go back up again."

They said to He Xiaoyong's woman, "We don't think there's anything the doctor can do. All they do every day is stand next to his bed for an hour or two, discussing what they might do. But when all is said and done, He Xiaoyong's still lying there with an oxygen tube up his nose and a blood-transfusion bottle hanging next to his arm. They're giving him the same medicine they gave him last week, and he isn't getting any better."

They concluded, "We think you ought to go see Mr. Chen over on the west side of town."

Mr. Chen on the west side of town was an old Chinese herbalist, an oracle, and a fortune-teller.

Mr. Chen said to He Xiaoyong's woman, "I've already prepared a prescription for him. But no matter how much effect the medicine has on his body, it still won't be strong enough to save his soul. If his soul escapes, there's no medicine on earth that can stop it from taking flight. When people's souls take flight, they almost always exit through the chimney. Here's what you have to do. Tell your son to go up on the roof, sit directly on top of the chimney, and call as loud as he can toward the Western Heaven, 'Dad, don't go! Dad, come back!' That's all he needs to say. No more and no less; just those two sentences. If he shouts for half an hour or so and He Xiaoyong's soul heeds the call, he'll turn around and come back, even if he's already taken flight. And if he hasn't yet taken flight, he'll stay right where he is."

He Xiaoyong's woman said, "He Xiaoyong doesn't have a son. All he has is two daughters."

Mr. Chen said, "Daughters don't count. As soon as you marry them off to another family, they're water under the bridge. If you sent one of your daughters up on the roof, her father's soul wouldn't be able to hear her, no matter how loud she shouted or how far the sound carried."

He Xiaoyong's woman said, "He Xiaoyong doesn't have a son. I haven't given him a son. All I've given him is two daughters. I don't know what crime I committed in my last life, or what he did in his last life, but we don't have a son in this life. If He Xiaoyong doesn't have a son, does it mean there's nothing we can do to save his life?"

He Xiaoyong's friends said, "Who says He Xiaoyong doesn't have a son? Isn't Xu Sanguan's Yile actually his son?"

AND SO IT WAS that He Xiaoyong's woman arrived at Xu Sanguan's door. As soon as the skinny woman caught sight of Xu Yulan, she began to cry. First she stood at the doorstep, wiping her eyes, which were already red from weeping, with a handkerchief. Then she sat down on the doorstep and began to sob in earnest.

Xu Yulan was alone, and when she saw He Xiaoyong's woman, she wondered what she could possibly be doing by her door. After the woman sat down on her doorstep and began to sob and wail, Xu Yulan began, "And who might this be? Who could be quite so shameless as all that? Rather than crying in the privacy of her own home, she cries on someone else's doorstep. And she doesn't just cry. She wails like a cat in heat."

He Xiaoyong's woman stopped sobbing long enough to say, "My fate is bitter. My husband, He Xiaoyong, was walking down the street minding his own business, not looking for any trouble, and for no reason at all, he got hit by a truck. He's been in a coma for seven days, and the doctors at the hospital can't do anything to save him. Mr. Chen on the west side says that only Yile can save his life, so I've come to beg you for a favor."

Xu Yulan picked up where the other woman had left off. "My fate is sweet. My husband, Xu Sanguan, has never been admitted to the hospital. He's over forty, and he's never known what it's like to sleep in a hospital bed. He's so strong, he can carry a hundred-pound sack of rice. The rice shop's almost a mile away, and he doesn't even need to stop for a break on the way home."

He Xiaoyong's woman broke once more into loud wails. "My fate is bitter. He Xiaoyong's lying in the hospital on the brink of death, and the doctors can't do anything to help him. Mr. Chen over on the west side can't help either. Only Yile can save him. If only Yile would climb up on our roof and call his soul back from the brink, he might live. If Yile doesn't call back his soul, he'll die for sure. And I'll be left a widow."

Xu Yulan said, "My fate is sweet. Everyone says Xu Sanguan will live for a very long time. They say you can see from his face that he'll be blessed with longevity. If you look at his hands, you'll see that my Xu Sanguan's life line runs long and deep. What does that mean? It means that even when he's over eighty, the King of Hell won't be able to pull him down to the netherworld, no matter how hard he tries. I'm going to live to a ripe old age as well, but I won't live as long as Xu Sanguan. He'll be around to see me off to the netherworld. What's the worst thing that can happen to a woman? To be widowed, that's what. How can you get through your days after you've been widowed? You have a lot less money than before, that's for sure. But there's worse yet. The kids don't have a father anymore, and there's no one around to protect them when they get into trouble. And when there's a big storm and you're scared of the lightning and the thunder, you won't have a shoulder to lean on anymore."

He Xiaoyong's woman's sobs grew increasingly jagged. She

said to Xu Yulan, "My fate is bitter. I'm begging you to show me some mercy. Let Yile call for He Xiaoyong's soul. If not for me, do it for Yile's sake. He is He Xiaoyong's son, after all."

Xu Yulan grinned. "Oh! If you had said that from the beginning, I might have let Yile go with you. But you never admitted it until now. And now it's just too late. Xu Sanguan would never agree now. Think about it. When I came to your house that first time, you yelled and screamed and cursed. He Xiaoyong even hit me. The two of you were riding high then, weren't you? You never imagined a day like today would come, did you? Xu Sanguan's right. You have bad karma, and you're getting exactly what you deserve. Our family has good karma. If you do right, good things will come to you. Look at us. We're doing better and better. Take a look at my blouse. This is raw silk. I sewed it for myself just last week."

He Xiaoyong's woman said, "We're getting what we deserve. We wouldn't take Yile because we wanted to save a little money. And we were wrong! He Xiaoyong did wrong, and I've suffered along with him. But that's not important anymore. I'm begging you to take pity on me. Please let Yile save his life. I hate him too, but I can't help that he's still my husband, for better or worse. My eyes are so swollen from crying that they hurt. What am I supposed to do if he dies?"

Xu Yulan said, "What will you do? You'll be a widow, of course."

XU YULAN said to Xu Sanguan, "He Xiaoyong's woman came by for a visit. Her eyes were so swollen from crying, they looked like lightbulbs."

Xu Sanguan asked, "What did she want?"

Xu Yulan said, "She was always very thin, but ever since He Xiaoyong's accident, she's wasted away to nearly nothing. She's as skinny as a pole. You could use her to hang your laundry out to dry."

Xu Sanguan asked, "What did she want?"

Xu Yulan said, "She hasn't combed her hair in days, and two of the buttons on her shirt were missing. One of her shoes was clean, but the other one was covered with mud. I wonder what she stepped in."

Xu Sanguan said, "I'm asking you a question. What did she want from us?"

"It's like this," Xu Yulan began. "He Xiaoyong's in the hospital, and he's about to die. The doctors can't do anything more, so she went to see Mr. Chen over on the west side. Mr. Chen couldn't do anything to save He Xiaoyong's life either. Mr. Chen said the only person who can save him is Yile. He said Yile has to climb up on their roof and call for He Xiaoyong's soul to come home. So she came by to look for Yile."

Xu Sanguan said, "Why doesn't she climb up on the roof herself? Why doesn't she have her two daughters climb up on the roof and call for his soul?"

"It's like this," Xu Yulan continued. "If she goes up there herself and calls for him, He Xiaoyong's soul won't be able to hear her voice. If his daughters go up there, he won't be able to hear them either. He'll only hear the call if it's his own son who's calling for him to come back. That's what Mr. Chen said, and that's why she came by to look for Yile."

"She's got to be kidding," Xu Sanguan said. "Dream on. When I wanted to give them back their son, the son I had raised on their behalf for over nine years, they wouldn't have any of it. Now that I've taken care of him for four more years, they're coming to ask for him back? Forget it. He Xiaoyong can go to hell for all I care. He doesn't do anyone any good anyway. Just let him die. Damn! So they want Yile to call back his soul? Even if Yile *could* bring him back, He Xiaoyong would still be a bastard."

Xu Yulan said, "Still, you have to feel bad for He Xiaoyong's woman. It's just about the worst thing that can happen to a woman. What do you do after the man of the house is gone? How can you go on living? What if something like that happened to me?"

"Shit," Xu Sanguan said. "I'm as healthy as they come. I've got more energy than I know what to do with. Look at these muscles. When I walk down the street, my muscles practically ripple under my shirt."

"That's not what I meant. What I'm saying is that sometimes you have to put yourself in other people's shoes. He Xiaoyong's woman came to our doorstep, sobbing and begging for mercy. It just wouldn't feel right if we didn't try to help her out. Forget what they did to us in the past. Because no matter what you think, his life is still in our hands, and it just isn't right to help someone into the grave."

Xu Sanguan said, "That's exactly what we should do. Help He Xiaoyong into the grave. We'd be ridding society of a pest. That truck driver did us all a favor."

Xu Yulan said, "You always say that those who do good get good in return. If you do something good, people stand up and take notice. If you let Yile call back his soul, everyone will say Xu Sanguan is a good man. They'll say: Even after everything He Xiaoyong's done to him, Xu Sanguan was still kind enough to save his life."

Xu Sanguan said, "They'll say that Xu Sanguan's a real idiot, a moron, a prize fool, a stupid fucking cuckold. They'll say Xu Sanguan's getting used to being a cuckold. They'll say he's liking it better and better."

Xu Yulan said, "No matter what you say, He Xiaoyong is still Yile's father."

Xu Sanguan jabbed a finger toward her face: "If you say that one more time, I'll bash your face in. I've raised that boy for thirteen years. If he's not my son, what is he? If I'm not his dad, who is?" Finally, he added, "Let me tell you something. Yile will call for that man's soul over my dead body. He Xiaoyong's soul won't be coming back as long as I'm here to stop it."

XU SANGUAN called Yile to come to him and said, "Yile, you're already thirteen years old now. When I was as big as you are now, my dad had already died and my mom had run off with another man. I couldn't live all by myself in town, so I walked a whole day to find my grandpa in the countryside. It wasn't actually that far—it should only have taken half a day to get there, but I got lost in the middle, and if I hadn't run into my fourth uncle, I don't know where I would have ended up. My fourth uncle didn't recognize me, but it was getting dark, and I was still a little kid, so he asked me where I was going. I said my dad had died and my mom had left with another man and I was looking for my grandpa. When my uncle realized that I was his brother's son, he knelt down and stroked my hair and began to cry. By then I could hardly walk anymore, so Fourth Uncle carried me home on his back.

"Yile, do you understand now why I care so much for my fourth uncle? It's because he picked me up and carried me to my grandpa's house that night. People have to keep to their conscience. Fourth Uncle's been gone for a few years now, but whenever I think of him, I feel like crying. You have to keep to your conscience. I've raised you for thirteen years now, and in those thirteen years there have been times when I've hit you or yelled at you. But you can't take those things to heart, because I did them for your sake. I don't know how many times I've been worried because of you. Because all else aside, I'm not your real dad. You know that. Now your real dad's in the hospital, and he's about to die because the doctors can't do anything to help him. Now Mr. Chen over on the west side—the Mr. Chen who's a fortune-teller and an herbalist—says you're the only person who can save He Xiaoyong. He Xiaoyong's soul has already left his body, but Mr. Chen says that if you climbed up on He Xiaoyong's roof, you might be able to call his soul back home.

"Yile, the way He Xiaoyong treated us was unforgivable, but people have to let bygones be bygones. Let's forget about the past for now. Right now his life is in danger, and we've got to help save it. He's a human being after all, and if someone's about to die, you have to do what you can, no matter what you think about him. And he is your real dad. Do it because he's your dad. Climb up on the roof and call for his soul.

"Yile, He Xiaoyong will recognize you as his own son now. And even if he didn't, I could never be your real dad.

"Yile, remember what I've told you today. You need to have a conscience. I'm not saying you need to pay me back for everything I've done for you. That's not what I mean at all. All I ask is that you come to see me as I saw my fourth uncle. That would be enough. After I get old and sick and die, if you would remember from time to time how it was that I raised you, and if you feel sad for a moment, maybe even shed a tear or two for me, that would be enough for me. That would make me very happy.

"Yile, follow your mom. Yile, listen to me. Go and call He Xiaoyong's soul back home. Yile, go on now."

CHAPTER TWENTY-FOUR

That day it seemed that everybody in town had heard that Xu Sanguan's Yile was going to climb up onto He Xiaoyong's roof, sit on top of the chimney, and call for He Xiaoyong's errant soul to come home. They crowded in front of He Xiaoyong's front door, standing and watching as Xu Yulan escorted Yile into the house to be greeted by He Xiaoyong's woman, who talked with them for a long time before pulling Yile by the hand behind her skinny frame toward a ladder leaning against the side of the house.

A friend of He Xiaoyong's was already on the roof, and another friend stood below, holding the ladder steady. Yile climbed up the ladder to the roof, and the man took his hand, leading him diagonally across the tiles to the chimney, where he helped him sit down squarely atop it. After Yile had taken up his high perch, he kept his hands on his legs and watched the man who had brought him there move back down toward the ladder. He grasped the edges of the roof tiles with the palms of his hands before finding a foothold on the top rung of the ladder.

Finally, like a man disappearing under water, he sank below Yile's line of sight.

Yile sat on the chimney and looked at the dank light reflected from the roofs surrounding him. A swallow let out a few piercing cries, circled above his head, and flew away. Seconds later a whole school of smaller swallows chirped out a much softer response. Their cries emerged from the eaves of the house just across from where Yile was sitting. Yile gazed out toward the mountains that rose and fell across the horizon. They were so distant that they resembled nothing so much as clouds or shadows, gray and blurry and insubstantial.

The people standing below craned their necks in anticipation of the moment when Yile would begin to call for He Xiaoyong's soul. They were looking up at him with their mouths all agape, waiting for a sound, for a cry, but no sound came. One by one they lowered their heads, rested their necks, and wondered what exactly was happening on the roof above. From Yile's perch, their anxious voices sounded like the twittering of magpies.

He Xiaoyong's woman shouted toward Yile, "Yile, start crying now. That's what Mr. Chen said you should do. Once you start crying, your dad's soul will hear you."

Yile looked down at the crowd of people below and saw them pointing and waving their fingers at him. He turned his head away from them and discovered that he was all alone on the roof. There wasn't anyone on any of the roofs around him. All the roof tiles in every direction were covered with green weeds that swayed back and forth in the wind.

He Xiaoyong's woman called out once again, "Yile, quick! Start crying. Why aren't you crying? Go on and cry."

Before Yile began crying, He Xiaoyong's woman herself started to cry. "Why isn't the kid crying? I thought we'd explained everything to him very clearly. What's wrong with him?" She called out once more, "Yile, cry. I'm begging you. Start crying."

Yile finally asked, "Why do you want me to cry?"

He Xiaoyong's woman said, "Your dad's in the hospital, and he's about to die. His soul has already flown away from his body, and it's getting farther and farther away. If you don't hurry up and cry, he'll be too far away to hear you. Quick, start crying."

Yile said, "*My* dad's not in the hospital. *My* dad's working at the silk factory. My dad's not going to die. He's pushing the cocoon cart at the factory. My dad's soul is safe inside his body. Who says my dad's soul has flown away?"

He Xiaoyong's woman said, "Xu Sanguan from the silk factory isn't your dad. Your dad's in the hospital. Your dad's He Xiaoyong."

Yile said, "Nonsense."

He Xiaoyong's woman said, "It's the truth. Xu Sanguan really isn't your dad. He Xiaoyong's really your dad."

Yile said, "Nonsense."

He Xiaoyong's woman swung around toward Xu Yulan. "All I can do now is beg. You're his mom after all. Say something to him. Make him cry. Make him call for He Xiaoyong's soul to come home."

Xu Yulan stood motionless for a moment before replying, "There are so many people watching. What exactly do you want me to say? I've already lost any face I might ever have had in their eyes. They're all laughing at me inside. What am I supposed to say to him? I'm not going up there."

He Xiaoyong's woman sank to the ground and began to frantically bow and scrape in Xu Yulan's direction. "I'm down on my knees in front of you. I've lost just as much face as you. And if they're laughing, it's me they're laughing at first and foremost. I'm on my knees. I'm begging you. Please go talk with Yile." Tears poured from her eyes as she pleaded with Xu Yulan.

Xu Yulan said, "Stand up. When you bow like that, I'm the one who loses face, not you. Stand up. I'll go talk to him." Xu Yulan stepped forward, raised her face to the roof, and called out, "Yile! Yile, turn this way. It's me, your mom. Please just cry a little bit, shout a few times. That's all you've got to do to bring He

Xiaoyong's soul home. When he's back, I'll take you home. Come on now."

Yile said, "Ma, I'm not going to cry. I'm not going to shout."

Xu Yulan said, "Yile, you've got to cry now. You have to shout. More and more people are coming to watch us, and I'm losing face. If any more people show up, I'll never be able to show my face again in this town. Go on and shout for his soul. After all, He Xiaoyong's your real dad."

Yile said, "Ma, how could you? How could you say he's my real dad? Don't you have any shame?"

"What did I do in my last life to deserve this?" Xu Yulan cried and wheeled around to face He Xiaoyong's woman. "Now even my son's saying I'm shameless. It's all because of what He Xiaoyong did to us. If he's going to die, let him. I don't care anymore. I really can't be bothered."

Since Xu Yulan refused to help, He Xiaoyong's friends said to his woman, "We'd better go get Xu Sanguan. Maybe if Xu Sanguan shows up, Yile will cry for him."

Xu Sanguan was at the silk factory pushing his cart when two of He Xiaoyong's friends came running up to him. "Yile refuses to cry or to shout for the soul. All he'll do is sit up on the roof and say that He Xiaoyong isn't his real dad, that you're the only dad he's ever had. When Xu Yulan tried to make him cry or call out, he told her that she was shameless. Xu Sanguan, would you come and see what you can do? This is a life-or-death situation."

Xu Sanguan listened to their description of the situation and set his silkworm cart to one side. "That's my boy."

When Xu Sanguan arrived at He Xiaoyong's house, he looked up at the roof and said, "You're a good son, Yile. You really are a very good son to me. I've raised you these thirteen years, and all my efforts have paid off. After what you said today, I'll be happy to take care of you for another thirteen years."

When Yile saw that Xu Sanguan had come, he said, "Dad, I've been up here long enough. Come get me down. I'm too scared to get down on my own. Dad, come up and get me down."

Xu Sanguan said, "Yile, I can't come up and get you just yet. You haven't cried and you haven't called out, so He Xiaoyong's soul hasn't come back yet."

Yile said, "Dad, I'm not going to cry. I won't shout either. I want to come down."

Xu Sanguan said, "Yile, listen to me. Just cry a little and call for him a couple times. That's all you have to do. I've already given my word that I'd help out, and when you promise something, you have to follow through. You have to keep your word. And after all, He Xiaoyong really is your dad."

Yile began to cry. "Everyone says you're not my real dad. Mom said you aren't my real dad either. Now you're saying the same thing too. That means I don't have a dad. I don't have a mom either. I don't have a family. All I have is me. I'm coming down on my own."

Yile stood and took a couple of strides across the roof until, frightened by the steepness of the incline, he stopped, sat back down on the tiles, and burst into noisy tears.

He Xiaoyong's woman shouted up toward the roof, "That's it, Yile, good job! You've finally started to cry. Now you can shout!"

"You shut up!" Xu Sanguan roared at He Xiaoyong's woman. "Yile's not crying for that bastard husband of yours. He's crying for me."

Xu Sanguan lifted his head up to look at Yile. "Yile, you're a good son. Once you've shouted, I'll come up and get you. Then I'm going to take you to the Victory Restaurant to eat fried pork livers."

Yile sobbed, "Dad, come up and get me."

Xu Sanguan said, "Yile, all you have to do is shout a few times. Once you shout, I'm going to be your real dad. Just shout a few times, and when you're done, that bastard He Xiaoyong will never be your real dad again. From now on I'm your real dad."

When Yile heard what Xu Sanguan said, he lifted his face to the sky and shouted, "Dad, don't go. Dad, come back."

When he was finished, he looked back down toward Xu Sanguan. "Dad, come up and get me."

He Xiaoyong's wife said, "Yile, shout it a couple more times."

Yile glanced down toward Xu Sanguan, who said to him, "Just two more times, Yile."

Yile shouted, "Dad, don't go. Dad, come back. Dad, don't go. Dad, come back."

Yile said to Xu Sanguan, "Dad, come up and get me."

He Xiaoyong's woman said, "Yile, you have to keep on shouting. Mr. Chen said you had to shout for half an hour. Yile, shout!"

"Enough already!" Xu Sanguan barked to He Xiaoyong's woman. "That Mr. Chen's a real bastard too. Yile's done his part. Now it's up to He Xiaoyong. If he lives, fine, and if he dies, he dies."

Then he said to Yile, "Yile, hang on. I'm coming up to get you."

Xu Sanguan climbed the ladder and clambered onto the roof, told Yile to hold on to his neck, and then carried him on his back down the ladder.

When they reached safety, Xu Sanguan lowered Yile to the ground and said to him, "Yile, stay right here and don't move."

Xu Sanguan proceeded to walk straight into He Xiaoyong's house. He emerged seconds later with a vegetable knife in hand. Standing by the door of He Xiaoyong's house, he lifted the blade to his face and sliced his own cheek. Then he stuck out his hand, rubbed it with the blood running from the gash, and announced to the crowd, "You saw what I just did, right? I cut my own face with this knife. From now on, if any of you"—he paused to point toward He Xiaoyong's woman—"and I mean you too. If any of you ever dares to say that Yile is not my real son, I'll do the same to you."

When he was finished speaking, he tossed the knife to one side and took Yile by the hand. "Let's go home."

CHAPTER TWENTY-FIVE

One summer day Xu Sanguan came home and said to Xu Yulan, "On the way back it seemed like no one who lives in our lane was at home. Everyone's in the streets. I've never seen so many people in the streets before in my entire life. There are people with red armbands, and people marching, and people writing political slogans, and people pasting up big-character posters. The walls on the main street are covered with big-character posters. They paste them up one on top of the other, thicker and thicker, until it looks like the walls are wearing cotton-padded jackets. And I saw the county secretary, that fat guy from Shandong. He used to think he was really something. Whenever I used to see him, he would be holding a nice cup of tea in his hand, but now he's got an old metal washbasin in his hand, and he keeps banging on it and cursing himself, saying he's a dog through and through."

Xu Sanguan said, "Have you heard? Do you know why the factories have shut down, and the stores are closed, and why there are no classes at the schools? You know why you don't have to go fry dough? Why some people have hung themselves from trees, and some people are locked up in 'cow sheds' and beaten half to death? Do you know why? Do you know why as soon as Chairman Mao says something, people take what he said and make it into a song, and paint his words on the walls, and on the pavement, and on cars and ferry boats, on their sheets and pillowcases, on cups and cooking pans, and even on bathroom walls and the sides of spittoons? Do you know how it was that Chairman Mao's name grew so long? Listen to this: He's the Great Leader Great Teacher Supreme Commander and Helmsman Chairman Mao May He Live Ten Thousand Years! That's fifteen words in all, and you have to say it in one breath, without missing a beat. You know why that is? Because the Cultural Revolution has arrived."

Xu Sanguan said, "I'm only just now starting to understand what this Cultural Revolution is all about. It's actually just a time for settling old scores. If someone offended you in the past, now's the time to write a big-character poster about him and paste it on a wall on the street. You can accuse him of being an unreconstructed landlord, or a counterrevolutionary, or whatever. You can say whatever you like. There aren't any courts or police these days anyway. There's just a lot of different crimes. You can pick any one you like, put it up on a poster, and sit back and watch everybody hound whomever you've accused to death. These days when I lie in bed, I think to myself, maybe I should find an enemy too, write a poster, and settle some old score. But the only enemy I ever had was that bastard He Xiaoyong, and he was hit by a truck and killed three years ago. I'm a good man, and I haven't made any other enemies all these years. That's good, because at least I don't have to worry about someone putting up a poster denouncing me."

Before he had finished, Sanle pushed open the front door and rushed in with a shout of alarm, "Someone put up a poster on the wall of the rice store saying that Mom is a 'broken shoe.'"

Xu Sanguan and Xu Yulan, frightened out of their wits, immediately ran over to the rice shop to see the poster on the wall. Sanle had not been mistaken. Among many other posters, there was indeed one that singled out Xu Yulan, saying that she was a "broken shoe," a shameless tramp, saying that she had become a prostitute at the age of fifteen, saying that you could sleep with her for just two *yuan* a night, saying that the men she had slept with would fill up ten whole trucks.

Xu Yulan pointed at the poster and broke into a string of curses. "It's your mama who's the real 'broken shoe'! Your mama's the real tramp. She's the one who's a whore. Ten truckloads? She's slept with so many men the whole earth couldn't swallow them all!"

Xu Yulan wheeled around to face Xu Sanguan and began to cry. "Only someone who's had no sons and no hope of grandsons, who's got boils growing on his head and running sores on his feet, only someone like that could be capable of spitting out this kind of venom."

Xu Sanguan said to the people standing next to him, "This is slander, pure and simple. It says Xu Yulan became a prostitute at fifteen. Bullshit! You think I wouldn't know if that were true? The night we got married, Xu Yulan left this much blood on the sheets." Xu Sanguan drew a circle in the air with his hands. "If Xu Yulan was a whore at fifteen, you think I would have seen any blood on our wedding night?" Seeing that the other people in the store hadn't replied, Xu Sanguan answered his own question, "Of course not!"

That afternoon Xu Sanguan called Yile, Erle, and Sanle to him and told them, "Yile, you're already sixteen now. And Erle's fifteen. Go out to the street and copy one of those posters. Doesn't matter which one. Just copy one of them, and then paste it over the poster about your mom. Sanle, you're still a snot-nosed little brat, so I guess all you can really do is carry a bucket of paste for the other two. Now remember, you can't just tear down a big-character poster. These days, if you tear one of those things down, you're a counterrevolutionary. Don't even think about tearing them down. Just copy out a new poster and paste it over the other one. I can't very well take care of this myself, because everybody will be looking. If you kids go, you won't draw as much attention. You brothers better go get the job done before it gets dark."

When night came, Xu Sanguan said to Xu Yulan, "Your three sons have pasted over that poster, so you can relax now. I doubt very many people saw it. There're so many posters out there that no one could possibly get around to all of them. And they're putting up new ones all the time. Before you can finish the first one, someone's put another one on top of it."

TWO DAYS LATER a group of people wearing red armbands came to Xu Sanguan's house and took Xu Yulan away. They were planning to hold a massive struggle session in the town square. They had already found a landlord, dug up a rich peasant, located a rightist, caught a counterrevolutionary, and gotten hold of a capitalist roader in a position of power. They had everyone they needed except a prostitute. They said they had spent three days looking for a prostitute, and since there was only half an hour left until the meeting was to begin, they had finally found one. They said, "Xu Yulan, come with us. We need your help. This is an emergency."

She didn't come back until later that afternoon. When she returned, the hair on the left side of her head was all gone, but the hair on the right remained untouched. They had given her a "yin yang" haircut, neatly shaving half of her hair at the part, so that it looked like a rice paddy midway through the harvest season.

When Xu Sanguan saw her, he let out an involuntary cry. Xu Yulan moved over to the window, picked up the mirror from the sill, and after seeing herself in the mirror, began to sob.

"Now that I look like this, how can I show my face? How am I going to live? When I was walking home, they were all pointing and laughing at me. Xu Sanguan, I didn't know how ugly I was yet. I knew they'd cut off half my hair, but I didn't know it would be this ugly. I didn't know until I looked in the mirror. Xu Sanguan, what am I going to do? Xu Sanguan, they cut off my hair at the struggle session. I heard the people below me laughing, and I saw my hair falling by my feet, so I knew they'd shaved my head, but when I tried to feel it with my hand, they slapped my face so hard my teeth hurt, and they said I wasn't allowed to touch. Xu Sanguan, how am I going to go on living? It would be better to die. I don't have anything against them, and they didn't have anything against me. I don't even know them. So why did they shave my head? Why didn't they just let me die? Xu Sanguan, why don't you say something?"

"What am I supposed to say?" Xu Sanguan said. Then he let out a long sigh. "There's not a whole lot we can do now. You've got a 'yin yang' head. Nowadays women with hair like that are supposedly either 'broken shoes' or whores. There's nothing much you can say, now that you've been made to look like that. No one will believe what you have to say for yourself. You couldn't wash yourself clean even if you jumped into the Yellow River. You can't go out anymore. You'll have to stay in the house."

Xu Sanguan helped shave off the other half of Xu Yulan's hair, then kept her inside the house. Xu Yulan herself was perfectly willing to stay in, but the people in red armbands were not willing to let her. They would come and take her away every few days, dragging her along to their struggle sessions. At almost every struggle session held in town, no matter how big or small, Xu Yulan was always standing to one side. Most of the time she was just playing a supporting role.

Xu Yulan said to Xu Sanguan, "They're not after me. They're attacking other people. I just stand to one side and keep the ones who are being attacked company."

Xu Sanguan told his sons, "Actually, they're not attacking your mom. Your mom is just keeping those capitalist roaders and rightists and counterrevolutionaries and landlords company. She just stands to one side and pretends to be participating. Your mom is just playing a supporting role. What do I mean by a supporting role? Well, she's like MSG. You can add MSG to any kind of dish, and it makes everything a little tastier."

Later, they made Xu Yulan bring a stool out into the busiest part of the shopping street and stand on top of it. She stood atop the stool with a wooden sandwich board around her neck. They had made the sign especially for her. It read simply: XU YULAN, PROSTITUTE.

They escorted Xu Yulan to her spot, watched as she put the sign around her neck and stood up on the stool, then left. After they left, they forgot all about her. She stood there all day, looking left and right, waiting for them to come back. When the sun went down and the streets emptied, she began to wonder if they had forgotten that they had left her there. Only then did she make her way home, carrying the stool in one hand and the sign in the other.

She was left to stand on the street all day long many times. When she got tired of standing, she would sit down on the stool and pound her legs and rub her feet until she was ready to stand once more on the stool.

The place where she stood was quite a distance from the nearest public toilet. When she had to go to the bathroom, she would walk two blocks to the public toilet next to the rice shop, with the wooden placard still dangling around her neck all the while. Everybody would watch as she walked by, clasping the placard and, with averted eyes, remaining as closely as she could to the side of the road. When she arrived at the toilet, she would take off her sign and lean it against the wall. When she was finished, she would replace the placard around her neck and move back to her spot.

Standing on the stool was very much like participating in a struggle session. She had to stand with her head bowed in front of her, because criminals were expected to bow their heads in just such a manner. Xu Yulan stood on the stool with her head bowed, staring at her feet. But if she stared at one spot for too long, her eyes would start to get sore, so every once in a while she looked up at the people walking up and down the street.

She noticed that no one paid any attention to her. Some of the people who went by would glance in her direction, but only a very few of them gave her a second look. This made Xu Yulan feel much better, and she told Xu Sanguan, "When I stand on the street, I'm just like a telephone pole for all anyone cares."

She said, "Xu Sanguan, I'm not afraid of anything anymore. I've suffered everything now. There's nothing else they can do to me. It's already come to this. What more could they do to me? Kill me? Fine, I'm really not afraid of dying. But sometimes I think about you, I think about the kids, and I start to feel frightened. If it wasn't for you and the kids, I really wouldn't be afraid of anything."

The thought of her three sons brought tears to her eyes.

"Yile and Erle ignore me. They won't even talk to me anymore. When I call to them, they pretend not to hear me. Sanle's the only one who still talks to me, who still dares to call me his mom. I'm out there every day suffering, and when I get home, you're the only one who's good to me. When my feet are swollen, you pour a basin of hot water for me to soak them in. When I come home late, you've kept some dinner under the quilt because you were afraid it would get cold. When I'm standing out there on the street, you're the one who brings me things to eat and water to drink. Xu Sanguan, as long as you're good to me, I'm not afraid of anything in the world."

Xu Yulan usually had to stand out in the street all day long, so Xu Sanguan would bring her something to eat and water to drink. At first Xu Sanguan wanted Yile to go, but Yile refused. "Dad, why don't you tell Erle to do it?"

Xu Sanguan called for Erle and told him, "Erle, we've all eaten, but your mom hasn't had anything yet. Why don't you take her something to eat?"

Erle shook his head. "Dad, why don't you have Sanle do it?"

Xu Sanguan got angry. He said, "I ask Yile to do it, and he passes the job on to Erle. I ask Erle to do it, and he passes the job to Sanle. And Sanle, the little brat, just puts the bowl down on the ground and disappears without a trace. When they want to eat, when they want clothes on their backs, when they want some money, they're my sons all right. But when it comes to taking their mom something to eat, it seems like I don't have any sons anymore."

Erle said to Xu Sanguan, "Dad, I don't want to go outside anymore. Whenever I go out, people who know who we are call me Two *Yuan* a Night. It's so embarrassing."

Yile said, "I'm not afraid of them calling me Two *Yuan* a Night. If they call me names, I just call them names right back and even louder than they did. And I'm not afraid of fighting either. If there are more of them than me, I'll just run. I'll head home and get a knife and run back and show them and say I'm a merciless killer and if they don't believe me, they can go ask Blacksmith Fang's son. Then it's their turn to run. It's not that I'm afraid of going out. I just don't feel like going out, that's all."

Xu Sanguan said, "I'm the one who should be afraid to go out. Whenever I go out, people throw little rocks at me, and spit at me, and other people want me to stop and publicly denounce your mom. If they did that to you kids, you could just pretend you didn't know or understand, but I'm too afraid of what will happen if I refuse to say anything. It's just as bad for me, if not worse. What are you kids afraid of? You kids were born into the new society, and you've grown up under the red flag. You're innocent. Look at Sanle. Isn't that little brat out all day long, playing in the streets? Though he's taken it a little too far today. It's getting late, and he still hasn't come home."

When Sanle came home, Xu Sanguan called him over for a talk.

"Where did you go? You left right after breakfast and haven't been home all day. Where were you? Who were you playing with?"

Sanle said, "I don't remember anymore. I went so many places that I can't remember. And I wasn't playing with anyone else, just by myself."

Sanle was willing to deliver the food to his mom, but Xu Sanguan worried that he was still too small for the responsibility. He had no choice but to bring her the food himself. He packed the rice in a little aluminum lunchbox and walked out into the street.

He could see Xu Yulan standing on the stool in the distance, head bowed, with the placard hanging from her neck. Her hair had started to grow out a little, and she looked like a little boy from a distance. Xu Yulan's clothes were in tatters, and her back was curved like the question marks that filled the big-character posters. Her hands hung limply in front of her, and because she kept her head at about the same height as her bent upper back, they dangled level with her knees.

Xu Sanguan, seeing the sorry state she was in, felt wave after wave of sorrow roll through him as he approached. When he arrived by her side, he said, "I'm here."

Xu Yulan's bowed head turned to look at Xu Sanguan, who showed her the little aluminum lunchbox.

"I've brought you some food."

Xu Yulan stepped down, sat on the stool, adjusted the placard, and took the aluminum lunchbox. She lifted the cover and set the lunchbox down on the stool beside her. When she saw that all there was in the box was rice, without even a little vegetables or meat, she said nothing, merely picking up the spoon and starting to eat. She stared at her feet as she chewed on the rice.

Xu Sanguan stood by her side, watching her silently eat her meal. After a moment he lifted his head to look at the people walking up and down the street.

A few people, noticing Xu Yulan sitting on the stool and eating, walked up to her, glanced inside the lunchbox, and asked Xu Sanguan, "What did you bring her to eat?"

Xu Sanguan hastily took the lunchbox from Xu Yulan's hand and showed it to them, saying, "Have a look. All there is is this rice. No meat or vegetables. You can see for yourself. I'm not giving her anything but rice."

They nodded. "That's right. Nothing in there but rice."

One of them asked, "Why don't you put something else in there? Plain rice is pretty tasteless without any vegetables or meat."

Xu Sanguan said, "I can't give her anything good to eat. If I gave her something good to eat"—he pointed in Xu Yulan's direction—"I'd be 'shielding the enemy.' When I make her eat plain rice without any extras, it's so I can 'struggle' against her too."

As Xu Sanguan spoke, Xu Yulan kept her head bowed to the ground, not even daring to chew on the rice she had in her mouth. It wasn't until they had moved into the distance that Xu Yulan began to chew again.

When Xu Sanguan saw that there was no one in the vicinity, he whispered to her, "I hid the good stuff under the rice. No one's looking now. Have a bite."

Xu Yulan dug through the rice with a spoon and saw that the bottom of the lunchbox was full of meat. Xu Sanguan had cooked her red-braised pork. She picked up a piece of the pork with her spoon, popped it into her mouth, bowed her head, and continued to chew.

Xu Sanguan whispered, "I made it for you in secret. Even the kids don't know."

Xu Yulan nodded, ate a few more spoonfuls of rice, and then put the cover back on the lunchbox. She told Xu Sanguan, "I don't want any more."

Xu Sanguan said, "You only had one piece of meat. Eat the rest of your meat."

Xu Yulan shook her head. "Give it to Yile and the rest of them. Bring it home and let Yile and the rest eat it." Then she stretched out a hand and pounded her legs with her fist. "My legs are numb from standing so much."

The way she looked brought the beginnings of tears to Xu Sanguan's eyes. He said to her, "There's an old saying that still rings true. The more you see, the more you learn about the world. I think I must have aged ten years in the last few months. It's true that 'you can know a man's face but not his heart.' We still don't know who's responsible for that poster. Who knows? You usually don't mince words, so you might have offended any number of people. From now on, you better be more careful. The ancients said that the more you say, the more you lose."

These words struck a chord in Xu Yulan. She burst out, "There was just that one time with He Xiaoyong, and now look at the state I'm in. You and Lin Fenfang did the same thing, but no one's ever bothered to 'struggle' against you."

Xu Yulan's words terrified Xu Sanguan. He looked hastily around to see if anyone was nearby, and when he was certain it was safe, he whispered, "You just can't say things like that. Don't *ever* say that to anyone else."

Xu Yulan said, "I won't say it again."

Xu Sanguan said, "You're already in hot water, and I'm the only one in the world who's trying to save you. If I got thrown in the water along with you, there'd be no one left to pull you out."

AROUND NOON Xu Sanguan usually emerged from the house with the aluminum lunchbox in hand. People who were familiar with him knew that he was on his way to deliver Xu Yulan her lunch, and they would always call out, "Xu Sanguan, making a delivery, eh?"

But one day a stranger stopped him on his way to Xu Yulan's spot and asked, "Aren't you Xu Sanguan? Is that the food you're bringing over to that woman named Xu Yulan? Let me ask you this. Have you held a struggle session at home? I mean to denounce Xu Yulan?"

Xu Sanguan held the aluminum lunchbox tightly to his chest, lowered his eyes to the ground, and nodded. "She's already been denounced all over town." Then he counted all the places she'd been struggled against on his fingers. "They denounced her at the factory, and at the school, and on the street, and she's been through five struggle sessions at the town square."

The man said, "She has to be struggled against at home too."

Xu Sanguan didn't know this man, and he wasn't wearing a red armband either. It was impossible to tell who he was or where he came from. Even so he had little choice but to listen and pay heed to what the man had said.

He said to Xu Yulan, "People are watching us, you know. Someone asked me today if we'd had a struggle session at home yet. He said we have to denounce you at home as well."

Xu Yulan had only just come home from the street. She lifted the "Xu Yulan, Prostitute" placard from around her neck and set it down on the floor behind the door. Then she replaced the stool she had stood on all day beside the table, picked up a rag, and started wiping the seat. She continued to wipe the stool without a glance in his direction as she listened, and when he was finished, she said, "Go ahead then."

That evening Xu Sanguan called to Yile, Erle, and Sanle and said, "Tonight our family's holding a struggle session. And who are we denouncing? Xu Yulan, of course. From now on you have to call her Xu Yulan. You're not allowed to call her Mom at a struggle session. You can't call her Mom until we're finished with the meeting."

Xu Sanguan had his three sons sit down in a row. He sat in front of them, and Xu Yulan stood to one side, although he had set out a stool for her too. The four of them sat on stools, while only Xu Yulan remained standing, head bowed, just as if she were still out on the street.

Xu Sanguan said to his sons, "Today we're denouncing Xu Yulan, so she really ought to remain standing. But since she's been standing all day on the street and her feet are swollen and her legs are numb, do you think we can let her sit down on a stool instead? All in favor raise your hands."

As he proposed the motion, Xu Sanguan raised his own hand. Sanle rapidly followed suit, while Yile and Erle exchanged glances before raising their hands.

Xu Sanguan said to Xu Yulan, "You may sit down."

Xu Yulan sat down on the stool.

Xu Sanguan said to his sons, "Each of you has to speak out. If you have something to say, don't hold back. If you don't have anything to say, keep it brief. But everyone has to say something so that if anyone asks, I can tell them in all honesty that everyone spoke at the meeting. Yile, you go first."

Yile turned and looked at Erle. "Erle, you go first."

Erle glanced at Xu Yulan, gazed toward Xu Sanguan, and finally looked over at Sanle. "Let Sanle go first."

Sanle's mouth dropped open, as if he were about to laugh but had thought better of it. He said to Xu Sanguan, "I don't know what to say."

Xu Sanguan looked at Sanle and said, "Well, I guess you wouldn't have had much to say anyway." He cleared his throat. "I'll start with a few words then. They say that Xu Yulan is a prostitute. They say she sees clients every night, that she charges two *yuan* a night. But I want you all to think about that. Who exactly is it that sleeps in the same bed with Xu Yulan every night?"

When he finished speaking, Xu Sanguan looked questioningly over at Yile, Erle, and Sanle. His three sons gazed silently back toward him.

Finally, Sanle broke the silence. "It's you! You sleep in the same bed as Mom every night."

"That's exactly right," Xu Sanguan said. "It's me. Every one of Xu Yulan's johns is me. But can you really call me a john?"

Xu Sanguan saw Sanle nod his head. Then he watched as Erle also nodded in agreement. Only Yile refrained from nodding.

Xu Sanguan pointed at Erle and Sanle and said, "Did I tell you two to nod? I wanted you to shake your heads. You idiots! You really think I'm her john? When I married Xu Yulan, I spent a lot of money on the wedding. I hired six men to play drums and gongs, and four men to carry the sedan chair. I had a three-table spread, and all the friends and relatives I could think of showed up at the party to eat and drink their fill. Everything about our marriage was on the up-and-up. That's why I'm not a john and she's not a whore. Though I should add that Xu Yulan did make one big mistake, and that mistake was He Xiaoyong." He glanced at Yile and continued, "You know all about Xu Yulan and He Xiaoyong's affair. That's what we're going to denounce at today's meeting."

Xu Sanguan turned to face Xu Yulan. "Xu Yulan, it's time for you to come clean to your sons about the affair."

Xu Yulan bowed her head and whispered, "How can I tell my sons about that? How could I even begin to talk about that with them?"

Xu Sanguan said, "Don't look at them as your sons. Just try to see them as the revolutionary masses who are denouncing you."

Xu Yulan looked up at her three sons. Yile sat with his head bowed. Only Erle and Sanle were looking at her. She swiveled her eyes back toward Xu Sanguan, who said, "Go on."

"I committed some crimes in my past life." Xu Yulan wiped her tears. "And I'm paying for it in this life. I must have offended He Xiaoyong in my past life, and he took his revenge on me in this one. He's dead and gone now, but I'm still paying."

Xu Sanguan said, "Enough of that."

Xu Yulan nodded, and lifted up both of her hands to wipe her face. "Actually, He Xiaoyong and I only did it once. I never thought that after just one time I would end up pregnant with Yile—"

Yile interrupted, "Don't talk about me. If you're going to confess, then speak for yourself."

Xu Yulan looked up at Yile, who was sitting ashen-faced across from her and avoiding her gaze. Her tears flowed once more as she continued. "I know I should apologize to you all. I know you all hate me. You've lost a lot of face because of me. But you can't blame me either. It was He Xiaoyong. He Xiaoyong took advantage of my dad leaving us alone when he went to the public toilet. He pushed me up against the wall. I tried to push him away. I told him I already belonged to Xu Sanguan. But he kept pressing me up against the wall. I tried my best to push him away, but he was stronger than me. I couldn't get him off me. I wanted to scream, but he squeezed my breasts and somehow I couldn't fight anymore. I just went limp."

Xu Sanguan saw Erle's and Sanle's eyes open wide with wonder. Yile kept his eyes to the floor, but his feet were sliding agitatedly back and forth across the floor.

Xu Yulan continued her story. "He dragged me to the bed, unbuttoned my shirt, unbuttoned my pants. I didn't have any strength left to resist him. He pulled one of my legs out of my pants leg, but didn't bother with the other one. Then he pushed his own pants down below his backside."

Xu Sanguan shouted, "Stop! Enough! Can't you see that Erle's and Sanle's eyes are just about ready to pop out of their heads? You're spewing venom. You're corrupting the younger generation."

Xu Yulan said, "You made me do it."

Xu Sanguan said, "I didn't tell you to talk about *that* stuff." He pointed toward Xu Yulan and shouted at Erle and Sanle, "This is your own mom! How could you have sat there listening to that stuff?"

Erle shook his head vigorously. "I didn't hear anything. Sanle was listening to it, not me."

Sanle said, "I didn't hear anything either."

"Forget it," Xu Sanguan said. "Xu Yulan's confessed more than enough. I think it's your turn to say something. Yile, you go first."

Only now did Yile lift his eyes from the floor and say to Xu Sanguan, "I don't have anything else to say. I hate He Xiaoyong the very most. And I hate her second most." He pointed at Xu Yulan. "I hate He Xiaoyong because he wouldn't recognize me as his son. And I hate her because I can't hold up my head in public."

Xu Sanguan signaled for him to stop talking. Then he looked over at Erle. "Erle, it's your turn."

Erle scratched his head with his hand and said to Xu Yulan, "Why didn't you bite him when he pushed you up against the wall? If you couldn't push him away, how come you didn't bite him? You say you didn't have any strength left to resist, but you must have had enough strength to bite him—"

"Erle!" Xu Sanguan shouted, so frightening the boy that he began to tremble. He gestured at him. "I thought you just said you didn't hear any of that stuff. If you didn't hear anything, then what the hell do you think you're talking about? If you didn't hear anything, then don't *say* anything either. Sanle, say something."

Sanle glanced at Erle, who was staring uneasily at Xu Sanguan, still flinching from the shock of being scolded by his father. Then Sanle glanced at Xu Sanguan, whose face was flushed with anger. By this time Sanle was so frightened, he didn't dare say a word. Instead, he sat with his mouth half open, lips poised to speak.

Xu Sanguan dismissed him with a wave of his hand. "Forget it. Don't say anything then. 'A dog's mouth doesn't produce ivory' after all. Today's struggle session is adjourned."

Yile said, "But I wasn't finished talking yet."

Xu Sanguan looked disapprovingly at Yile. "What else do you have to say?"

Yile said, "I had only got up to the part about who I hated. You didn't let me talk about who I love. The person I love most, of course, is our Great Leader Chairman Mao. And the one I love second most"—Yile gazed at Xu Sanguan—"is you."

Xu Sanguan stared back at Yile without so much as blinking. After what seemed like a long while, tears spilled from his eyes, and he said to Xu Yulan, "Who says Yile isn't my son?"

Xu Sanguan raised his right hand to his eyes to wipe away the tears. After he had been wiping for a moment, he raised his left hand to his eyes as well and continued to rub away his tears.

Finally, he gazed benevolently at his three sons. "I've also made a serious mistake in my life. It was with Lin Fenfang. You know, Fatty Lin."

Xu Yulan said, "Xu Sanguan, why are you bringing that up?"

"Because I want to tell them." Xu Sanguan gestured in Xu Yulan's direction. "It was like this. Fatty Lin broke her leg so I went to visit her. Her husband wasn't home, and so we were alone in the house. I asked her which leg was broken. She said it was the right one. I asked her if it hurt. First I touched her calf, and then I touched her thigh, and then I touched her even higher up—"

"Xu Sanguan." Xu Yulan said his name. "You have to stop right there. If you keep on going, you'll poison their minds."

Xu Sanguan nodded and looked at his three sons. All three of the boys had their eyes glued to the floor. He continued. "I did it just one time with Lin Fenfang. And your mom did it just once with He Xiaoyong. The reason I told you all of this tonight is because I want you boys to know that I'm actually just as bad as your mom. Both of us made serious mistakes. That's why you shouldn't hate her for it." He pointed toward Xu Yulan. "If you hate her, you have to hate me too, because she and I are birds of a feather."

Xu Yulan shook her head and said to her sons, "He's not the same as me. He only did it with Lin Fenfang because I hurt his feelings first."

Xu Sanguan, shaking his head, said, "It's all the same, really."

Xu Yulan addressed Xu Sanguan. "We're not the same. If the

incident with He Xiaoyong had never happened, you never would have touched Lin Fenfang."

Xu Sanguan couldn't help but agree. "Well, that's true. But," he added, "we're still the same."

LATER Chairman Mao began to talk. Chairman Mao was saying things nearly every day. When he said, "We must fight with words and not weapons," everyone put down the knives and clubs in their hands. When Chairman Mao went on to say, "We must take the revolution back to the classroom," Yile, Erle, and Sanle put on their book bags and went back to school, where classes had resumed. When Chairman Mao said, "We must make the revolution serve production," Xu Sanguan went back to work at the silk factory, and Xu Yulan got up every morning to fry dough. Xu Yulan's hair was getting longer and longer, almost long enough to cover her ears.

Sometime after that Chairman Mao stood atop the rostrum at Tiananmen, held up his right hand, and waved toward the west, addressing millions and millions of students assembled on the square: "It's necessary that educated youth be removed to the countryside to be reeducated by middle and lower peasants."

So it was that Yile, carrying a bed mat, a Thermos, and a washbasin, marched at the back of a column of students, all of whom were just as young as he. They marched under a red flag, singing anthems, happily climbing onto buses, happily boarding ferries, waving good-bye to the tears of their mothers and fathers on their way to their new homes in the countryside.

After Yile was sent down to the countryside, he would often sit all alone on a hillside as dusk approached, wrapping his arms around his knees and staring blankly at the fields all around him. When the other students who had been sent down saw him sitting there, they would ask, "Yile, what are you doing?"

Yile would say, "I'm thinking about my mom and dad."

When this story about Yile made its way back to town, Xu Sanguan and Xu Yulan both cried.

By that time Erle had also graduated from school. Soon he too would move away, carrying only a bed mat, a Thermos, and a washbasin, as he and yet another column of students marched under the red flag on their way to their new homes in the countryside.

Xu Yulan said to Erle before he left, "Erle, when you get to the countryside and things get really rough, just climb up a hill and think about your mom and dad, and remember us."

One day Chairman Mao sat on the sofa in his study and said, "You may keep one child by your side." And so it was that Sanle stayed by his parents' side, graduated from high school at age eighteen, and started work at the machine tools factory in town.

CHAPTER TWENTY-SIX

One day a few years later Yile came back to town from the countryside. He was as skinny as a twig, his face was grayish yellow, and he held a broken old basket in his hands, filled with a bundle of leafy vegetables. This was his present for his parents. He hadn't come home for a visit for over six months, and when he knocked on the front door, Xu Sanguan and Xu Yulan stared at him for a moment before realizing that this was actually their son.

Yile's pallid and wasted look brought them up short with surprise, because he hadn't looked nearly so bad last time he came home. Granted, he had been thinner and darker than when he had first left home, but he had been in good spirits, and when he left, he had carried a crock that could fit nearly a hundred pounds of rice away with him on his back. He walked away with his back bent against the weight, his feet sounding out hollowly against the pavement as he went. He didn't have a rice crock in the countryside, so he had been storing his rice in a cardboard box, but when the weather turned humid, the bottom of the box rotted away, turning the rice at the bottom a yellowish-green color.

After he came back home, Xu Sanguan said to Xu Yulan, "Do you think Yile might be sick? When he's not lying down, he just sits around the house. He's not eating much either, and it seems like he's stooping all the time."

Xu Yulan put her hand on Yile's forehead to see if he was running a fever.

"He's not sick. If he was sick, he'd be running a fever. I think he just doesn't want to go back down to the countryside. It's too hard on him down there. Let him stay in town for a few more days and rest up. After he's rested for a few days, I'm sure he'll start to feel better."

Yile stayed in town for ten days. During the daytime he always sat by the window, with his arms draped over the windowsill and his chin resting on his arms, looking outside at the lane. Usually, he stared at the walls of the houses across the way. The walls were nearly a hundred years old, and green weeds grew from the cracks between the bricks, fluttering in the breeze. Sometimes a few women who lived in the area would stop beneath his window and chatter for a while. When they said something interesting, Yile would smile and move his arms into a more comfortable position.

By that time Sanle had already become a regular worker at the machine tools factory and had a bed at the factory dormitory. They lived five to a room, but Sanle was happy to stay at the factory, because he could be with people his own age. When Yile came home, Sanle would come by every day after dinner and spend some time with the family. Whenever Sanle came over, Yile was lying in bed. Sanle said to him, "Yile, the more other people sleep, the fatter they get. The more you sleep, the skinnier you seem to be."

The only times Yile became the least bit animated was when

Sanle came home. He would smile and talk with him, and there were even a few times when they went out together for a walk. But after Sanle left, Yile would once again lie down in bed or sit motionlessly by the window, as if he had been glued in place.

Xu Yulan, seeing that Yile kept hanging around the house and seemed not to have the slightest intention of going back down to the countryside, said to him, "Yile, when are you planning to go back? You've been home for ten days already."

Yile said, "I don't have any energy now. It wouldn't do any good for me to go back now, because I just don't have the energy to work in the fields. Let me stay for a few more days, okay?"

Xu Yulan replied, "Yile, it's not that I want to make you go back. But think about it. Of the people who were sent down with you, quite a few have already gotten their transfers and been allowed to come back to town. There are even four people who came back up from the countryside working at Sanle's factory. You have to work hard and get on your brigade chief's good side. That way you can come back to town for good."

Xu Sanguan agreed. "Your mom is right. We don't want to kick you out. If it were up to us, you could stay here your whole life if you wanted, and we'd be happy to have you. But as things stand now, you'd better go back and get to work. If you stay at home too long, people in your brigade will get to talking, and your brigade chief will be that much less likely to give you a transfer. Yile, go back down for now, and after a year or two of hard work, you can earn your way home for good."

Yile shook his head. "I really don't have the energy. If I went back now, I just couldn't work very hard anyway."

Xu Sanguan said, "You know, energy isn't like money. The more you use money, the less you have. But the more energy you put out, the more you'll have. If all you do is hang around the house all day, it's no wonder you don't feel very energetic. But if you go back and work every day, sweat a little every day, your energy will come back, and pretty soon you'll feel stronger and stronger."

Yile continued to shake his head. "It's been more than six months since I last came home. Erle got to come back home twice already in that time, and I didn't get to come at all. Can't you let me stay a little longer?"

"Nothing doing," Xu Yulan said. "You're going back tomorrow."

Yile went back to the countryside after ten days at home. The morning he was to leave, Xu Yulan came home as soon as she was finished frying dough. She brought two pieces of fried dough home for Yile. "Eat them while they're hot. You can leave after you've eaten."

Yile sat listlessly by the window looking at the fried dough and shook his head. "I don't feel like eating. I don't feel like eating anything. I just don't have any appetite."

Then he stood up, folded the change of clothes he had brought back with him from the countryside, and stuffed them into an old book bag, which he proceeded to sling over his shoulder. "I'm leaving."

Xu Sanguan said, "Eat the fried dough before you go."

Yile shook his head. "I just don't feel like eating anything right now."

Xu Yulan said, "You have to eat something. You have a long way to go today."

Xu Yulan told Yile to wait a moment and went into the kitchen to hard-boil a couple of eggs. When they were done, she wrapped them in a handkerchief and handed them to him. "Yile, take these with you. You can eat them if you get hungry on the way."

Yile, still holding the eggs in his hand, walked out the front door. Xu Sanguan and Xu Yulan went to the front door to watch him go. Xu Sanguan saw that he was walking with his head bowed, moving slowly and carefully down the lane and almost leaning against the wall for support as he went. He was so thin, his shoulder bones stuck sharply out from his shirt, and the clothes that had once been a little too small for him now hung so loosely around his frame that it seemed there was no body underneath. When Yile reached the telephone pole, Xu Sanguan saw him lift his hand to his face and wipe his eyes. Xu Sanguan wondered if he was crying. He said to Xu Yulan, "I'm going to go see him off."

When Xu Sanguan caught up to him, he saw that Yile really was crying. He said to him, "Your mom and I can't do anything about it either. We just want you to do well down there so you can get a transfer and come back as soon as possible."

With his father walking by his side, Yile stopped wiping the tears on his face. He shifted the book bag, which was slipping off his shoulder, across his back. "I know."

The two walked ahead without exchanging any more words. Xu Sanguan walked faster than Yile and had to stop every few steps to wait for him to catch up before he continued down the street. When they came to the front entrance to the hospital, Xu Sanguan said, "Yile, wait here for a little while." He walked into the hospital.

Yile stood outside the door waiting, but after a few minutes he sat down on a pile of bricks, his book bag dangling again from his shoulder, the two hard-boiled eggs still held in one hand. He started to feel like eating a little something, so he took one of the eggs, tapped it lightly against a brick, peeled off the shell, and put it in his mouth. He slowly chewed on the egg, eyes fixed on the hospital's front entrance. He ate very slowly, but by the time he had finished one egg, Xu Sanguan still hadn't emerged from the door of the hospital. He turned his eyes away from the door, put his book bag on his knees, folded his arms on top of the book bag, and then cradled his head with his arms.

After a few more moments Xu Sanguan returned. "Let's go."

They walked west until they reached the ferry pier. Xu Sanguan told Yile to sit down in the waiting room and went off to buy his ferry ticket. When he was finished, he sat down next to Yile to wait for the boat, which was due to depart in half an hour.

The room was crowded with people, the majority of whom were peasants who had come up to town early that morning to sell produce and were now on their way home. They had piled their carrying poles on the floor and sat holding their baskets, now emptied of produce, in their hands, smoking cheap cigarettes, and cheerfully chatting among themselves.

Xu Sanguan pulled thirty *yuan* from his front pocket and stuffed it into Yile's hand. "Take this."

Yile, taken aback by the sight of his father suddenly handing him so much money, asked, "Dad, that's for me?"

Xu Sanguan said, "Take it. Now. Put it somewhere safe."

Yile looked down at the money. "Dad, I'll just take ten *yuan*, all right?"

Xu Sanguan said, "Take all of it. I earned it selling blood just now. Take all of it. Some of it's for Erle too. Erle's far away from town, but he's pretty close to where you are, so you can give him ten or fifteen the next time he comes to see you. Tell him to use it wisely. You two are far away from home, so we can't look after you. You two brothers have to take good care of each other."

Yile nodded and took the money.

Xu Sanguan continued, "Don't waste this money on unnecessary things. Be careful with it, and spend it wisely. If you feel tired, but you don't have any appetite, buy yourself something good to eat to give yourself strength. And when Spring Festival comes around, buy two packs of cigarettes and a bottle of liquor and give them to the chief of your production brigade. That way, when the time comes, you'll be able to come back to town much sooner. Got that? Use it wisely. The best steel is for the blade and not the handle."

It was time for Yile to get on the boat, so Xu Sanguan stood and escorted Yile over to the gate where they collected the tickets. He watched him board the ferry, then shouted, "Yile, remember what I told you. The best steel is for the blade, not the handle."

Yile turned back toward Xu Sanguan and nodded his head. Then he ducked his head and walked through the low door into the cabin.

Xu Sanguan was left standing by the gate. He stood by the gate until the ferry began to move down the river, and only then did he turn to make his way home.

LESS THAN A MONTH after Yile went back to the countryside, the chief of Erle's production brigade came to town. He was well over fifty years old, bearded, and when he smoked cigarettes, he liked to attach the butt he had just smoked to the tip of a fresh cigarette in order to conserve tobacco. In the half hour that he spent at Xu Sanguan's house, he smoked four cigarettes, starting three of them with the end of the cigarette that had just preceded it. After he had ground the fourth cigarette out on the floor and placed the butt in his pocket, he stood and told them that he had plans to eat lunch somewhere else, but that he would be back for dinner at Xu Sanguan's place.

As soon as Erle's brigade chief left, Xu Yulan sat down on the doorstep and began to wipe tears from her eyes. As she rubbed her face, she said, "It's the end of the month, and all we have left in the house is two *yuan*. How can you have someone over to dinner on just two *yuan*? When you have company, you have to serve them fish and meat, and you need to supply wine and cigarettes as well. All you can get for two *yuan* is a pound of meat and half a fish. What am I going to do? 'Even the cleverest maid is in trouble when there's no rice in the larder,' so how am I supposed to have someone for dinner when there's no money to feed him? And this is no ordinary guest. This is Erle's brigade chief. If there isn't very much to eat, Erle's brigade chief won't be pleased, and if Erle's brigade chief isn't pleased, it's going to be tough on Erle. Not only will he lose all hope for a transfer back to town, but he'll also have a harder time of it in the production brigade. It's the brigade chief who's coming to dinner, and we have to wine him and dine him and give him some nice presents as well. How can I manage with just two *yuan*?" Xu Yulan swung around to face Xu Sanguan inside the room. "Xu Sanguan, I'm going to have to ask you to sell some blood."

Xu Sanguan sat for a moment nodding his head, and then said to her, "Go get me a bucketful of water from the well. I'll need to drink water before I sell blood."

Xu Yulan said, "There's water in that cup over there. Drink the water in the cup."

Xu Sanguan said, "There isn't enough water in the cup. I have to drink a lot of water."

Xu Yulan said, "There's water in the Thermos too."

Xu Sanguan said, "The water in the Thermos is too hot. I asked you to get me some water from the well. Now I want you to do it."

Xu Yulan nodded her assent, stood, and rushed to the well. When she returned, Xu Sanguan told her to put the bucket on the table and asked her to bring him a bowl. He proceeded to down bowl after bowl of water. After the fifth bowlful, Xu Yulan began to worry that he'd hurt himself. "Stop drinking. I'm afraid you'll hurt yourself."

Xu Sanguan, paying her no mind, drank two more bowls of well water. Then, clasping his stomach with both hands, he stood carefully up from the table and took a few mincing steps forward. He paused for another moment by the doorway before stepping into the lane.

Xu Sanguan went to the hospital to see Blood Chief Li. "I've come to sell blood again," he said to him.

Blood Chief Li was by this time already well into his sixties. His hair had gone completely white, and his back was hunched. He sat at his desk smoking cigarettes, coughing, and spitting a seemingly incessant flow of phlegm onto the floor. As he spat, his cotton-soled shoes would slide back and forth across the floor in a futile effort to wipe the floor clean of phlegm. He looked at Xu

Sanguan for a moment and said, "You just sold me some blood the day before yesterday."

Xu Sanguan said, "I was here a month ago to sell blood."

Blood Chief Li smiled. "You came a month ago, so I remembered who you were. Don't think I'm getting old. My memory's still sharp. If I see something or hear about something, doesn't matter how trivial, I always remember."

Xu Sanguan smiled and nodded. "Your memory is really good. Mine is terrible nowadays. Even about the most important things. I'll go to sleep and wake up having forgotten all about whatever it was that happened the day before."

Blood Chief Li, warmed by these words, leaned contentedly back in his chair. "You're quite a few years younger than me, but it sounds like your memory isn't nearly as good as mine."

Xu Sanguan said, "How could I compare with you?"

Blood Chief Li said, "Well, you have a point there. My memory's certainly better than yours. To tell you the truth, there're a lot of twenty- and thirty-year-olds who can't compare with me."

Xu Sanguan watched as his face broke into a delighted grin and then asked, "Then will you let me sell blood?"

"Nothing doing." Blood Chief Li's smile disappeared immediately. "Are you trying to kill yourself? You need to rest for at least three months after each and every time you sell blood. You're not permitted to sell blood until three months after the previous time."

Xu Sanguan, left at a loss, stood silent for a moment. Then he said, "I really need the money. Our Erle's brigade chief—"

Blood Chief Li cut him short. "Everyone who comes to see me really needs the money."

Xu Sanguan said, "But I'm begging you—"

Blood Chief Li cut him short. "Don't beg me. Everybody who comes here begs me."

Xu Sanguan began again. "I'm begging you. Our Erle's brigade chief is coming over for dinner, and all we have left is two *yuan*—"

Blood Chief Li waved his hand. "Don't waste your breath. I'm not going to listen to you anyway. Come back in two months."

Xu Sanguan began to cry. "If I come back in two months, the damage will already be done. Erle's life will be ruined. What's going to happen to him if we offend his brigade chief?"

"Who's Erle?" Blood Chief Li asked.

"My son," Xu Sanguan replied.

"Ohhhh." Blood Chief Li nodded.

It seemed to Xu Sanguan that Blood Chief Li's expression had softened, so he wiped his tears and continued. "If you let me sell just this one time, I guarantee this will never happen again. Please—just this once."

"Nothing doing." Blood Chief Li shook his head. "This is for your own good. Who would have to bear the responsibility if you ended up selling away your life?"

Xu Sanguan said, "I would take full responsibility."

"What the hell are you talking about?" Blood Chief Li asked. "If you were dead, you would be in no position to take any kind of responsibility. And I would be following you down the road to hell. You know why? It's called medical malpractice. The higher-ups would be down here in a second flat."

Blood Chief Li, noticing that Xu Sanguan's legs were trembling, paused to ask, "Why are you shaking like that?"

Xu Sanguan said, "I really have to take a piss."

At that moment someone walked into the room, an empty carrying pole slung over one shoulder and a live chicken in the other hand. As soon as he walked into the room, he called out to Xu Sanguan, who failed to recognize him at first. "Xu Sanguan, don't you recognize me anymore? I'm Genlong."

Xu Sanguan realized that it was indeed Genlong. "Genlong, you look completely different. How did you get so old all of a sudden? Your hair's gone completely gray. I thought you were still only forty."

Genlong said, "Life's harder down in the country, so we folks look a little older than people in town. And you've got some gray yourself, you know. You look a lot different than you used to, but I could still tell it was you."

Genlong handed the chicken to Blood Chief Li. "This is a laying hen. She laid an egg with a double yolk just this morning."

Blood Chief Li accepted the gift, beaming so widely that his eyes seemed to disappear into the creases fanning across his face: "Aiyo! You're too good to me, Genlong, you're just too kind."

Genlong addressed Xu Sanguan. "So you're here to sell blood too? What a coincidence, running into you like this again. It's been, what, ten years now?"

Xu Sanguan said to Genlong, "Genlong, help me out. See if you can get Blood Chief Li to let me sell some blood."

Genlong turned to look inquiringly over at Blood Chief Li.

Blood Chief Li said, "It's not that I don't want to let him sell some blood. But he already sold some just a month ago."

Genlong nodded and explained to Xu Sanguan, "You need to rest for three months after every time you sell."

Xu Sanguan said, "Genlong, I'm begging you. Ask him on my behalf. I'm really desperate for the money. I'm doing this for the sake of my son."

When Genlong heard him out, he turned again toward Blood Chief Li. "I'm begging you too. Do it as a favor to me. Let him sell some blood. Just this once."

Blood Chief Li slapped his desktop. "If it was anyone else but Genlong, I'd never allow it. But of all my friends, Genlong has the most pull around here. If Genlong asks for a favor, well, Genlong gets what he wants."

After Xu Sanguan and Genlong sold their blood, they went together to the hospital lavatory to clear the urine from their bellies. Then they went to the Victory Restaurant, sat at a window by the river, and ordered fried pork livers and yellow rice wine. After they ordered, Xu Sanguan asked, "Ah Fang's doing fine, right? How come he didn't come today?"

Genlong said, “Ah Fang’s in bad shape.”

Xu Sanguan was badly startled. “What happened to him?”

“His bladder burst,” Genlong said. “We usually drink a lot of water before we sell blood, but that one time he simply drank too much and his bladder burst. We didn’t even get far enough that day to sell any blood. Before we even got to the hospital, Ah Fang said his stomach was hurting. I told him to rest for a little while by the side of the road. We went over to the front steps of the movie theater. But as soon as he sat down, he started screaming with pain. It scared me so much I didn’t even realize what was going on. After a while he just fainted. Luckily, we were right near the hospital. I didn’t find out that his bladder had burst until I brought him to the hospital.”

Xu Sanguan asked, “But he pulled through, didn’t he?”

“Oh, he’s alive,” Genlong said. “But he’s in bad shape. He’ll never be able to sell blood again.”

Genlong asked Xu Sanguan, “But how are you doing?”

Xu Sanguan shook his head. “Two of my sons got sent down to the countryside. Sanle’s the only one who’s doing well—he’s working at the machine tools factory. It’s really hard on the other two. All the kids whose parents have any kind of pull spent just a year or two down there before they got transferred back to town. But what do I have to offer? You know just as well as I do that I’m just a cart-pusher at the silk factory. I don’t have any pull at all. We’ll just have to see if the two of them can help themselves out. If they’re lucky, and they get on well with the brigade chief, there’s a chance they could be reassigned to a job in town sooner rather than later.”

Genlong said to Xu Sanguan, “Why didn’t you have them sent down to our production brigade? Ah Fang’s the production brigade chief. He’s still the brigade chief now, even in the shape he’s in. If your sons were in our production brigade, we could have looked after them. And when it came time to issue transfers, of course, they’d be the first to go home.”

Genlong paused and lifted a hand to his forehead. "Why am I feeling so dizzy?"

"You're right." Xu Sanguan eyes widened. "How come I never thought of that?"

He watched as Genlong bent forward and rested his forehead against the tabletop. "Genlong, are you all right?"

"I'm fine. It's just that I feel a little dizzy."

Xu Sanguan's thoughts turned once again to his own problems. He sighed. "If I had only thought of that earlier. Now I suppose it's just too late."

He saw Genlong shut his eyes. "But even if I had thought of having them sent there, it might not have done any good. We couldn't very well tell the authorities where we wanted them assigned."

When he realized that Genlong hadn't responded, he leaned over and gave him a prod. When his motion still didn't produce any response, he called his name: "Genlong, Genlong."

When Genlong still didn't move, Xu Sanguan started to feel frightened. He looked around to see that the restaurant was packed with other people. The noise of talking and eating was deafening, and cigarette smoke and cooking steam cast a gray pall over the room. Waiters were squeezing through the crowd, carrying platters of food. Xu Sanguan prodded Genlong once more, and when there wasn't any response, he shouted to the waiters, "Come help! I think Genlong's dead."

The restaurant went suddenly quiet. The waiters hastily squeezed their way over to the table. One of them shook Genlong by the shoulders, while the other rubbed his face. The waiter rubbing his face said, "He's not dead. His face is still warm."

Another waiter appeared, lifted Genlong's face from the table, and told the assembled onlookers, "Looks to me like he's almost dead."

Xu Sanguan asked, "What do we do now?"

Someone said, "Take him to the hospital."

After they had taken him to the hospital, the doctor said he had suffered a cerebral hemorrhage. When they asked him what a cerebral hemorrhage was, the doctor told them that one of the blood vessels in his head had burst. Another doctor standing to one side added, "Wasn't just one blood vessel, from the looks of it."

Xu Sanguan sat on a chair in the hospital corridor for three hours and did not stand up until Genlong's woman Guihua arrived. He hadn't seen Guihua for more than twenty years, and the Guihua standing in front of him bore no resemblance at all to the young woman he remembered. This Guihua looked as strong as a man. It was already late autumn, but Guihua had come to town in bare feet, with her pants legs rolled up around her knees. And since she had come directly to the hospital when she heard the news, without stopping to wash up at home, her feet were coated with mud from the fields. Her eyes were red and swollen. Xu Sanguan thought to himself that she must have been crying the whole way into town.

After Genlong's woman arrived, Xu Sanguan left the hospital and went home. As he walked home, a feeling of emptiness washed over him. His body felt terribly heavy, as if he were carrying a hundred-pound sack of rice, and his legs trembled with every step forward. The doctor said Genlong had suffered a cerebral hemorrhage, but Xu Sanguan knew better. Genlong had gotten sick because he had sold too much blood. Xu Sanguan told himself, *The doctor must not have known that Genlong had just sold some blood. Otherwise he wouldn't have said that it was a cerebral hemorrhage.*

As soon as Xu Sanguan arrived home, Xu Yulan screamed, "Where have you been? You had me worried to death! Erle's brigade chief is coming over for dinner, and you just disappear! Did you sell blood?"

Xu Sanguan nodded. "I sold blood. But Genlong's dying."

Xu Yulan stuck out her hand. "Where's the money?"

Xu Sanguan gave her the money. She hastily counted the notes, and only when she was finished did she register what Xu Sanguan had just said. "Who did you say is dying?"

"Genlong." Xu Sanguan sat down on a stool. "The man who went to sell blood with me. The Genlong from my grandpa's village."

Xu Yulan didn't know who Genlong was and didn't know why he was about to die. She slipped the money into her inside pocket, and before Xu Sanguan could finish his sentence, she bounded out of the door to the market to buy meat, fish, cigarettes, and liquor.

Xu Sanguan, left alone in the house, sat for a while in his chair, but he soon felt so fatigued that he lay down in bed. He thought to himself, *If I'm feeling so tired from just sitting in my chair, maybe I'm about to die too.* Just as the thought crossed his mind, he felt his chest constrict. After a moment or two of this suffocating feeling, he felt dizzy. He remembered that Genlong's illness had begun with a spell of dizziness. Genlong had put his head down on the table, and when he had called to him, he didn't answer.

Xu Sanguan was still lying in bed when Xu Yulan came back from the store. When she saw that he was in bed, she said, "You stay where you are. You're still weak from selling blood. Just stay put, and I'll take care of everything. You can rest until the brigade chief shows up."

Erle's brigade chief arrived around dusk. He was greeted by a table heavily laden with food.

"So much food! Why, the table's almost overflowing. You're really much too polite. And such fine liquor as well!"

When he caught sight of Xu Sanguan, he continued, "You look thin. You look thinner than when I saw you this afternoon."

Xu Sanguan's heart sank with these words, but he forced himself to smile. "Yes, I've lost weight. Have a seat, chief."

"I've seen people lose weight over the course of six months or a year. But this is the first time I've ever seen someone lose so much weight in one day." The brigade chief sat down at the table. When he noticed that there was a new carton of cigarettes on the table, he cried out in spite of himself, "And you bought a whole carton of cigarettes? I couldn't possibly smoke so much in one night!"

Xu Yulan said, "Brigade chief, this carton of cigarettes is for you. You can take whatever you don't finish home with you."

Erle's brigade chief nodded cheerfully and just as cheerfully picked up the bottle of spirits and twisted open the cap with his right hand. He filled his own cup with liquor and was about to pour some for Xu Sanguan when Xu Sanguan hastily lifted his cup from the table. "I don't drink."

Erle's brigade chief said, "That may be so, but you're going to drink with me tonight. I don't like to drink alone. It's no fun that way."

Xu Yulan said, "Xu Sanguan, you better have a drink or two with the brigade chief."

Xu Sanguan had no choice but to pass the cup over to Erle's brigade chief, who filled it to the brim, handed it back to him, and declared, "Now then! Bottoms up!"

Xu Sanguan said, "I'll just have a sip."

"That won't do," the brigade chief said. "You've got to down it all in one gulp. This is a test of our friendship. Friends drink when they're together. Acquaintances merely sip."

Xu Sanguan drank the whole cup in one gulp. His body immediately began to feel warm, just as if someone had struck a match in his belly, and he felt his strength beginning to seep back into his body, and with it a sense of relaxation. He picked up a piece of meat with his chopsticks and put it in his mouth.

Xu Yulan said to Erle's brigade chief, "Brigade chief, every time Erle comes home, he tells us what a good man you are, how kind, how easy you are to get along with, and how well you look after him."

Xu Sanguan, thinking of the bitterness with which Erle

cursed his brigade chief whenever he came home, picked up where Xu Yulan left off. “He tells us that everyone really appreciates how well you take care of them.”

Erle’s brigade chief gestured toward Xu Sanguan, “Well, it’s all true.” He lifted his cup. “Bottoms up!”

Xu Sanguan, forced to follow his lead, downed his liquor in one gulp.

Erle’s brigade chief wiped his mouth. “I don’t mean to brag, but you won’t find a better brigade chief for at least a hundred miles around. I always apply the same principle in whatever I happen to be doing. My watchword is that if everything’s aboveboard, no one’s going to rock the boat.”

Xu Sanguan began to feel dizzy, and he remembered Genlong, and that Genlong was in the hospital. When he thought about how serious Genlong’s condition was, he began to feel that he would be in the hospital himself before too long. His head spun faster and faster, and his heart was racing and thudding inside his chest. His legs seemed to be trembling as well. And within a few seconds the trembling had spread to his shoulders.

Erle’s brigade chief said to Xu Sanguan, “Why are you shaking like that?”

Xu Sanguan said, “I’m cold. I feel cold.”

“You’ll warm up after a few more drinks.” He lifted up his cup. “Bottoms up!”

Xu Sanguan shook his head. “I really shouldn’t have any more.” As he spoke, he thought to himself, *One more, and I’m a dead man.*

Erle’s brigade chief lifted Xu Sanguan’s cup and forced it into his hands. “Come on now, all in one gulp!”

Xu Sanguan shook his head. “I really can’t drink any more. I’m in pretty bad shape. I’ll pass out. The blood vessels in my head will burst.”

Erle’s brigade chief pounded the tabletop. “So what? That’s what drinking is all about. You’ve got to drink, even if it kills you.

You know why? Because it's better to harm yourself than to hurt a friend's feelings. If you really think of me as a friend, you'll drink this cup."

Xu Yulan said, "Go on, Xu Sanguan. The brigade chief is right. It's better to harm yourself than to hurt a friend's feelings."

Xu Sanguan knew what Xu Yulan meant but could not say aloud. He had to do it for Erle's sake. Xu Sanguan decided to drink. He would drink for Erle's sake. He would drink so that Erle could be transferred back to town. He gulped down the liquor.

When this third cup of liquor slid down his throat, his stomach began to pitch like the high seas in the midst of a storm. He knew he was going to vomit. He rushed out the front door, let out a moan, and began to retch. His stomach quivered as he expelled the liquor, and the pain was so sharp that he couldn't stand up straight. When he was finished vomiting, he knelt on the ground for a minute before slowly rising to his feet. He wiped his mouth and, with tears still streaming down his face, returned to his seat.

As soon as Xu Sanguan returned, the brigade chief poured him another glassful of liquor. "Drink! Better to overdo it than hurt a friend's feelings. Have another drink."

Xu Sanguan repeated to himself, *Do it for Erle. Even if it kills you. Drink.* He took the cup into his hands and drained it in a gulp.

Xu Yulan, seeing the state he was in, grew frightened. "Xu Sanguan, I think you've had enough. Something might happen to you."

Erle's brigade chief cut her off with a wave of his hand. "Nonsense! Nothing's going to happen to him." He poured another glass and handed it to Xu Sanguan. "The most I ever drank at one go was two quarts of liquor. I couldn't drink any more after the first quart, so I stuck my finger down my throat and vomited it all up. Once I had cleared my stomach out, I was ready for another quart."

Discovering that the first bottle of spirits was already empty, he said to Xu Yulan, "Go buy another bottle."

That night the brigade chief drank until he too began to feel intoxicated. He stood and walked unsteadily to the front door. Then he turned to one side and began to pee into the street. When he had finished peeing, he swung slowly around, gazed blearily toward Xu Sanguan and Xu Yulan, and announced, "That's all for tonight. We can drink some more next time I come by."

After Erle's brigade chief left, Xu Yulan helped Xu Sanguan to bed, removing his shoes and his shirt and covering him with the quilt. After she tucked him in, she went to clear the table.

Xu Sanguan lay with his eyes shut, disturbed only by the occasional hiccup. After a few minutes his hiccups slowly turned into snores.

He slept until late the next morning. When he awoke, his whole body ached. Xu Yulan had already gone to fry dough. Xu Sanguan slowly picked himself out of bed. His head ached so badly, he thought it might split. He sat by the table and drank a glass of water. Then he remembered Genlong. How was Genlong doing? He had to go to the hospital and find out.

When he arrived at the hospital, the bed Genlong had been lying in the day before was empty. Pleasantly surprised that Genlong had been discharged from the hospital so soon, he asked the other patients in the ward, "Where's Genlong?"

"Who's Genlong?" came the reply.

"The man who came in yesterday with a cerebral hemorrhage."

"He died."

Genlong dead? Xu Sanguan stood with his mouth hanging open, gazing at the empty bed. There weren't even any sheets on the bed, just a burlap mattress cover. There was a bloodstain on the burlap that had been there for so long, it had begun to turn black.

Xu Sanguan emerged from the hospital and sat on a pile of bricks outside the door. The winter wind sent chills through his body. He stuffed his hands inside his sleeves and hunched his shoulders so that his collar would shield his neck. He sat and remembered Genlong. And Ah Fang. He remembered the first time the two men had taken him to sell blood. He remembered how they had taught him to drink water before selling blood, and how they had taken him to eat fried pork livers and drink yellow rice wine afterward. He remembered Genlong, and when he was finished remembering, he sat and cried.

CHAPTER TWENTY-SEVEN

After Yile returned to the countryside, he grew weaker and weaker by the day, until even the effort of lifting his own arm would leave him panting. At the same time his body began to feel colder and colder. He covered himself with whatever he could find, but he still couldn't get warm, so he put on a cotton-padded jacket, got under his quilt, and went to sleep. And still when he woke up in the morning, his feet would be icy cold.

This went on for two months. Yile lay in bed, sleeping for whole days on end, eating cold rice and drinking cold water, until he grew so weak that he couldn't even speak.

It was at this point that Erle came to visit. Erle had departed from his own production brigade that afternoon, traveling by foot for three hours before he arrived. It was almost dark by the time he got there. Erle stood outside Yile's door, knocking and calling his name. Yile heard him arrive, and he wanted to get up to answer the door but simply did not have the strength. He wanted to say something, but he could not speak.

After Erle called his name, he pressed his face to the door

frame and peeked inside. He saw Yile lying in the dark, gazing at the door. His lips were moving, but no sound emerged. Erle shouted to him, "Open the door! It's snowing out here, and the northwest wind is howling, and the snow is coming down my neck. I'm just about frozen stiff. Let me in! You know I'm here, so why won't you open the door? I can see you looking at me. I can see your mouth moving, and I saw your eyes. What? Are you laughing at me? This isn't any time to joke around. I'm just about freezing to death out here. Goddamnit, stop fooling around! My feet are going numb. Don't you hear me stamping my feet? Yile, open the goddamn door!"

Erle kept on shouting until the sky had gone completely dark and Yile had been swallowed up by the encroaching color of night. And yet Yile refused to get up and open the door. Erle began to feel frightened. He wondered if something was wrong with his brother. He wondered if Yile had poisoned himself with pesticides. He decided to kick open the door. Smashing his foot twice against the lock, the door gave way. Then he ran to the bed and touched Yile's face. Yile's face was so hot that it scared him half to death. He thought to himself, *Yile must be running a fever of 104 degrees, at the very least.*

When Yile spoke, his voice was terribly weak. "I'm sick."

Erle swept the quilt aside and took Yile into his arms. "I'm taking you home. We can take the night ferry home."

Erle, struck by the realization that Yile was seriously ill, decided that any further delay might be dangerous. He immediately slung Yile over his back, went out the door, and began to jog toward the ferry pier. The closest ferry pier was nearly three miles away from Yile's production brigade. Erle carried Yile on his back through the snow and the wind for more than an hour before they reached the pier. The pier was sunk in darkness, and Erle could only just make out the little open shelter near the pier by the weak gleam of the moonlight reflecting on the snow. The road curved around to the left of the shelter, and a long flight of stone steps led down to the river on the right.

They reached the pier. The shelter had been built to shield ferry passengers from the rain, the snow, and the heat of summer. Erle carried Yile over to the shelter and laid him out on a concrete bench that was exposed on all sides to the elements. Then he noticed that Yile's hair and his back were completely coated with snow. He brushed the snow off Yile's back with one hand, then wiped the snow from the top of his head. Yile's hair was soaked, and the moisture had trickled down his neck as well. His entire body trembled as he told Erle, "I'm cold."

Erle, on the other hand, was so hot from the journey to the pier that sweat ran down his back. It was not until Yile spoke that he realized that the snow was swirling into the shelter from all sides, windblown. He took off his padded jacket and wrapped it around his brother. Yile continued to tremble. Erle asked him, "When will the ferry come?"

He could barely hear what Yile said in reply. Erle bent his ear next to Yile's mouth before he was able to understand. "Ten o'clock."

Erle thought to himself, *It couldn't be much later than seven now. If we stay out here in the open for another three hours, Yile will freeze to death.* He shifted Yile to the ground instead of the bench so that not quite as much snow and wind would reach him.

"You sit right here. I'm going to run back and get your quilt."

Erle sprinted toward Yile's production brigade, running as if his life depended on it, not daring to delay a single second. But because he was sprinting through snow, he tumbled repeatedly to the ground. Waves of pain coursed through his right arm and his buttocks as he continued to run. When he finally reached Yile's place, he stood for a moment to catch his breath, picked up the quilt, and then began to sprint back to the pier.

By the time he regained the shelter, Yile seemed to be nowhere in sight. Erle, shocked, shouted, "Yile! Yile!" Suddenly he caught sight of something dark and indistinct lying on the ground in front of him. It was Yile lying in the snow. The padded jacket had slid to one side, and only a corner of the cloth still covered Yile's chest. Erle called to his brother as he reached down and took him into his arms. Yile did not respond. Erle, on the verge of panic, stroked his face. Yile's face was as cold as his hand.

Erle screamed, "Yile, Yile, are you dead?"

He saw Yile's head move and, reassured that he was not yet dead, broke into a smile. "Goddamnit," he said, "you really scared me that time." Then he told him, "I went to get your quilt. You won't be as cold that way."

Erle spread the quilt across the ground, then rolled his brother inside it. Then he wrapped the padded jacket around the quilt. He sat down on the concrete floor of the shelter and took this bundle, with Yile inside it, into his arms. Finally, he leaned his back against the concrete bench so that Yile could lean against his chest.

"Yile, are you still cold?"

Then Erle sensed his own exhaustion. He nestled his head against the concrete bench, feeling that his arms, which were still wrapped tightly around Yile, might fall to his sides any minute. And a moment later they did. Yile felt like a stone pressing against him. He let his hands dangle by his sides for a moment to rest, then propped himself up on the concrete so as to distribute the burden away from the rest of his body.

Erle's shirt was moist with sweat, and after a short while the sweat went icy cold. The northwest wind whistled down his neck, and his whole body began to shiver. Drops of water began to tumble from his head onto his body, and when he reached up to pat his hair, he realized that the snow on his hair was melting. Patting his clothes, he realized that the snow that had accumulated there was melting as well. His icy sweat was seeping out from underneath his clothes, and the snow melt was soaking into them. It was not long before he was drenched through to his skin.

The night ferry did not arrive until well after ten o'clock. Erle carried Yile on his back onto the boat, which was nearly empty.

He walked back to the stern. The engine was directly by the stern, behind some wooden planks. Erle set Yile down in a chair that he leaned against the planks, which were pleasantly warm from the heat emitted by the engine.

The boat arrived in town just before dawn. It was snowing there too, and the streets were coated with a thick layer of icy flakes. Erle hoisted Yile onto his back once more. Because Yile was still wrapped in the heavy cotton quilt, the two boys together were nearly as big as a three-wheeled bicycle cart. The footprints Erle left in the snow wobbled through the streets, sometimes deep and sometimes shallow, their uneven imprints glittering coldly under the electric street lamps.

WHEN ERLE ARRIVED home with Yile on his back, Xu Sanguan and Xu Yulan were fast asleep. They heard the front door being banged open from the outside and, emerging from the bedroom to see what was happening, watched as an enormous mountain of snow tumbled through the door and into the house.

Yile was taken to the hospital immediately. By the time the sun rose, the doctor informed them that Yile had contracted a form of hepatitis and that his condition was extremely serious. There was nothing more that they could do for him in town. The only recourse was to send him, as soon as was humanly possible, to the big hospital in Shanghai. Any delay, he added, might be life-threatening.

Before the doctor had even finished speaking, Xu Yulan began to cry. She sat in a chair outside the ward, tugging Xu Sanguan's sleeve and weeping.

"If he's this sick now, he must have already been sick the last time he was home. We shouldn't have made him leave. But we didn't know he was sick. If we had known, we could have taken care of him, and things would never have gotten so serious. Now they have to send him to Shanghai, and if he doesn't go, there's no guaranteeing that he'll survive. How much is it going to cost to send him to Shanghai? We don't even have enough money for an ambulance. Xu Sanguan, what are we going to do?"

Xu Sanguan said, "Don't cry. No matter how much you cry, it's not going to make Yile any better. If we don't have the money, we'll just have to find another way. We can borrow. We can borrow a little from everyone we know. We can always find enough money that way."

Xu Sanguan went to Sanle's factory first. When he found Sanle, he asked him how much money he had. Sanle told him they had just given out the payroll four days earlier, so he still had a good twelve *yuan*. Xu Sanguan asked him for ten.

Sanle shook his head. "If I give you ten, how am I going to eat for the rest of the month?"

Xu Sanguan said, "You can eat the northwest wind for all I care."

Sanle began to chuckle.

Xu Sanguan shouted, "Don't fool around with me! Your brother Yile's about to die, and you're laughing?"

Sanle stared at him, stupefied. "Dad, what did you say just now?"

Then Xu Sanguan realized that he had yet to inform Sanle why he needed to borrow the money in the first place: Yile was suffering from an advanced case of hepatitis. He hastily explained the situation to Sanle, who gave him the entire twelve *yuan*.

"Dad, take all of it. You go back to the hospital, and I'll meet you there as soon as I tell the people at the factory that I'm not coming in for work."

After Xu Sanguan collected the twelve *yuan* from Sanle, he paid a visit to Blacksmith Fang. He sat down next to Blacksmith Fang in his foundry. "We've known each other almost twenty years now, no? In all that time I've never asked you for anything, but today I'm finally going to have to ask a favor of you."

After Xu Sanguan explained the situation, Blacksmith Fang took a ten-*yuan* note from his pocket and handed it to Xu Sanguan. "All I can give you right now is ten *yuan*. I know it's not nearly enough, but that's all I can afford right now."

After leaving Blacksmith Fang's, Xu Sanguan spent the rest of the morning visiting eleven other families around town. Of the eleven families, eight were willing to lend him some money. Around noon he came to He Xiaoyong's house. After He Xiaoyong's death, Xu Sanguan had encountered his widow only very rarely. When he arrived at the doorstep, she and her daughters were just sitting down to lunch inside. Since the loss of her husband, He Xiaoyong's woman's hair had gone gray.

Xu Sanguan addressed her from the doorstep. "Yile's seriously ill. The doctor says he has to be sent to Shanghai for treatment or else he'll die. We don't have enough money to pay for it. Do you think you could lend us something to help out?"

He Xiaoyong's woman gazed toward Xu Sanguan for a moment. Then she turned wordlessly back to her meal.

Xu Sanguan stood quietly for a moment before trying a second time. "We'll pay you back as soon as we can. We can even write a promissory note."

He Xiaoyong's woman glanced at him once more, turned back inside, and continued to eat her lunch.

Xu Sanguan spoke for a third time. "I know I did you wrong before, and I'm sorry for it. Now I'm begging you, for Yile's sake. Because when it comes down to it, Yile is—"

He Xiaoyong's woman addressed her daughters. "How about it? Yile is your big brother, after all. You can't just stand and watch a drowning man go under. How much money do you girls have? Give the man whatever you have." He Xiaoyong's woman gestured toward Xu Sanguan.

Her two daughters stood up from the table and went upstairs to get some money. He Xiaoyong's woman, in turn, reached inside her clothes and pulled out a bundle wrapped neatly in her handkerchief. Setting it down on the tabletop, she unfolded the cloth, revealing one five-*yuan* note and one two-*yuan* note, along with some small change. She picked out the two bills, tucked the change back into the handkerchief, and put the bundle back in her pocket. At the same time her daughters came downstairs and handed her their money.

He Xiaoyong's woman collated the bills, counted them, stood, and handed the notes to Xu Sanguan. "That's seventeen *yuan* all together. Count it."

Xu Sanguan accepted the money, counted it, and put it in his pocket. Then he told her, "I've been to see thirteen different people this morning, and of all those people, you came up with the most money. Let me pay my respects to you."

Xu Sanguan made a deep bow, turned, and left. He had collected sixty-three *yuan* that morning. He gave all the money to Xu Yulan and told her to take Yile to Shanghai.

"I know this won't be enough to cover everything, but I'll find a way to come up with the rest. All you have to do is take good care of Yile and leave the rest to me. Once I've come up with the money, I'll come and find you in Shanghai. You should get going as soon as possible. This is a matter of life and death."

THE AFTERNOON after Xu Yulan had set off for Shanghai, Erle got sick. He had caught a nasty cold carrying Yile home from the countryside on his back. Now he was laid up in bed, coughing incessantly. What scared Xu Sanguan was that he was coughing so violently that he sounded as if he were vomiting instead. When he put his hand on Erle's forehead, he felt as if he were holding it against an open flame.

Xu Sanguan took him to the hospital without any further delay. The doctor said Erle had a bad flu and that his bronchial passages were also infected. Fortunately, his lungs were still clear, and there was nothing wrong that a few shots of streptomycin couldn't fix.

Xu Sanguan called Sanle to his side and said, "I'm leaving Erle in your hands. Stay home from work for a few days and look after him. Make sure he gets enough rest and enough to eat. I know you can't cook, and I won't have any time to cook for you either, because I have to find a way to collect enough money for Yile. You'll just have to get your meals from the canteen at the factory. Here's ten *yuan*. Take it."

Then Xu Sanguan went once again to pay a visit to Blood Chief Li. When Blood Chief Li saw Xu Sanguan walk into the room, he smiled. "You're here to sell blood *again*?"

Xu Sanguan nodded. "My son Yile has hepatitis, and they had to send him to the hospital in Shanghai. My son Erle is sick in bed at home too. I'm desperate this time."

"Don't even bother talking to me"—Blood Chief Li waved him away—"because I'm not listening."

Xu Sanguan stood before him on the verge of tears.

Blood Chief Li continued, "Are you trying to kill yourself, selling blood at this pace? You've been here almost every month, no? If you're really so tired of living, you'd do better to find yourself a nice quiet spot where there's a tree to hang yourself from."

Xu Sanguan said, "Look, I'm begging you. Help me out for Genlong's sake."

"Damn!" Blood Chief Li exclaimed. "When Genlong was still alive, you asked me to do it on Genlong's account. I'm still supposed to help you on his account now that he's dead and gone?"

Xu Sanguan replied, "Genlong hasn't been gone for very long. I'll bet his corpse isn't even cold yet. Can't you do it out of respect for him?"

Blood Chief Li chuckled despite himself. "You really have no shame, do you? Thickest skin I ever saw. So out of respect for your thick skin, I'm going to give you a little suggestion. Even if *I* won't let you sell any blood, you can always go somewhere else. Try another hospital. *They* won't know that you've just sold blood somewhere else. They'll be happy to take your blood. Get it?" Blood Chief Li saw Xu Sanguan nodding his head. "That way, you can sell as much blood as you want. And you can sell your life away along with it, for all I care."

CHAPTER TWENTY-EIGHT

Xu Sanguan put the ailing Erle to bed at home, told Sanle to look after him, slung a blue floral-print cloth bundle across his back, stuffed two *yuan* and thirty *fen* into his front pocket, and set off for the ferry pier.

He was on his way to Shanghai, but before he got there, he would pass through Lin's Pier, North Marsh, Westbank, Hundred-Mile, Tongyuan, Pine Grove, Big Bridge, Anchang Gate, Jing'an, Huang's Inn, Tiger's Head Bridge, Three Ring Cave, Seven-Mile Fort, Yellow Bay, Willow Village, Changning, and New Village. And of these places, only Lin's Pier, Hundred-Mile, Pine Grove, Huang's Inn, Seven-Mile Fort, and Changning were county seats. He would go ashore in all six of these towns to sell blood. He would sell his blood all the way to Shanghai.

Around noon that day Xu Sanguan arrived at Lin's Pier. He walked along the little river that cut through town, between buildings and houses that clustered above the banks with their foundations spilling into the water below. Xu Sanguan unfastened the buttons of his cotton-padded jacket, letting the wintry sunlight shine onto his chest. His time-bronzed skin flushed a deep red in the cold wind. When he saw a set of stone-hewn steps leading down to the water, he went and sat by the river's edge. A jumble of boats were moored on either side of the river; the steps where he sat offered the only unobstructed access to the stream along the embankment. There must have been a heavy snowfall in Lin's Pier not long before, for Xu Sanguan saw that the cracks in between the stone steps were filled with veins of unmelted snow that glittered in the sun. Looking across the water at the windows of the houses, Xu Sanguan could tell that the people of Lin's Pier were eating lunch, because steam had fogged their windows opaque.

He took a bowl out from his bundle, skimmed it below the water's surface, and drew a bowlful. The water from around Lin's Pier looked a little greenish in the bowl. He took a sip. The bone-piercingly cold water rolled down into his gut, and his body shivered. He wiped his mouth with his hand, then arched his neck to the sky and drank all of the water in a single gulp, clasping himself with his arms to steady the violent shivers that began almost as soon as he had finished. After a little while he felt his stomach slowly regain its usual temperature, so he skimmed another bowlful of water, drank it, and once again steadied himself against a fit of trembling.

The people of Lin's Pier, sitting by their windows eating steaming bowls of lunch, noticed Xu Sanguan. They opened their windows and stuck their heads outside to gaze at this almost fifty-year-old man sitting at the bottom step of the stone pier, drinking bowl after bowl after bowl of wintry cold river water and shivering violently with each gulp.

And so they said to him, "Who are you? Where are you from?" "I've never seen anyone so thirsty in my life." "Why are you drinking from the river? It's winter, you'll get sick that way." "Come on up here, come up to my house, I'll give you something to drink. We have boiled water, and we have tea leaves. We'll make you a pot of tea."

Xu Sanguan looked up at them and smiled. "I don't want to bother you, thanks. You're nice folks, and I wouldn't want to trouble you. I have to drink a lot of water, so it'll be less trouble to drink from the river."

They replied, "We have plenty of water, you can drink all you want. If one pot isn't enough for you, then you can have two pots or even three for that matter."

Xu Sanguan stood, bowl in hand and faced the window through which the invitation had been issued. "I don't want to use up all your tea. Give me a little salt. I've already had four bowls of water, but the water's too cold, and I can hardly drink any more. Give me a little salt, and then I'll feel like drinking some more water."

They found this request somewhat odd. "What do you need salt for? If you can't drink any more, then you won't be thirsty anymore anyway."

"I'm not thirsty. I'm not drinking because of thirst."

Some of them laughed. One of them said, "If you're not thirsty, why are you drinking so much water? And why drink cold water from the river? If you drink that much river water, you'll get a stomachache for sure."

Xu Sanguan looked up at them. "You seem like nice folks, so I'll tell you. I'm drinking so much water so that I can sell my blood."

"Selling blood?" they asked. "Why do you have to drink water to sell blood?"

"The more you drink, the more blood there'll be. If you drink enough water, you can sell two bowls of blood."

As he spoke, Xu Sanguan tapped the rim of his bowl and laughed, his wrinkled face folding into a smile.

"But why do you want to sell your blood?"

Xu Sanguan replied, "Yile's sick. I mean, he's seriously ill. It's hepatitis. They've already taken him to a big hospital in Shanghai—"

"Who's Yile?" someone interrupted.

"My son," Xu Sanguan said. "He's seriously ill, and only the big hospital in Shanghai can save him. I don't have any money, so I have to sell my blood. If I can sell blood all the way to Shanghai, I might be able to make enough to pay the medical bill by the time I get there."

At this point Xu Sanguan began to cry. He smiled wordlessly as tears rolled down his face. Xu Sanguan's speech had left them speechless, and they could only gaze back at him. Finally, Xu Sanguan lifted his arm toward them. "You seem like kind-hearted folks. Do you think you could give me some salt?"

They all nodded. After a little while one of them brought him some salt wrapped in a piece of paper, while someone else gave him three pots full of hot tea. Xu Sanguan, looking toward the salt and the hot tea, said, "So much salt. I can't use all of it. Tell you the truth, what with the tea, I don't think I'll need any salt after all."

They said, "If you can't use the salt now, take it with you, and you can use it next time you sell blood. Have some tea now before it gets cold."

Xu Sanguan nodded, put the packet of salt in his pocket, sat back down on the stone steps, skimmed half a bowl of river water, picked up one of the teapots they had proffered, and poured it into the bowl. Then he drank this concoction in one gulp and wiped his mouth.

"That tea really tastes good." Xu Sanguan drank three more bowls of tea.

They exclaimed, "You really know how to drink!"

Xu Sanguan smiled bashfully. "I'm really just forcing it down." He glanced at the three teapots on the steps. "I have to leave now, but I don't know who these teapots belong to. Who should I give them back to?"

They said, "You go on. We'll collect them ourselves."

Xu Sanguan nodded and looked around at the people in the windows and the people standing next to him on the steps, and he bowed in their direction. "You've all been so good to me, and I have nothing to give you in return, except my respects."

Soon afterward, Xu Sanguan arrived at the Lin's Pier County Hospital. In the blood donation room at the end of the clinic corridor sat a man about the same age as Blood Chief Li. He sat beside a desk, one arm draped across the tabletop, staring across the hall into a bathroom without a door.

When Xu Sanguan saw that his white coat was every bit as filthy as Blood Chief Li's, he said, "You must be the blood chief around here. Your white coat's all black in front and around the sleeves. The front's like that because you're always sitting in front of a desk, and the sleeves are dirty because you rest your arms on top of the desk. You're just like our Blood Chief Li. And the back of your coat's black too, because you sit on a stool all day long."

Xu Sanguan sold his blood at the Lin's Pier County Hospital, then ate a plate of fried pork livers and drank two shots of yellow rice wine at the restaurant in town. Then he began to walk through the streets of Lin's Pier. The cold winter wind chilled his face, slipped down his collar, and down his neck. He began to feel the chill. Wrapped in the cotton-padded jacket, he felt his body suddenly go cold. He knew it was because he had sold his blood, because he had sold all the warmth in his body. He felt the wind slide down his chest and to his belly, and his stomach muscles contracted from the cold. He grasped hold of his collar, pulling it forward so that it would wrap around his neck. He looked as if he were pulling his body down the road with his collar.

Bright sunlight played across the road that ran through Lin's Pier. Xu Sanguan's shivering body moved through the sun's rays. He walked past one street and came to another, where he caught sight of a few young men leaning against an old sunlight-bathed wall, squinting as they absorbed the warmth, hands stuffed snugly inside their sleeves. They were talking among themselves, shouting, laughing. Xu Sanguan stood for a moment in front of them, then moved into their midst, standing against the wall and squinting his eyes against the bright sun.

Xu Sanguan saw them turn to look at him, so he said, "It's warm here, and there's not so much wind."

They nodded and watched him huddle against the wall, hands still tightly clasped around his collar. They whispered, "Look at his hands." "He's holding his collar so tight it looks like someone's trying to strangle him." "Or like he's being throttled with a rope. What do you think?"

Xu Sanguan, overhearing this comment, smiled in their direction. "It's just that I'm afraid the wind will come in through my collar." He released one side of the collar and pointed toward his neck with his free hand. "This is like a window in a house. You wouldn't leave a window open during the winter, would you? If you left the windows open, everybody inside would freeze to death."

They erupted into laughter at this explanation. Then someone said, "Well, I've never seen anyone as afraid of the cold as you. And we all heard your teeth chattering even though you're wearing such a thick coat. Look at us. None of us are wearing a padded coat, and our collars are all open."

Xu Sanguan said, "Just a minute ago my collar was open too. Just a minute ago I drank eight bowls of water from the river."

They said, "You think you might be running a fever?"

Xu Sanguan replied, "I don't have a fever."

They said, "Oh no? Then why are you talking nonsense?"

Xu Sanguan said, "I'm not talking nonsense."

They said, "You're definitely running a fever. You're feeling unusually cold, right?"

Xu Sanguan nodded. "That's right."

"Then you're feverish," they said. "People feel cold when they're running a fever. Feel your forehead. I'll bet it's really hot."

Xu Sanguan smiled as he looked back toward them. "I'm not running a fever, I'm just cold, that's all. It's because I just sold—"

They interrupted, "If you're feeling cold, it's got to be because you have a high fever. Feel your forehead."

Xu Sanguan smiled but didn't lift his arm to feel his forehead.

They continued to urge, "Go ahead, feel your forehead. You'll know right away if you have a fever or not. It's not like it's such a big chore. Just lift up your arm."

Xu Sanguan lifted his hand to his forehead as they looked on.

"It's hot, isn't it?"

Xu Sanguan shook his head, "I don't know. I really can't tell because my forehead's the same temperature as my hand."

"I'll try then." One of them walked over and placed his hand on Xu Sanguan's forehead. He turned to the others and said, "His forehead's really cold."

Someone else said, "You just took your hand out of your pocket, it's probably too warm to tell. Try putting your own forehead next to his instead." So he pressed his own forehead against Xu Sanguan's, waited for a moment, turned back toward them, and slowly rubbed his hand across his own forehead. "Maybe I'm the one running a fever. My forehead's a lot warmer than his." Then he added, "You try."

One after another they walked over and pressed their foreheads against Xu Sanguan's forehead, until they were compelled to agree with what he had said in the first place. "You're right. You're not running a fever. We're the ones who're running fevers."

They stood around him in a circle, laughing. When they were finished laughing, someone started to whistle. Then a few more of them started to whistle, and they moved away together, whistling. Xu Sanguan watched them go until he couldn't see them anymore and the sound of their whistling faded to silence. Then he laughed quietly to himself as he sat down on a rock at the base of the wall, his body surrounded by the sunlight. He felt a little warmer than he had a moment before. His hands had started to go numb from the cold, so he released his collar and stuck his fingers into his pockets.

XU SANGUAN took a river ferry to North Marsh, and from North Marsh he went on to Westbank, where he took another boat to Hundred-Mile. It had been three days since he had left home, and three days since he had sold blood at Lin's Pier. Now he planned to go to the hospital at Hundred-Mile and sell blood. In Hundred-Mile he walked down the street that ran along the river. The street was lined with muddy piles of melting snow, and when the wind blew into his face, his skin felt as dry and taut as the preserved fish hanging from the eaves of the houses along the way. He held his drinking bowl in one hand and the little packet of salt inside the wide sleeves of his padded jacket. He ate the salt crystals as he walked, and whenever his mouth began to pucker from the saltiness, he would climb down the stone steps to the river, skim the surface, and drink a couple of bowls of icy water. Then he continued down the road, eating fresh pinches of salt as he went.

That afternoon, just after he emerged into the street from selling blood at the Hundred-Mile hospital, and just before he managed to cross over to a restaurant on the opposite side of the street to eat a plate of fried pork livers and drink two shots of yellow rice wine, he discovered that he could no longer walk. His limbs shook like bare tree branches in a violent wind, whipping back and forth until it seemed that they would snap, and he clasped onto his body with his hands in an effort to stop the trembling. Then his legs buckled underneath him, and he tumbled to the pavement.

Someone on the street walked toward him to ask what was wrong, but Xu Sanguan was shivering so violently that the man couldn't make out what he had said in reply. Someone else suggested that they take him to the hospital: "Lucky for him it's just a few steps away." Another man hoisted him up on his back and began to carry him toward the hospital door.

But with that Xu Sanguan's voice grew more clear. "No, no, no, no," he repeated over and over again. "I don't want to go. I don't want to go to the hospital."

They said, "You're ill, you're seriously ill, I've never seen anyone in my life shake as hard as you're shaking right now. We have to get you to the hospital."

But still he repeated, "No, no, no, no."

So they asked him, "Then tell us what's wrong with you. Did you come down with something just now, or is it some kind of chronic illness? If it just hit you all of a sudden, we should definitely get you to the hospital."

They saw his lips tremble and his mouth move, but none of them could tell exactly what he was trying to say to them. Someone asked, "What's he trying to tell us?"

"We can't tell. It doesn't matter anyway. Let's just bring him to the hospital."

With this, his speech once again grew more distinct: "I'm not sick."

His words were clear enough, but someone else asked, "He says he's not sick, but if he weren't sick, why would he be shaking like that?"

He said, "I'm cold."

This too was distinct enough to be understood. They said, "He says he's cold. You think he might have the hot-and-colds? If he has the hot-and-colds, it's no use going to the hospital anyway. Maybe we should just take him to an inn instead. He doesn't talk like he's from anywhere around here."

When Xu Sanguan heard them say they would take him to an inn, he fell silent and simply let them convey him to the nearest available place. They set him down in a dormitory room with four beds and piled all four of the quilts on top of him. Despite being smothered under four quilts, Xu Sanguan's body continued to tremble. They stood over him and asked, "Feeling any warmer?"

Xu Sanguan shook his head. His head, protruding from underneath the quilts, seemed very far away.

When they saw his head shake, they said, "If you still feel cold even under four quilts, it must be the hot-and-colds. Once you get a case of the hot-and-colds, you feel cold whether you have four quilts or ten, because the cold is on the inside and not on the outside. You'll feel better if you have something to eat."

They looked on as the quilts themselves began to quiver. After a little while Xu Sanguan extended one hand from underneath the quilts, clasping a ten-*fen* note. "I'd like to eat some noodles."

They went to buy him a bowl of noodles and then propped him up in bed to eat. Having swallowed the noodles, Xu Sanguan felt his body regain a little of its warmth. And after a moment he was able to speak more clearly, so he told them he didn't really need to use all four of the quilts. "I'm begging you. Take two of them away. I can hardly breathe."

That night Xu Sanguan shared the room with a man who arrived after dark. Well into his sixties, he was wearing a tattered cotton-padded jacket, and his dark, ruddy face was cracked and seamed by the winter wind. He walked into the room cradling two little piglets in his hands. Xu Sanguan watched as he laid the piglets out on top of the bed. The piglets began to cry. The sound was sharp and thin at the same time. The piglets lay draped across the bed, their feet bound together with string.

The man said to them, "Sleep, sleep now, it's time to go to sleep." As he spoke, he covered their little bodies with a quilt, then borrowed under the covers at the other end of the bed.

After he had lain down, he noticed Xu Sanguan looking at him. "It gets awfully cold in the middle of the night. I'd rather let them sleep with me than risk that they freeze to death during the night."

He saw Xu Sanguan nod in reply and let out a friendly chuckle. He told Xu Sanguan that he was from the country outside of

North Marsh, that he had two daughters who were already married and three sons who were still single. He had two grandsons too. He had come to Hundred-Mile to sell the piglets. "Prices are higher here in Hundred-Mile, so I can make a little more money." Finally he added, "I'm sixty-four years old this year."

"I would never have guessed it," Xu Sanguan said. "Sixty-four and still going strong."

With this, the other man chuckled again. "My eyes are still good, I can still hear pretty well, and there's nothing in particular the matter with me. It's just that I'm not as strong as I once was. I still work in the fields every day, and I can do just as much work as any of my three sons, but I'm not as strong as I once was. When I get tired, my back starts to hurt."

When he noticed that Xu Sanguan was lying underneath two quilts, he asked, "Are you sick or something? You've got two quilts, but you're still shivering like a leaf."

Xu Sanguan said, "I'm not sick, I'm just cold, that's all."

"There's another quilt over there. Want me to put it on top of you?"

Xu Sanguan shook his head, "No, I'm already feeling much better. I was really cold after I sold blood this afternoon, but I'm much better now."

"You sold blood today?" he continued. "I sold blood once too. When my youngest was ten, he had an operation and needed to have a blood transfusion, so I sold my own blood to the hospital, and they gave it to my youngest. After I sold the blood, I felt really weak."

Xu Sanguan nodded. "If you sell just once or twice, you feel weak. If you keep on selling blood, all the warmth in your body escapes, and you just can't get warm."

As he spoke, he poked his hand out from under the quilts and pointed his finger toward the other man.

"I've sold blood three times in three months, two bowls each time. That's four hundred milliliters, as they would say in the hospital. I already sold all my strength. All I had left was my warmth. But the other day I sold blood in Lin's Pier, and today I sold two bowls here in Hundred-Mile, so now even the little warmth that I had left is gone."

When he finished speaking, he breathed heavily from the exertion.

The old man from the countryside around North Marsh said, "If you keep on selling blood like this, won't you end up selling them your life along with it?"

Xu Sanguan said, "In a few more days I'm going to sell some more in Pine Grove."

The old man said, "First you sold your strength. Now you've sold your warmth. What's left but your life?"

"If that's what it takes, I'm willing." Xu Sanguan explained, "My son has hepatitis. He's in a hospital in Shanghai. I have to find enough money to pay for his treatment. If I stopped selling blood for even a few months, there would be no way to pay his hospital bill."

He paused to catch his breath.

"I'm almost fifty now, and I've had a taste of pretty much everything life has to offer. Even if I were to go, it wouldn't really be much of a loss. But my son's only twenty-one, and he hasn't really lived yet. He hasn't gotten himself a woman, hasn't known what it is to be a man. If he were to go now, it would be too unfair."

The old man nodded repeatedly as he listened to Xu Sanguan's speech. "You're right, you know. When you've lived to be our age, you've pretty much learned all there is to know about what it is to be a man." The two pigs began to squeal. The old man said, "I bumped them just now when I moved my feet."

Xu Sanguan was still shivering under the covers.

The old man continued, "You look like a city person. I know you city people like to keep clean, but we don't care as much about all that down in the country. What I'm trying to say is . . ." He paused for a moment. "What I'm trying to say is that if you don't mind too much, I'll put the pigs in bed with you. They'll help keep you warm."

"Why should I mind? That's awfully kind of you. Why don't you put one of them over here? One should be enough."

The old man stood, hoisted one of the piglets, and set it down by Xu Sanguan's feet. The piglet had already fallen asleep and seemed not to notice its passage from one bed to the other. But when Xu Sanguan pressed his icy feet against its side, the piglet suddenly squealed and curled itself into a quivering ball under the quilts.

The old man asked apologetically, "Think you'll still be able to sleep?"

"My feet are too cold. Woke the little creature up."

The old man said, "Pigs are just animals after all. It'd be better if you had someone to share the bed with you."

"I can feel his warmth. I'm feeling a lot warmer already."

FOUR DAYS LATER Xu Sanguan arrived in Pine Grove. By this time his face was gaunt and yellow with fatigue, his limbs were weak, his head felt dizzy, his vision was blurred, and his ears had begun to ring. His bones ached, and when he swung his legs forward to walk, they seemed to flutter underneath him.

When the blood chief at the Pine Grove Hospital saw Xu Sanguan standing in front of him, he waved him away before Xu Sanguan had even finished a sentence. "Go take a piss. Your face is so yellow, it looks gray, you can hardly get out a word before you start to pant, and you expect me to buy some of your blood? I'd say you better go get yourself a blood transfusion instead."

Xu Sanguan left the hospital and sat down in a sunny corner sheltered from the wind. He sat for nearly two hours with the sun's rays shining into his face and across his body. When his face grew hot from the sun, he stood up and went back to the blood donation room at the hospital.

The blood chief saw him walk in but didn't recognize him as

the same man who had come in earlier. "You're all skin and bones. A nice gust of wind, and you'd be flat on the ground. But you do have good color. Your face is nice and ruddy. How much blood do you want to sell?"

"Two bowls," Xu Sanguan replied, pulling a bowl out from his sleeve to show him.

The blood chief said, "You can fit about ten ounces of rice in two bowls like that. How much blood that works out to, I don't know."

"Four hundred milliliters," Xu Sanguan offered.

"Go to the end of the hall and have the nurse in the clinic take your blood."

A nurse wearing a white face mask drew four hundred milliliters of blood from Xu Sanguan's arm and then watched as he slowly steadied himself and stood to leave. As soon as he had managed to stand up, though, he tumbled to the floor. The nurse cried out in alarm, and they carried him to the emergency room. The doctor on duty in the emergency room laid him out on a gurney and began to examine him. He rubbed his temples, held his hand against the arteries on his wrist, lifted his eyelids, and then checked his blood pressure. When he saw that Xu Sanguan's blood pressure had fallen to sixty over forty, he said, "He needs a blood transfusion."

And so it was that the four hundred milliliters of blood Xu Sanguan had just sold to the hospital found its way back into Xu Sanguan's bloodstream. Only after the doctor supplemented this first transfusion with an additional three hundred milliliters of someone else's blood did Xu Sanguan's blood pressure return to one hundred over sixty.

When Xu Sanguan came to and discovered to his fright that he was laid up in the hospital, he immediately slid out of bed and made his way toward the exit. But they stopped him before he could get away and told him that although his blood pressure had returned to normal, he needed to stay an extra day for further observation because the doctors hadn't yet been able to determine the reason for his illness.

"I'm not sick! I just sold too much blood."

He told the doctor that he had sold blood a week ago at Lin's Pier and again three days later in Hundred-Mile.

The doctor gazed at him aghast and, after a moment of silence, spat out a question. "So you're suicidal?"

"No, no, I'm not suicidal. It's my son—"

The doctor cut him short with an abrupt wave of his hand. "Get out of here."

The hospital in Pine Grove charged Xu Sanguan for seven hundred milliliters of blood, plus emergency treatment, which amounted to roughly the same sum he had earned from his last two blood-selling transactions.

Xu Sanguan went to find the doctor who had accused him of being suicidal and complained, "I sold you four hundred milliliters of blood, and you sold me seven hundred milliliters. Let's forget about the blood that you gave back to me for now. But I never asked for someone *else's* blood. Let me give those three hundred milliliters back to you."

The doctor said, "What in the world are you trying to say?"

"I want you to take back three hundred milliliters of blood."

The doctor said, "You're *sick*."

Xu Sanguan said, "I'm not sick. It's just that I sold too much blood and got cold. You sold me seven hundred milliliters of blood. That's about four bowls. And now I don't feel cold anymore. In fact, I feel kind of hot, too hot, really. So I want to return three hundred milliliters to you."

The doctor pointed one finger at his own head. "I meant that you are mentally ill."

Xu Sanguan said, "I'm not mentally ill. I just want you to take back the blood that isn't mine." He looked around at the people who had gathered in a circle to listen and pleaded, "People should be even-handed when it comes to doing business. When

I sold you my blood, everything was aboveboard. So how come you never even asked me how much blood I wanted back?"

The doctor said, "We saved your life! You were in shock. If we had waited to tell you what we were going to do, you'd be dead by now."

Xu Sanguan nodded. "I know you were trying to save my life. And it's not like I want you to take back all seven hundred milliliters. All I want you to do is take back the three hundred milliliters that don't belong to me. I'm almost fifty years old now, and I've never taken anything that doesn't belong to me."

When he looked back toward the doctor, he realized that he had already left and that the people standing around him had broken into a gale of laughter. He realized they were making fun of him, then fell silent, stood for a moment, turned, and left the hospital.

It was almost dusk. Xu Sanguan walked through the streets of Pine Grove for a long time, until he came to the banks of the river. He walked until the railing by the water blocked his path forward. He stopped and watched as the setting sun dyed the river red. A tugboat approached from far in the distance, its wood-burning engine chugging noisily as it moved down the waterway. Xu Sanguan watched it pass, watched as the waves rippling from from its stern slapped noisily against the stone piles along the embankment.

He stood for a while until he began to feel the chill. Then he squatted down next to the trunk of a tree. After he had squatted for a while, he extracted all his money from inside the lining of his jacket and began to count. The total was thirty-seven *yuan* and forty *fen.* He had sold blood three times but had only two bowls' worth of blood money to show for it. He carefully folded the bills and put them back in his inside pocket. He felt wronged. Tears welled up in his eyes, and a cold wind blew the tears down to the ground, so that by the time he tried to wipe his eyes, they were already dry. He sat for a little while longer and then got up and continued to walk. He thought to himself that it was still a long way to Shanghai. He knew he would still have to pass through Big Bridge, Anchang Gate, Jing'an, Huang's Inn, Tiger's Head Bridge, Three Ring Cave, Seven-Mile Fort, Yellow Bay, Willow Village, Changning, and New Village before he got there.

Xu Sanguan decided that he could no longer afford to take passenger ferries. He figured that it would cost him three *yuan* and sixty *fen* to get to Shanghai from Pine Grove by boat. Since he had sold blood twice to no avail, he couldn't spend his money so carelessly anymore. And that was how he decided to hitch a ride on a concrete river barge loaded with silk cocoons manned by two brothers called Laixi and Laishun.

Xu Sanguan had caught sight of them as he stood on the stone steps by the river. Laixi was standing at the prow brandishing a bamboo pole used for pushing the boat down the river, while Laishun stood at the stern waving a long oar. Xu Sanguan waved and asked where they were headed. They said they were going to Seven-Mile Fort. There was a silk factory in Seven-Mile Fort to which they would deliver their cargo of cocoons.

Xu Sanguan said to them, "We're going in the same direction. I'm going to Shanghai. Do you think you could give me a lift to Seven-Mile Fort?" By the time he explained himself, the barge had already glided past him.

Xu Sanguan ran along the bank of the river in pursuit of the barge. "One more person won't sink the boat. And I can help you row. Three people rowing is bound to be easier than just two. And I can help out with your food expenses. It's cheaper for three to eat than two—everyone can eat an extra bowl or two of rice, and you don't need any more vegetables."

The two brothers realized that Xu Sanguan was talking sense, so they brought the barge to a halt against the banks and let him climb aboard.

Xu Sanguan didn't know how to row, and almost as soon as he took the oar from Laishun, it slid out of his hands and into the water. Laixi hurriedly brought the boat to a halt with his bamboo pole, while Laishun bent over the stern and fished the oar from the water when it floated up on the current.

Having retrieved the oar, Laishun pointed at Xu Sanguan and yelled, "You said you could help row, but all you know how to do is drop the damned oar in the river. What else did you say just now? You said you could do this and help us with that, which is the only reason we let you on in the first place. So that's what you call rowing? I wonder what else can you do?"

"I said I could eat with you, because it's cheaper for three to eat than two."

"I have no fucking doubt that you can eat!" Laishun shouted.

Laixi broke into laughter at the prow. "Well, you can cook for me. That's a start."

Xu Sanguan went up to the little brick stove on the deck. There was a wok on top of the stove and a bundle of kindling next to it. Xu Sanguan began to cook.

When night came, Laishun and Laixi moored the barge by the bank, opened an iron hatch on the deck, crawled down into the cabin, and wrapped themselves in a single quilt. Noticing that Xu Sanguan was still outside, they called up to him, "Come down and get some sleep."

Xu Sanguan, seeing that the cabin was even smaller than a single bed, demurred. "I won't crowd you two. I'll sleep up here."

Laixi said, "It's wintertime. If you sleep outside, you'll freeze to death."

Laishun added, "If you freeze to death, we'll be in trouble too."

"Come on down," Laixi continued. "We're all on the same boat, so we have to take the good and bad together."

Xu Sanguan knew he was right: it really was very cold outside, and when he remembered that he would have to sell still more blood at Huang's Inn and could not afford to get sick, he slid down into the cabin and lay down between them. Laixi passed a corner of the quilt to him, and Laishun pulled enough of the fabric in his direction to cover him.

Xu Sanguan said to them, "You two are brothers, but somehow Laixi always sounds nicer than Laishun when he's saying something."

The two brothers' chuckles quickly gave way to snores. Xu Sanguan was squeezed between them, and their shoulders jutted into his shoulders. And after a little while their legs were draped across his legs, and after a while longer their arms were sprawled across his chest. Xu Sanguan lay pressed beneath them, listening to the motion of the water. The sound was extremely clear and distinct. He could even hear the sound of drops of water splashing above the current, and he felt as if he were actually sleeping submerged in the river itself. The sound of the river brushing his ears kept him awake for a long time, so he thought about Yile and wondered how he was doing in the hospital in Shanghai. He thought about Xu Yulan, and he thought about Erle lying sick in bed at home, and he thought about Sanle watching over Erle.

After a few nights in the tiny cabin Xu Sanguan's bones ached. During the day he sat on deck pounding his back, kneading his shoulders, and swinging his arms back and forth.

When Laixi saw him, he said, "The cabin's too small. You didn't sleep well."

Laishun said, "He's getting old, and his bones are brittle."

Xu Sanguan felt old. He knew he was no longer a young man. *Laishun's right, I* am *getting old. It's not that the cabin's too small. When I was young, I could sleep in a crack in the wall and not feel a thing.*

The boat continued to move. They passed through Big Bridge, through Anchang Gate, and through Jing'an. The next stop was Huang's Inn. The sun had been shining for two days, and the snow on the banks of the river was beginning to melt. A few patches of snow still clung to the roofs of the farmhouses they passed on either side of the river. The fields around the houses sat barren and idle, and they only rarely saw people at work in the paddies, but there were quite a few people walking on the road along the river, carrying shoulder poles and baskets and chattering loudly among themselves.

Within a few days Xu Sanguan and the two brothers had become quite friendly with one another. They told Xu Sanguan that transporting their load of cocoons would take them ten days all told. And for their efforts they would receive six *yuan*, or a mere three *yuan* each.

Xu Sanguan said to them, "You might as well sell blood then. You can make thirty-five *yuan* each time." He continued, "Your blood is like water in a well. It'll never run dry, no matter how much you draw."

Xu Sanguan told them everything Ah Fang and Genlong had told him years before. When he was finished, the brothers asked, "But won't your health go bad after you sell blood?"

"No," Xu Sanguan replied, "but your legs will probably feel a little weak for a while. It's a lot like the moment after you've finished with a woman."

The brothers chuckled uneasily.

Noticing their befuddlement, Xu Sanguan asked, "You understand what I'm talking about, right?"

Laixi shook his head, and Laishun said, "Neither of us has ever had a woman, so we don't know what it feels like when you're done."

Xu Sanguan also chuckled. "Well, selling blood is one way to find out."

Laishun addressed Laixi. "Why don't we give it a try? We'll make lots of money, and we'll find out what it feels like. Why not kill two birds with one stone?"

When they arrived at Huang's Inn, Laixi and Laishun tied the boat to a wooden mooring on the bank and followed Xu Sanguan to the county hospital to sell blood.

As they walked, Xu Sanguan told them, "There are four kinds

of blood. The first kind is O, the second is AB, the third is A, and the fourth is B—"

Laixi broke in, "How do you write those?"

Xu Sanguan said, "They're foreign letters. I don't know how to write them either. I only know the first one, O. You draw a circle. My blood type is a circle."

Xu Sanguan led them through the streets of Huang's Inn until they found the hospital. Then they went to the stone steps by the river. Xu Sanguan took a bowl from out of his pocket and handed it to Laixi. "Before you sell your blood, you have to drink a lot of water. If you drink a lot of water, you can water down your blood. Think about it. If your blood is watered down, there will be that much more to sell, right?"

Laixi took the bowl and asked, "How much should I drink?"

"Eight bowls."

"Eight bowls?" Laixi was astonished. "Won't your stomach burst if you drink eight bowls of water?"

Xu Sanguan replied, "I can drink eight bowls, and I'm almost fifty. Add your ages together, and the two of you still wouldn't be as old as I am. Can't you drink as much as an old man?"

Laishun said to Laixi, "If he can drink eight bowls, then we should be able to manage nine or ten."

"No way," Xu Sanguan said. "The very most you should drink is eight. Any more than that, and your bladder'll burst, just like Ah Fang—"

"Who's Ah Fang?"

"You don't know him. Drink. Each of us can drink one bowl first, and then we'll take turns."

Laixi bent down and skimmed up a bowl of water to drink. As soon as he started, he clasped his chest and exclaimed, "Too damn cold! It's so cold my stomach's twitching."

Laishun said, "Of course winter water is cold. Give me the bowl. I'll go first." After one sip, Laishun also called out, "No way! No way. It's too cold. I can't take it."

Then Xu Sanguan remembered that he had yet to give them any salt. He fished the packet from out of his pocket and passed it to them. "Eat a little salt first. When your mouth gets dry, you'll be able to drink."

The brothers took the packet and began to eat the salt. After a while Laixi said he was ready to drink. He skimmed another bowlful of water and took three gulps. Then he started to shiver. "You're right. When your mouth's all salty, it's easier to drink it."

He drank a few more gulps. When the bowl was dry, he passed it to Laishun and sat trembling with his arms wrapped around his own shoulders. Laishun took a few gulps but managed to finish the bowl only after letting out a long string of curses and exclamations.

Xu Sanguan took the bowl and said to them, "I'll go first after all. Watch how it's done."

The brothers sat on the stone steps and watched as Xu Sanguan tapped a bit of salt into his palm and popped it into his mouth. His mouth twitched. Then he fished up a bowlful of water and drank it in one gulp. He drank two bowls in a row, stopped, poured more salt into his palm, and popped it into his mouth. He repeated these motions until he had swallowed eight bowls of water, never once wiping the water from around his mouth or allowing himself to shiver. Only when he was finished did he finally wipe his mouth, wrap his arms around his shoulders, and shudder with the cold. Then he burped three times. After burping three times, he sneezed three times.

When he finished sneezing, he turned to the brothers and said, "I've drunk enough. Your turn."

Each of the brothers drank five bowls, then declared, "I can't drink any more. Any more water, and my stomach will freeze solid."

Xu Sanguan, realizing that "a man can't get fat from a single bite of food," let them stop there. That they had been able to drink five bowls of icy river water on their first try was enough. He stood and led them to the hospital.

When they got there, Laixi and Laishun sold their blood first. He was happy to discover that they too had type O blood. "The three of us all have circle type blood."

After they had sold their blood at the Huang's Inn County Hospital, Xu Sanguan brought them to a restaurant by the river. He sat in front of the window, and the brothers sat at his flanks. "You can be thrifty at other times, but at a time like this you have to spend a little extra. Do your legs feel weak now that you've sold blood?" He saw them nod. "That's what it feels like after you've been with a woman. Your legs go weak. At times like this you have to eat a plate of fried pork livers and two shots of yellow rice wine. The pork livers build up the blood, and the wine gives it life." As he spoke, he began to tremble.

Laishun said to him, "You're shaking. When you're done with a woman, do you shake after your legs go soft?"

Xu Sanguan chuckled and gestured in Laishun's direction. "I see what you mean. But this time it's only because I've been selling blood the whole way here." Xu Sanguan crossed two fingers to make the character for ten. "In the last ten days I've sold blood four times. If you did it with a woman four times in one day, weak legs and trembling would be just the start of it. You'd start to feel cold chills too."

Noting that the waiter was winding his way toward their table, he lowered his voice.

"Put your hands on the table. Don't let them hang underneath the table like people who've never been to a restaurant before. You want to look like you always come to places like this, if only for some wine. Straighten up and hold your heads high. You have to do this with style. When you order, make sure to slap the table and speak up. That way they won't dare cheat you, or skimp on the food, or water down the wine. When the waiter comes over to our table, just follow my lead."

The waiter came over to the table and asked what they wanted. Xu Sanguan was no longer shivering. Rapping the table for emphasis, he barked, "A plate of fried pork livers and two shots of yellow rice wine." He waved his right hand back and forth through the air and added, "Warm the wine up for me."

The waiter took his order and turned to Laishun.

Laishun pounded on the table with his fist until it rocked back and forth. Then he demanded with a shout, "A plate of fried pork livers and two shots of yellow rice wine."

Laishun forgot what he was supposed to say next. He looked toward Xu Sanguan, but Xu Sanguan merely twisted his head in Laixi's direction. The waiter had already begun to take Laixi's order.

Laixi tapped the table with his fingertips, but he used a voice every bit as earsplitting as Laishun's as he called out to the waiter, "A plate of fried pork livers and two shots of yellow rice wine."

Laixi also forgot what he was supposed to say next.

The waiter asked, "Should I warm the wine up for you?"

The two brothers turned questioningly toward Xu Sanguan. Xu Sanguan once again waved his right arm back and forth through the air, proclaiming in a magisterial tone, "Of course."

After the waiter left, Xu Sanguan lowered his voice. "I didn't tell you to scream. I just wanted you to speak up. What were you shouting about? It's not like this is a fight or something. And Laishun, next time you should use your fingers, not your fist. Otherwise you might just break the table in two. And don't ever forget the last part about warming up the wine. As soon as they hear you say the last part, they'll know that you're a regular at a restaurant. That's the main thing."

After they ate the fried pork livers and drank the wine, they returned to the boat. Laixi untied the rope from its mooring and pushed the boat away from the embankment with the bamboo pole while Laishun stood at the stern rowing with the oar. When they maneuvered the boat beyond the bank and out into the middle of the river, Laishun called out, "On to Tiger's Head Bridge."

His body rocked back and forth as he rowed, and the oar sang as it first divided, then danced above the river's flow. Xu Sanguan sat at the prow of the barge, just behind Laixi, watching the bamboo pole move gracefully through his hands. Whenever they reached a bridge, Laixi would prop the pole against the foundations, ensuring a smooth passage through the passageway beneath the arch.

The afternoon light faded, and the sunlight no longer shone quite as warmly across their faces. As they rowed past Huang's Inn, a fresh breeze began to blow, and the reeds on either side of the river rustled and sang. As Xu Sanguan sat on the barge's prow, waves of cold shivered through his body. He wrapped himself in his cotton-padded jacket, his hands grasping his knees so that he curled himself into a kind of ball.

Laishun, still rowing at the stern, shouted at him, "Go down into the cabin. We don't need you to help out up here anyway. Might as well go take a nap in the cabin."

Laixi added, "Go on down to the cabin."

Xu Sanguan, noting the gusto with which the breathless and sweat-drenched Laishun was throwing himself into his rowing, said, "You sold two bowls of blood, but you look so energetic that you'd never know."

Laishun said, "When we first started out, my legs felt a little weak, but not now. Ask Laixi if his legs are still weak."

"They were a while ago, but not now."

Laishun said to Laixi, "When we get to Seven-Mile Fort, let's sell two more bowls of blood. What do you think?"

"Sure. It's thirty-five *yuan*, right?"

Xu Sanguan said to them, "You two are still so young. I really can't keep up with you. I'm getting old. I'm sitting here shivering from head to toe. I'm going down to the cabin to sleep."

As he spoke, Xu Sanguan opened the cabin hatch, covered himself with the quilt, lay down, and fell asleep. By the time he awoke, it was already dark outside, and the barge was nestled against the riverbank. Emerging from the cabin, he saw the brothers standing by a tree. He watched by the light of the moon as they struggled to break a branch as thick as a man's arm from the trunk. After they pulled it free, they realized that it was too long, so they snapped it in half with their feet, picked up the thicker of the two halves, and walked back to the side of the boat. Laixi placed one end of the branch in the ground and held it steady as Laishun picked up a rock and began to pound it into the ground. After five strokes, only about six inches of the branch protruded from the soil. Laixi fetched a rope from the deck of the barge and tied it around the branch.

When they noticed that Xu Sanguan was standing on deck, they said, "You're up."

Xu Sanguan gazed past them. It was pitch dark, save for a few scattered lights in the distance. "Where are we?"

Laixi replied, "I don't know where we are, but we're not in Tiger's Head Bridge yet."

They lit the stove, cooked dinner on the moonlit deck, and ate steaming bowls of rice in the cold winter breeze. When Xu Sanguan finished eating, his body began to feel warmer. "I'm warmer now. Even my hands are warm."

The three men lay down to sleep in the cabin. Xu Sanguan was still in the middle, under their quilt, his body pressed close to their bodies. Though the three men were crowded together, the two brothers were very happy. Having earned thirty-five *yuan* in a single day for their blood, they suddenly felt that earning money wasn't nearly as hard as they had once thought. They told Xu Sanguan that they had decided not to work the barge anymore, that when they had finished their work in the fields, they would no longer need to earn whatever extra cash the boat would afford them, because working the barge was too hard and left them too exhausted. If they needed extra money, they would sell their blood instead.

Laixi said, "This selling blood business is really great. Besides the money itself, you also get to eat fried pork livers and drink yellow rice wine. Usually we wouldn't even think of going to a restaurant and eating such delicious fried pork livers. When we get to Seven-Mile Fort, we're going to sell blood again."

"Don't even think about it. You can't sell blood again when you get to Seven-Mile Fort." Xu Sanguan jabbed the air with his fingers for emphasis. "When I was young I was just the same. I thought selling blood was like shaking money from a tree. When I ran out or needed a little extra, I could always give the tree a shake, and the money would come tumbling down. But that's not how it is at all. I still remember the first time I ever went to sell blood. Two friends of mine showed me how it was done. One was named Ah Fang, and the other was Genlong. Where are they now? Ah Fang's a wreck, and Genlong died selling blood. Don't you two even think about selling too much blood. Each time you sell, be sure to rest up for at least three months before you go again, unless you absolutely need the money. If you keep on selling blood, you'll ruin your health. Remember what I'm telling you now, because I've been there and back."

Xu Sanguan stretched out his arms, gave them each a light slap. "This time out I sold blood at Lin's Pier, and then I sold some more just three days later at Hundred-Mile. When I went to sell blood four days later at Pine Grove, I passed out. The doctor said I was in shock. That means I was completely out of it. So they gave me a transfusion of seven hundred milliliters of blood. That and the money they charged to save me meant that the first two times I sold blood were a complete waste. I ended up buying blood back instead of selling it. I almost died in Pine Grove."

Xu Sanguan sighed deeply. "I don't have any choice in the matter. I have to keep on selling blood because my son's seriously ill in the hospital in Shanghai, and if I don't find a way to collect the money, the doctors will stop giving him the shots and medicine that he needs. But my blood's gotten thinner over the years. I'm not like you two. One bowl of your blood is as good as two of mine. I was planning to sell some more at Seven-Mile

Fort and at Changning, but now I don't dare, because if I sell blood one more time, I'll probably sell my life along with it.

"I've earned about seventy *yuan* so far. I know that won't be enough to cure my son. So I guess I'll just have to find some other way to earn the money when I get to Shanghai."

Laixi said, "You say one bowl of our blood is as thick as two of yours. Does that mean that one bowl of our blood is worth more than two of yours? We all have round blood, right? When we get to Seven-Mile Fort, why don't you buy a bowl of our blood? We'll sell you one bowl of our blood, and that way you'll be able to sell *two* bowls to the hospital."

Xu Sanguan thought this was a good idea, but he replied, "How could I possibly take your blood away from you?"

Laixi replied, "If we don't sell it to *you*, we'll just end up selling it to someone else."

Laishun added, "It's better to do business with a friend than a stranger, after all."

"You need to row the barge. You need to save some strength for yourselves."

"I have an idea," Laixi said. "We can conserve our strength. We'll each sell one bowl to you. If we each sell you one bowl, you'll be buying two bowls all together. That way when you get to Changning, you'll be able to sell four bowls."

Xu Sanguan smiled. "The most you can sell at a time is two bowls." Then he added, "All right then. I'll buy just one bowl of your blood, but I'm only doing it on account of my son. Anyway, I can't afford two bowls of blood. If I buy one bowl of your blood, I'll be able to sell two when I get to Changning. That means I'll have earned an extra bowl's worth of blood money."

Just as Xu Sanguan finished speaking, the brothers' snores began to resonate through the cabin. Their legs once more crossed atop his own. They made his back hurt and his waist ache, but he was warm because of the heat of their young bodies. And so he lay there as the wind whistled outside the little cabin, sweeping whorls of dust down from the deck, through the hatch that led to the cabin, and onto his face and shoulders. He could see a few pale stars through the hatch, and though he could not see the moon, he saw the way the moonlight frosted the night sky. He lay for a while looking at the sky, then closed his eyes, listening to the sound of the water beating against the hull, so close that it seemed to be slapping against his own ears.

Five days later they arrived in Seven-Mile Fort. The silk factory at Seven-Mile Fort was about a mile outside of town, so they made straight for the hospital. When they arrived at the front door of the hospital, Xu Sanguan called them back. "Don't go in yet. Now that we know where the hospital is, we should go to the river." He added, "Laixi, you haven't drunk any water yet."

Laixi said, "I shouldn't drink anything this time. If I'm going to give you some blood, then I can't drink any water."

Xu Sanguan slapped his own head. "As soon as I saw a hospital, all I could think about was drinking water. I almost forgot that this time you're selling the blood to me—" Xu Sanguan stopped short. "Laixi, I still think you should really drink a little bit of water. They say you should never take advantage of your brother."

Laishun said, "You aren't taking advantage of anyone."

Laixi said, "I'm not going to drink any water. If you were in my place, I'm sure you wouldn't drink any either."

Xu Sanguan was forced to agree. If he had been in Laixi's place, he wouldn't drink any water either. "If I can't convince you to the contrary, all I can do is let you do what you think best."

The three men proceeded to the blood donation room inside the hospital. When the blood chief at Seven-Mile Fort Hospital heard them out, he pointed his finger toward Laixi and said, "So you're selling your blood to me." He pointed in Xu Sanguan's direction. "And then you want me to sell it back to him?"

When he saw them nod, he burst into laughter and pointed at his own chair. "I've sat in this chair for thirteen years now. I've seen thousands of people come to sell their blood. But this is the first time I've ever had someone ask to buy and sell blood at the same time."

Laixi said, "Maybe this is a good omen. Maybe it means you'll be in luck this year."

"That's right," Xu Sanguan added. "Nothing like this has ever happened anywhere else either. Laixi and I aren't even from the same town, but we happened to meet on the road. And it just so happens that he wants to sell blood and I want to buy some. It's one in a million that we ran into each other, and now we've been lucky enough to run into you. Maybe the good luck is catching."

The blood chief of Seven-Mile Fort unwittingly nodded his head. "Certainly is a real coincidence. Who knows? You might be right. Maybe I'll get lucky too." Then he shook his head, "Then again, it's hard to say. Maybe this year will be disastrous. They say that coming across something strange is sometimes inauspicious. You must have heard the old saying. If a bunch of frogs crosses the street in front of you, or it starts to rain bugs, or if your chicken crows at dawn instead of the rooster, it's sure to be a bad year."

Xu Sanguan and the brothers discussed these matters with the blood chief of Seven-Mile Fort for well over an hour before he finally consented to Laixi selling his blood to Xu Sanguan. When they finished the transaction, the three men emerged from the hospital gate, and Xu Sanguan said, "Laixi, we'll take you to a restaurant to eat a plate of fried pork livers and two shots of yellow rice wine."

Laixi shook his head. "I only sold one bowl of blood today. I can do without eating the pork livers, and I can do without the wine."

Xu Sanguan said, "Laixi, you can't be stingy with blood money. You sold blood, not sweat. If it was sweat, you could drink a bowl or two of water to make up for what you lost. But to restore your blood, you need to have the fried pork livers. Eat. Listen to me. I've been through all this before."

Laixi said, "It's really not a problem. Didn't you say selling blood is just like sleeping with a woman? If people had to eat fried pork livers every time they did it, where would that leave you?"

Xu Sanguan shook his head. "Selling blood isn't the same thing as doing it with a woman."

Laishun said, "It's the same thing."

Xu Sanguan said, "What do you know about it?"

Laishun said, "That's what you told us."

Xu Sanguan said, "I may have said that, but it wasn't true."

Laixi said, "I'm fine now. My legs feel a little rubbery, as if I walked a really long way, but that's all. If I rest for a little while, they won't feel rubbery anymore."

Xu Sanguan said, "Listen to me. You still have to eat the fried pork livers."

As they spoke, they came to the spot by the riverside where the barge was moored. Laishun jumped on deck, and Laixi, after untying the rope from a wooden post, also hopped aboard.

Laixi, standing on the deck, said to Xu Sanguan, "We have to deliver the cocoons to the factory now, so we can't take you any farther down river. We live in the Eighth Production Team just outside of Tongyuan. If you're ever in Tongyuan, come stay with us. We're friends now."

As Xu Sanguan stood on the bank watching them push off into the current, he said, "Laishun, take good care of Laixi. Don't you believe him when he says he's just fine. He's running on empty. Don't let him exhaust himself. Tire yourself out a little instead. Don't let him push the barge. And if you get tired and can't row anymore, just stop and rest by the side of the river. Don't let him switch places with you."

"I hear you," Laishun said.

The barge had already moved out toward the middle of the river when Xu Sanguan addressed Laixi. "Laixi, if you really refuse to eat some pork livers, then make sure you get a good night's sleep. You know the saying: if you can't get enough to eat, there's nothing to do but sleep. Sleep helps you recover your strength."

The brothers rowed away, waving toward him as they moved farther and farther into the distance. Xu Sanguan waved until he could no longer see the boat, then turned to climb the steep stone steps of the embankment back to the street.

That same afternoon Xu Sanguan left Seven-Mile Fort on a ferry to Changning, where he sold four hundred milliliters of blood. He did not ride the boat after Changning because there was a bus from Changning to Shanghai, and although it was much more expensive than the ferry, he wanted to reach Yile as quickly as possible and to see Xu Yulan. He counted the time on his fingers. Fifteen days had gone by since Xu Yulan had departed with Yile for Shanghai, yet he had no way of knowing whether Yile's illness had taken a turn for the better or worse. He boarded a bus, and as soon as it began to move, his heart began to pound wildly in his chest.

Xu Sanguan left Changning in the morning and arrived in Shanghai the same afternoon. By the time he found the hospital where Yile was being treated, it was already dusk. He walked into the room where Yile had been staying and saw that there were six hospital beds, five of which were occupied by other patients. One of the beds was empty.

He asked, "Where can I find Xu Yile?"

They pointed toward the empty bed and said, "Right there."

A huge roaring sound filled his head. Suddenly, he remembered Genlong. The morning Genlong had died, he had sprinted back to the hospital, but Genlong's bed had been empty, and they had told him that Genlong was dead. *Maybe Yile is dead too,* he thought to himself. He stood transfixed, then began to sob. His sobs were as loud as screams, and his hands repeatedly swept streams of tears away from his face and onto the hospital bed.

A shout rang out behind him. "Xu Sanguan, you're finally here!"

Xu Sanguan stopped crying and turned to see Xu Yulan helping Yile back into the hospital room. His tears gave way to laughter, and he said to himself, *Yile isn't dead. I thought Yile was dead.*

Xu Yulan said, "What the hell are you crying about? Yile's feeling much better now."

Yile really did look much better. He could even walk by himself now. When he had settled back into his bed, he looked up at Xu Sanguan, smiled, and called his name: "Dad."

Xu Sanguan rubbed Yile's shoulders. "Yile, you're so much better now. Your color is much better. You don't look so pale and gray anymore, and your voice is louder, and you seem to be in good spirits, but your shoulders are still much too skinny. Yile, just now I came in and saw your bed was empty, and I thought you were dead." As he spoke, tears once more streamed from his eyes.

Xu Yulan gave him a little push. "What are you crying about this time, Xu Sanguan?"

Xu Sanguan wiped his tears away. "Just now I was crying because I thought Yile was dead. Now I'm crying because I know he's alive."

CHAPTER TWENTY-NINE

Xu Sanguan walked down the street. His hair was white, and he had lost seven teeth, but his eyes were still good and he could see things just as clearly as he always had. And he knew his ears were still good because he could hear things that were happening very far away.

Xu Sanguan was over sixty years old. His son Yile had been allowed to return to town eight years earlier. Erle had followed him back home two years later. Now Yile worked at the food-processing plant, and Erle was a buyer at the department store next to the rice shop. Within a few years Yile, Erle, and Sanle had all gotten married, had children, and moved to their own houses. And these days their three sons brought their wives and kids back to the family home to see them only on Saturdays.

Now that Xu Sanguan was no longer responsible for the children, and the money that he and Xu Yulan earned was for their use alone, they rarely lacked for cash. There were no longer any patches on their clothes. Their life was like Xu Sanguan's health, which, as he often told people he happened to run into on the street, "is very good."

Which is why when he walked down the street, Xu Sanguan's face was awash in smiles and the wrinkles that covered his face rippled like river water. The sun shone on his face, etching the ripples in light and shadow. That was how he looked as he walked with a smile out of the house and strolled past the snack shop where Xu Yulan made fried dough for breakfast every morning, past the department store where Erle worked, past the movie house that had once been a theater, past the elementary school, past the hospital, past Five Star Bridge, past the clock shop, past the butcher's shop, past Heavenrest Temple, past a newly opened boutique, past two trucks parked next to each other, and past the Victory Restaurant.

But just as he passed the Victory Restaurant, he smelled the aroma of fried pork livers escaping from the open window above the kitchen along with a gust of oily cooking smoke. He had walked past the restaurant, yet the smell stopped him in his tracks, and he stood stock-still, nostrils flaring and mouth widened in an effort to better savor the aroma.

And so it was that Xu Sanguan began to crave a plate of fried pork livers accompanied by a couple of shots of yellow rice wine. His craving grew more and more intense, and he began to feel another craving. He began to feel like selling some blood. He remembered when he had sat at the table by the window with Ah Fang and Genlong, remembered when he had sat in a restaurant with Laixi and Laishun in Huang's Inn, fingers drumming on the tabletop, calling loudly to the waiters: a plate of fried pork livers, two shots of yellow rice wine, and warm that wine up for me.

Xu Sanguan stood by the door of the Victory Restaurant for nearly five minutes before making up his mind to go to the hospital to sell blood. He turned to leave. It had been fifteen years since he sold blood. Today he would sell blood once again, but this time he was going to sell blood just for himself. This would be the very first time he had sold blood for himself. He thought that in the past he had always eaten fried pork livers and drunk yellow rice wine because he had sold blood. Today it would be the other way around. Today he would sell blood so that he could eat fried pork livers and drink yellow rice wine. He walked past the two trucks, walked past the new boutique, walked past the Heavenrest Temple, past the butcher's shop, past the clock shop, past Five Star Bridge, and finally came to the hospital.

The man who sat behind the desk in the blood donation room was no longer Blood Chief Li, but a young man who looked as if he were not yet thirty years old. When the young blood chief looked up he saw that the man who walked into the office had white hair and was missing three of his four front teeth.

When he heard that this same old man had come to sell blood, he waved his hand dismissively. "You want to sell blood? An old man like you? Who needs your blood?"

Xu Sanguan said, "I may be old, but my health is very good. So what if my hair is gray and I've lost a few teeth? My eyes are fine, I have a lucky mole on my forehead, and my ears are as good as they ever were. I can even hear what people whisper to each other in the street from inside my house."

The young blood chief said, "I don't care about your eyes, ears, or anything else, for that matter. Do me a favor. Turn around and march yourself right out of here."

Xu Sanguan said, "Old Blood Chief Li never said things like that."

The young blood chief said, "My name isn't Li. My name is Shen. And Blood Chief Shen can say whatever he pleases."

Xu Sanguan said, "When Blood Chief Li was still here, I came here all the time to sell blood."

The young blood chief said, "But Blood Chief Li is dead now."

Xu Sanguan said, "I know he's dead. He died three years ago. I stood by the gates of Heavenrest Temple and watched them carry his body to the crematorium."

The young blood chief said, "Get out of here! I'm not going to buy your blood. You're just too old. There's more dead blood than living in your veins. No one could possibly want any of your blood. The only person who might be able to use your blood is the lacquer man." The young blood chief chuckled. "You want to know why the lacquer man could use your blood? Because just before they lacquer a piece of furniture, they prime the wood with a coat of pig's blood." The young blood chief burst into laughter. "Understand now? The only thing your blood is good for is furniture. So turn left on your way out of the hospital, and it won't be long before you come to the lacquer shop under the Five Star Bridge. The boss is named Wang. He's famous for his lacquer. Why don't you try selling some of your blood to him? He just might be buying."

Xu Sanguan listened in silence, then shook his head. "I'll forget what you've just said to me and let it go at that. But you should know that if my three sons had been here to hear all of that, they would have broken your jaw."

With these words, he turned to leave. He walked out of the hospital and into the street. It was noon and the streets were full of people who had just left work for lunch. Wave after wave of young workers rolled by on their bicycles, while flocks of children with book bags slung over their shoulders flew down the sidewalk. Xu Sanguan also moved down the sidewalk, but his heart was brimming with grief and resentment. Stung to the core by what the young blood chief had said, he moved down the sidewalk, lost in thought. He was an old man now, his blood was more dead than alive, no one would want his blood anymore, and it was good only for lacquer. This was the first time in forty years he had not been allowed to sell his blood. And in those forty years, he had overcome every family calamity by selling his blood. Now that no one wanted his blood, what would he do if some calamity were once again to befall his family?

Xu Sanguan began to cry. He walked with his shirt open,

letting the wind blow onto his chest and across his face, allowing the big, cloudy tears to fall from his eyes, roll slowly down his cheeks, run into his neck, and slide onto his chest. He lifted his hand to wipe his face, and the tears rolled onto his hand, across his palm, and slid down the back of his hand. His tears kept sliding down as his feet moved across the sidewalk. He held his head high, straightened his back, and his legs stepped forward with energy and spirit. His arms swung back and forth without the slightest hesitation. But his face was suffused with sadness. Rivulets of tears crisscrossed like rain streaming across a windowpane, or the hairline cracks crawling up the sides of a fragile antique bowl, or the dense profusion of branches reaching out from an old tree, irrigation canals spreading across the fields, a network of streets extending across a town. Tears wove a net across his face.

He wept in silence as he walked down the street, moving past the elementary school, past the movie theater, past the department store, past the shop where Xu Yulan fried breakfast crullers, past his own front door. He kept right on walking, walking past one street and then another, until he passed by the Victory Restaurant. And he kept on walking even then, past the clothing store, past Heavenrest Temple, past the butcher's shop, past Five Star Bridge, until he came to the entrance to the hospital. Still he continued to walk, past the elementary school, past the movie theater, until he had circled the streets of the town once, then twice, and people on the streets began to stop and take notice of this man weeping silently as he walked through the streets of the town.

People who knew him called out as he walked past, "Xu Sanguan, Xu Sanguan, Xu Sanguan, Xu Sanguan, Xu Sanguan, why are you crying? Why won't you say anything? Why won't you listen to us? Why are you walking in circles? What's the matter with you?"

Someone said to Yile, "Xu Yile, quick! Look! Your dad's crying and walking through the streets."

Someone said to Erle, "Xu Erle, there's an old man crying in the street. Lots of people are gathering around to watch. You'd better have a look. Isn't that your dad?"

Someone said to Sanle, "Xu Sanle, your dad's crying on the street. He's crying so hard it looks like someone must have died."

Someone went and told Xu Yulan, "Xu Yulan, what are you doing? Still cooking? Drop everything! Come right away. Your old man Xu Sanguan's crying in the streets. We tried to talk to him, but he wouldn't even look at us, and we asked him what was the matter, but he wouldn't tell us anything. We don't know what's going on. Come quick!"

Yile, Erle, and Sanle ran out into the street and stood in their father's way just as he was about to cross Five Star Bridge.

"Dad, what are you crying for? Who's been upsetting you? Tell us what's going on."

Xu Sanguan leaned back against the railing of the bridge and sobbed, "I'm old. No one wants my blood anymore. The only one who might be able to use it is the lacquer man."

His sons said, "Dad, what are you talking about?"

Xu Sanguan continued along his earlier train of thought. "What will happen if we run into trouble again? How will we manage?"

"What are you trying to say?"

Xu Yulan arrived just at this moment, grabbed hold of Xu Sanguan's sleeves, and said, "What's the matter with you? You were just fine when you went out, and now you're crying like a baby."

When Xu Sanguan saw that Xu Yulan had arrived, he lifted his head and wiped away his tears. "Xu Yulan, I'm an old man now. I'll never be able to sell blood again. No one wants my blood anymore. What'll happen to us if something goes wrong?"

Xu Yulan said, "Xu Sanguan, you don't have to sell your blood anymore. We have enough money, and that's not going to change. What do you need to sell your blood for? And why did you go to sell blood today anyway?"

Xu Sanguan said, "I wanted to eat a plate of fried pork livers. I wanted to drink two shots of yellow rice wine. I thought I could eat pork livers and drink wine if I sold some blood."

Yile said, "Dad, don't cry out here in the street. If you want to eat some fried pork livers and drink yellow rice wine, I'll give you the money. Just don't cry out here. If you cry in public, people will think we don't treat you right."

Erle said, "Dad, are you telling me that you've been making a scene all afternoon over some stupid pork livers and wine? And for that you've made us lose any face we might once have had?"

Sanle said, "Dad, don't cry. If you really have to cry, why don't you cry at home? Don't cry out here. It just doesn't look right."

Xu Yulan wheeled around toward her three sons, and with her finger jabbing the air for emphasis, she shouted:

"What is with you three? Have your consciences been eaten by dogs? How can you talk that way about your dad? It was all for you. Each and every time he sold his blood was for you. Every *fen* he made selling blood he spent on you. You were *raised* on his blood. During the famine, when all we could get to eat was corn flour gruel and you three were nothing but skin and bones, he sold blood just so that you could eat some noodles. You three seem to have forgotten all about that. Then there was the time Erle was sent to work in the countryside. Your dad sold blood not once but twice. And all of that just so he could get on Erle's brigade chief's good side. Your dad treated him to lavish meals, bought him all kinds of gifts, just so you could get sent back home a little earlier. But you don't remember any of that, do you, Erle? And Yile, what you just said hurts the most of all. How could you, of all people, talk to your dad that way? You've always been his favorite son. And he's not even your real dad. Even so, he's always been so good to you. When you had to go to the hospital in Shanghai, he sold blood everywhere he could along the way, because we didn't have any money for the hospital bill. You're supposed to wait at least three months each time you sell blood, but to save *your* life, your dad put his own life in danger. He sold blood after three days, then sold it again five days later. And he almost died in Pine Grove because of it. But you seem to have forgotten about that. What is with you three? I really think your consciences must have been eaten by dogs."

As Xu Yulan's voice faded to a whisper, tears slid down her face as well. She took hold of Xu Sanguan's hand.

"Xu Sanguan, let's go. Let's go eat fried pork livers and drink yellow rice wine. We've got plenty of money now." She fumbled in her pocket and extracted a wad of bills. "Look, these two are five-*yuan* bills, and here's a two-*yuan* note, and here's another one. And there's more where that came from. You can eat whatever you want."

Xu Sanguan said, "All I want is fried pork livers and yellow rice wine."

Xu Yulan brought him to the Victory Restaurant, sat him down at a table, and ordered a plate of fried pork livers and two shots of yellow rice wine. When she was finished ordering, she picked up the menu and showed it to Xu Sanguan.

"There are a lot of other dishes here too. All of them are really good. Which ones do you want to try? Just tell me."

"All I want is pork livers and rice wine."

Xu Yulan ordered a second plate of fried pork livers for him, and then a third, accompanied by a whole bottle of yellow rice wine. When everything had been delivered to their table, she asked him once again what else he would like to eat. This time he shook his head.

"That's enough. Any more dishes and I really wouldn't be able to finish the meal."

The table in front of Xu Sanguan was laden with three plates of fried pork livers, a bottle of yellow rice wine, as well as four extra shots of rice wine. He laughed as he ate the pork livers and drank the wine and said to Xu Yulan, "This is the best meal of my whole life."

He laughed as he remembered what the young blood chief

had said to him in the hospital. As he ate, he related to Xu Yulan exactly what he had said.

When Xu Yulan had heard his story, she began to curse. "*His* blood is the pig's blood, not yours! Not even the lacquer man would want *his* blood. Only a ditch or a drainage pipe could use *his* blood. Who does he think he is? I know who he is! He's that idiot Shen's kid. His dad's an idiot. The man's so stupid, he can't even tell the difference between one *yuan* and five. And I know who his mom is too. She's a real slut. Who knows whose bastard that Shen really is! Why, he's even younger than Sanle, and yet he dares to talk like that to you! Back when we had Sanle, this Shen wasn't even a twinkling in his mother's eye, and now he thinks he's on top of the world."

Xu Sanguan said to Xu Yulan, "That's why people say pubic hair doesn't come out till after your eyebrows do, but gets even longer in the end."

TRANSLATOR'S AFTERWORD

The extent to which Yu Hua—perhaps the most notorious agent provocateur of the Chinese literary avant-garde that flourished in the years around the Tiananmen movement of 1989—has become part of the mainstream was brought home to me on a recent visit to Beijing. Flipping through the cable TV channels, I suddenly stumbled across an "Arts and Entertainment"–style documentary featuring Yu Hua's life and work. Replete with impressionistic black-and-white televisual reenactments of episodes from his youth in Haiyan, a small provincial city on China's prosperous southeastern seaboard, the show narrates Yu Hua's meteoric rise from "barefoot" dentist to fame as one of the very best-selling and most critically acclaimed figures in the Chinese literary establishment through a series of vignettes. We are shown his birth in 1960, the travails of a childhood spent amid the all-encompassing political chaos of the Cultural Revolution, his formative and easy familiarity with the funereal world of the hospital morgue where both his parents worked as doctors, the five years he spent pulling teeth by day and obsessively reading the masterpieces of modern literature by night, and, finally, the triumphal moment when one of his first short stories, sent unsolicited to a literary magazine in the far-off capital city of Beijing, elicited the phone call from an influential editor that would eventually catapult him to the forefront of the literary scene, and make him a major figure in the post-Mao transformation of China's literary and cultural terrain.

Yu Hua never mentioned the documentary to me when we had dinner a few nights later, and I didn't bring it up. I suspect he didn't care for the way in which the show neglected the very thing that remains most important to him: the power and precision with which he wields words as a means of engaging critically with the world around him. And I was at considerable pains to reconcile this slick televised portrait with the man I had first met one night in the early 1990s after having been drawn (and sometimes repulsed) by the clinical lyricism and musical violence of his angular and modernistic prose. Such was the sensitivity to the "rustle of language" and the almost *Mitteleuropäer* morbidity of sensibility evinced by his early work, that I was more amused than surprised when a skinny and slightly unkempt Yu Hua, almost immediately upon entering my hotel room in a converted traditional courtyard residence in Beijing for the first time, lit a cigarette, got down on all fours in search of an annoying buzzing sound of which I had been completely unaware, and unceremoniously unplugged the mini-refrigerator.

BEIJING, where Yu Hua now lives and works, is a noisier city than it once was. One traverses the city's seemingly endless expanse of concrete housing blocks on newly constructed elevated expressways lit on both sides by glowing neon and the billboarded icons of transnational commerce: Toshiba, IKEA, Motorola. As we ate in a glitzy new Cantonese seafood restaurant, Yu Hua's son played a portable video game and clamored for McDonald's. Karaoke pop music and the blare of the television news seeped from another room, mixing with the loud conversation and shrill cell phone ring-tones of well-dressed entrepreneurs. Unplugging, in other words, is no longer an option. For writers of Yu Hua's generation, often referred to as the "experimentalists," the crucial questions have changed, irrevocably. The socialist orthodoxy and stale humanist verities against which they struggled mightily in the '80s have long since been dethroned. The cultural insularity they so pointedly punctured by way of the importation and creative appropriation of modernist, magical realist, and postmodernist models has become less a problem than a virtual impossibility. Literary censorship is now largely market-driven, and formal experimentation simply doesn't sell. The question that remains is this: How can a writer make his or her voice heard above the din? How do specifically *literary* signals penetrate the pervasive noise of commercial culture, media babble, and globalized culture that has inundated urban China in the new century? What position can Chinese writers occupy in an aggressively capitalist era in which the nouveau-riche entrepreneur is insistently exalted as the most alluring sort of culture hero? It is only in the context of these questions that we can understand Yu Hua's transformation into a best-selling author, and the local significance of his *Chronicle of a Blood Merchant* as a work of literary imagination and social critique.

FOR YU HUA, growing up in the narrow, stone-cobbled and moss-edged lanes of his native Haiyan, writing was a way out. The lives of the salaried writers employed by the local party-sponsored "Cultural Palace" seemed positively bourgeois compared to the drudgery of pulling teeth. Perhaps even more important, the translations of global modernist fiction that were just beginning to trickle into local book markets in the mid-1980s as a result of the post-Mao program of "reform and opening," seemed to offer a means of shirking the ideological and intellectual drudgery of everyday life, of imagining "one kind of reality" (as he titled an early novella) in which conventional ways of seeing the world no longer held sway. The Japanese Nobel Prize–winner Yasunari Kawabata's lyrical attention to the world of things was an early and abiding influence. (Whenever he managed to find a rare Chinese translation of Kawabata's works, Yu Hua once told me, he would buy two copies: one to read, and the other to keep pristinely intact on his bookshelf.) Yu Hua's initial encounter with Franz Kafka's tortuously Byzantine narratives of modern life, and especially his unflinching attention to spiritual and corporeal violence, was equally revelatory. The efforts of Jewish writers such as Bruno Schulz and Isaac Bashevis Singer to understand the horrors of inhumanity spoke to Yu Hua's own concern with the question of how he might most effectively represent the cataclysms of recent Chinese history. The labyrinths of Jorge Luis Borges exercised a profound fascination as well, for they pointed Yu Hua toward narrative convolution and philosophical uncertainty rather than the straight story lines and invariant verities of socialist dogma. And it was his intense dissatisfaction with the class-coded and stereotypical attributes of the stalwart heroes and reactionary villains he had grown up reading and watching in revolutionary novels and films that attracted him to the radical experiments of the French new novelist Alain Robbe-Grillet, whose characters are deliberately emptied of any pretense of humanity or psychological depth—for the flatter the characters, Robbe-Grillet felt, the more quickly the illusionism and stale conventions of realism could be revealed as a cheap, if powerful, ideological ploy.

By the late 1980s, Yu Hua had begun to produce a series of shockingly audacious short stories and novellas in which he not only cut up his own characters in confrontationally graphic detail, but also relentlessly skewered and dissected the norms and conventions of almost every fictional genre, from premodern tales of "scholars and maidens" to martial arts fiction, from ghost stories and detective fiction to epics of the revolutionary struggle. Yu Hua's narrator could linger for pages over a loving description of a madman sawing off his own nose ("1986"), or an unbearably visceral evocation of a young girl being hacked to pieces and sold to cannibals ("Classical Love"). His stories dispensed with the linear plot lines of realist fiction, preferring instead to loop back upon themselves, interlock into complex mosaics, or deliberately and seemingly inexplicably replay the same passage over and over again.

These heady experiments grew out of the cultural ferment and unrest of the years just before and after the Tiananmen movement of 1989. And Yu Hua was by no means alone in making these sorts of antiauthoritarian gestures in the literary journals of the day. He and a group of similarly avant-garde young authors such as Ge Fei and Su Tong (all of whom had still been children during the high tide of the Cultural Revolution in the late 1960s) came to dominate China's literary scene in the early 1990s. If post-Mao writers had struggled to rescue humanism from the ashes of a failed socialist past throughout the 1980s, enthused Chinese critics believed, the experimentalists of the 1990s would go even further, exposing the pitfalls of the humanist thinking and grand historical narratives their predecessors had relied upon as a means of cultural protest. If earlier artists had reclaimed European modernism after years of literary repression and isolation under socialism, other critics declared, Yu Hua and his contemporaries represented the arrival of a new global postmodernism on Chinese soil. The problem, these critics argued, was not so much the depredations of Maoism *in particular*, but the dangerous arrogance of any intellectual or political or literary system—even those as seemingly benign as humanism or nationalism or realism—that dared claim to tell the whole story, the only true story, in the name of the people. The nihilistic energy of Yu Hua's fiction—and its refusal to behave like conventional fiction—thus came to be seen as a necessary refusal, a deconstructive gesture, and a sign of the times.

What this account missed, however, was Yu Hua's deep affinity for the work of another Chinese master, Lu Xun, whose fiction and impassioned political advocacy had helped launch the epochal May 4th Movement for literary and cultural revolution in 1919. Widely acknowledged as the "father of modern Chinese literature" for his groundbreaking importation and appropriation of Western literary forms, Lu Xun's unique brand of realist short fiction was inflected by the language and procedures he had learned as a failed medical student in Japan around the turn of the century. Medicine, he later wrote, could heal only bodies. It was the task of literature to minister to their sick minds. Eager to eviscerate what he saw as the deep-seated flaws of the Chinese national character (flaws that seemed by the 1920s to have resulted in China's subjection to aggressive imperial powers such as England, Germany, France, the United States, and Japan), Lu Xun wielded his pen like a scalpel, cuttingly remarking on the cultural follies and moral failings of his fellow Chinese. What made Lu Xun a great writer, however, was not only his tremendous linguistic invention and uncompromising social conscience, but also the way he fretted about his inability as a member of the educated elite to truly reach or represent the masses. Relentlessly self-critical, he took pride in his willingness to turn his scalpel inward, to dissect his own failings even more unsentimentally than he did his "patients" and their pathologies.

The extent to which Yu Hua poked mordantly ironic fun at Lu Xun in his early fiction—one character in his "One Kind of Reality" is quite literally dissected by a wisecracking team of organ harvesting doctors after having been executed for murder—should not obscure their underlying affinities. At the most superficial level, they both grew up in and write almost exclusively about small-town life in Zhejiang province, near Shanghai. As a teenager in Haiyan, Yu Hua was so enamored with the ambiance of Lu Xun's first masterpiece of short fiction, "Diary of a Madman" (in which traditional Confucian culture is ingeniously represented by a cannibalistic cabal plotting the demise of an enlightened, or perhaps merely paranoid, narrator), that he set it to music, with each Chinese character of the original text being assigned a random musical pitch. (Yu Hua still likes to say that it is quite possibly the longest and most impossible song ever written.) Like Lu Xun, Yu Hua returns obsessively to the violent spectacles of China's tumultuous modern history. As in Lu Xun's fiction, the incalculable sufferings of poverty, war, and revolution come to life for the reader in Yu Hua's fiction as a sort of "theater of cruelty" visited upon the bodies of his characters. And as with Lu Xun, it is the operating theater and the hospital that more often than not serve as a symbolic site of cruelty, official ineptitude, and state malpractice. This is certainly true of *To Live*—the 1992 novel that catapulted Yu Hua to national fame, prompting a successful film adaptation by the internationally renowned director Zhang Yimou. The climax of that story—which relates the epic transformations of modern Chinese history through the eyes of a ne'er-do-well gambler called Fugui and his family—wrenchingly relates the entirely preventable death by bleeding of a pregnant woman in a hospital at the height of the Cultural Revolution.

While the sheer absurdity and cruelty of the vicissitudes Fugui and his family so resiliently suffer throughout the novel are reminiscent of Yu Hua's early work, *To Live* represented a decisive turn away from avant-garde writing toward a more pointedly populist style. By 1992, the vogue for challenging, intellectually serious fiction had begun to cool, and China's headlong push for wholesale marketization had begun to transform the way people thought about and, more importantly, bought and sold their culture. Ironically, the avant-garde of which Yu Hua had been such a prominent part, fell victim not so much to state repression as to the vagaries of the emergent capitalist marketplace. Literary journals and publishing houses, which had been subsidized by the authorities, were now forced to fend for themselves. Television dramas, Hong Kong and Taiwanese pop music, Hollywood blockbusters, and entertainment fiction rapidly came to dominate urban cultural markets. The intricately constructed narrative labyrinths and earnest cultural critique of the pre- and immediately post-Tiananmen years suddenly seemed hopelessly old-fashioned at best and willfully elitist at worst. The era of mass culture had arrived with a vengeance. Perhaps the best anecdotal emblem of this cultural sea change was the appearance in 1996 of a soapy six-part television miniseries of dubious artistic merit called *China Models.* Each episode, it turned out, had been ghostwritten by a critically acclaimed proponent of highbrow literary writing in China, including one segment penned by Yu Hua himself.

It would be too simplistic, however, to argue that a book like *To Live* was merely a capitulation to mass culture. For not unlike Lu Xun before him, Yu Hua has willingly become what we would now refer to as a public intellectual. He writes serious essays on literature, Western classical music, and the visual arts for the popular press. He has been active in producing musicals on Beijing's vibrant drama scene. He frequently weighs in on issues of public concern on television and via the Internet. Since *To Live,* his fiction has gravitated toward gripping stories of ordinary men and women living through extraordinary travails. And in experimenting with and finally adopting a reconstructed realist style—one characterized by its stripped-down, almost cinematic brevity, earthy humor, and raw emotional appeal—he has also made a conscious decision to narrow the gulf between elite intellectuals and their audience, a gulf that Lu Xun self-consciously despaired of ever being able to overcome.

All of these tendencies come together in the *Chronicle of a Blood Merchant,* Yu Hua's most successful novel to date, first published as *The Chronicle of Xu Sanguan's Blood Selling (Xu Sanguan mai xue ji)* in 1995. The novel's deceptively simple scenario takes for its inspiration a subculture, born of rural poverty and a network of blood plasma collection stations in public hospitals, which has existed for more than thirty years in the Chinese countryside, engendering its own protocols, ritual codes of conduct, and belief systems. The disturbing revelations of official corruption and mismanagement within this system, as well as the widespread contamination of blood reserves with the HIV virus, came to light only several years *after* Yu Hua's novel was published. Yu Hua's novel, in this sense, seems eerily prescient. That many rural communities, especially in the drought-stricken central province of Henan, have come to subsist almost entirely on their "blood money" is chilling enough. And the appalling fact that these "blood villages" have also become "AIDS villages"—in which it is conservatively estimated that tens and perhaps hundreds of thousands of peasants have contracted HIV through selling their own blood—cannot help but shadow our reading of Xu Sanguan's distinctly unhygienic encounters with bumbling "blood chiefs" and venal medical officials.

But Yu Hua's account of the prehistory of this public health holocaust is neither journalistic nor strictly ethnographic. And although Yu Hua faithfully chronicles Xu Sanguan's life from the early days of socialism in the 1950s, to the disastrously ambitious economic collectivization of the Great Leap Forward in 1958 and the three years of famine that resulted, followed by the factional violence of the Cultural Revolution (1966–76) and the relative prosperity of the post-Mao years, the novel isn't necessarily, or exclusively, historical in its focus. There's more than a whiff of the morality play here, for starters. Attentive as always to the musical aspects of his material, Yu Hua has staged his story as the sort of traditional Chinese opera that townsfolk like Xu Sanguan and his country cousins would heartily enjoy. Performances take place in an impromptu manner, in the street or at market or in the midst of a temple fair. Props are minimal, settings suggested in a few broad brushstrokes. Characters, playing more or less to type, appear onstage, explaining themselves directly to the audience and each other in soliloquy. Public life arranges itself into a series of dramatic gestures and emotionally charged tableaux; private life is virtually an impossibility, carried out against the backdrop of a disapproving crowd through furtive kindness or tender mercy, as when Xu Sanguan secretly brings his wife a morsel of meat as she stands in ritual humiliation on a busy street corner. The language of the original, finally, has the plain-speaking concision, bawdy humor, and sharp cadence of street opera, and Yu Hua's themes—sustenance, suffering, blood money, blood ties, and bonds bought and paid in blood—are nothing if not elemental and operatic.

Few Chinese readers would miss the way in which the story—if only metaphorically—also engages with the wrenching social and economic dislocations of contemporary Chinese life. In a dizzyingly hyper-capitalistic climate in which the private sector has made a startling and often unregulated comeback, state workers such as Xu Sanguan have been rendered redundant, government officials have routinely exploited their political capital and connections to accumulate financial advantage for themselves and their families, and the infrastructure of socialism (medical care and public education) has been gutted by official corruption and privatization, Xu Sanguan's career as a blood merchant poses a series of disturbing and politically pointed questions. Where does capital come from? What if the only capital you have is your own body? What does it mean to sell your lifeblood for a living? And what happens when there is no longer a market for your "labor"? It is in this specific sense that Xu Sanguan has become an emblematic figure for those who have inevitably been left behind by marketization, a scruffy reverse mirror image of the new entrepreneurial class so insistently touted as the masters of the future by the Chinese media in recent years.

Perhaps the most important question Yu Hua asks in this novel is this: Is there any difference between self-possession and being dispossessed? And the answer, if there is any for the taking, has perhaps to do with the way in which Yu Hua's characters redeem themselves (and are repaid) not in blood money, but in an altogether more writerly sort of currency: words. Xu Sanguan's wondrous verbal cookery during the famine is not just about conjuring a perversely empty pleasure from out of desperate privation. The words that he feeds his hungry children after fifty-seven days of eating gruel are a possession, a symbol of his own self-mastery, and a gift: of love, of imagination, of solidarity. What sustains Xu Sanguan and Xu Yulan through betrayal and tribulation is not so much the quasi-contractual blood bonds that brought them together but the stories they tell to each other, their neighbors, and their three children about the forgivably messy ways their lives have tangled and interwoven. And what ultimately counts most for Yile and his father is not so much blood but a simple term of address, a signal that cuts through the noise, an inaccurate yet redemptive fiction: "Dad."

ABOUT THE AUTHOR

Yu Hua was born in 1960 in Zhejiang, China. He finished high school during the Cultural Revolution and worked as a dentist for five years before beginning to write in 1983. He has published three novels, six collections of stories, and three collections of essays. His work has been translated into French, German, Italian, Dutch, Spanish, Japanese, and Korean. In 2002 Yu Hua became the first Chinese writer to win the prestigious James Joyce Foundation Award. His novel *To Live* was awarded Italy's Premio Grinzane Cavour in 1998, and *To Live* and *Chronicle of a Blood Merchant* were named two of the last decade's ten most influential books in China. Yu Hua lives in Beijing.

ABOUT THE TRANSLATOR

Andrew F. Jones is the translator of Yu Hua's first collection of short fiction in English, *The Past and the Punishments,* as well as a collection of literary essays by Eileen Chang. He is associate professor of modern Chinese literary and cultural studies at the University of California, Berkeley, and the author of *Yellow Music: Media Culture and Colonial Modernity in the Chinese Jazz Age.*